THE POLISH TRIANGLE

JONATHAN CULLEN

LIQUID MIND PUBLISHING

Liquid Mind Publishing

liquidmindpublishing.com

ALSO BY JONATHAN CULLEN

The Days of War Series

The Last Happy Summer

Nighttime Passes, Morning Comes

Shadows of Our Time

The Storm Beyond the Tides

Sunsets Never Wait

Bermuda Blue

Port of Boston Series

Whiskey Point

City of Small Kingdoms

The Polish Triangle

Love Ain't For Keeping

Sign up for Jonathan's newsletter for updates on deals and new releases!

https://liquidmind.media/j-cullen-newsletter-sign-up-2-jody/

Enjoying the Port of Boston series? Pre-Order the latest installment, *Love Ain't For Keeping*, coming to Amazon on August 1, 2023!

https://www.amazon.com/Love-Aint-Keeping-Boston-Crime-ebook/dp/B0BGQHSZ58/

My homeland – heroic spirit of the Polish people, that by miracle lives amid hunger and cold...

— Maria Konopnicka

CHAPTER 1

September 1970

I HAD JUST ARRIVED at Harrigan's apartment when I heard the call. The two-way was faint and staticky, the reception bad from all the brick buildings. But it was clear enough. *Shots fired.* My hand shook as I turned the squelch, and it wasn't from the coffee. There was urgency in the dispatcher's voice.

Officer down.

Just then Harrigan came out the front door, his suit pressed and black skin gleaming from a fresh shave. He walked with a swagger that I sometimes took for slowness, a consequence of his childhood on St. Kitts in the Virgin Islands.

I hit the horn. Startled, he ran toward the car, moving clumsily with a briefcase in one hand, a mug in the other.

"Lieutenant?" he asked as he got in.

"Officer down!"

He was barely in his seat when I turned on the sirens and pulled into traffic. We raced to the location, swerving around cars and buses. Morning was the worst time to get anywhere in the city. Harrigan

1

braced himself for the ride, clutching the side of the door, having already spilled coffee on his pleated pants.

"What happened?" he asked.

"A bank robbery, I think."

I reached for a cigarette, fumbling to light it.

"Any idea who?"

Not knowing if he meant the suspects or the victim, I shook my head. Anytime an officer was hurt on duty, the entire force held its breath.

We sped down Massachusetts Avenue, where the leaves on the trees were already starting to turn. Soon the Citgo Sign peered above the buildings, and we were almost there. Blowing through the last two lights, we went under an overpass and came into Kenmore Square.

In the distance, I saw a dozen emergency vehicles: police cruisers, ambulances, and fire trucks. People were watching from the sidewalks; a helicopter hovered overhead. Several officers stood in the middle of the intersection, attempting to direct traffic through a square that was a chaotic juncture of two wide boulevards and several smaller roads.

With no place to park, I stopped in the street, and we jumped out. We ran toward the scene, but there was so much activity it was hard to know where the scene was. On the corner, I saw Edmund McNamara, the barrel-chested chief of police, standing beside a Delta 88 with some police officials. Easy to spot in a crowd, he wore a fedora, something that had been out of fashion since Eisenhower was president.

I ran toward him, Harrigan trailing behind, and by the time I got there, I was out of breath.

"Chief," I said.

"They hit the Shawmut Bank," he said, nodding to a small two-story building on Beacon Street with a stucco façade. "Sergeant Duggan has been shot—"

"Giraffe?"

McNamara frowned as he nodded, probably unaware of the nickname.

"How is he?" I asked.

Pausing, he looked at the men around him; a local precinct captain, two detectives from Area B, and a few others I didn't know.

"We don't have an update yet. They rushed him to City Hospital."

It was a diplomatic answer, but I understood why. Things changed quickly after an incident, and giving no information was better than giving the wrong information.

I looked around, stunned, dizzy from exertion. Jerry Duggan was a fellow officer, but he was also a friend, a 6' 6" half-Irish, half-Italian giant who was raised in public housing in Charlestown. We had joined the department the same year and even lived together as rookies. With five kids at home, he worked mostly nights, priding himself on never having missed a Little League game or a school recital.

"Brae," the chief said, startling me. "This is Paul Shine...FBI..."

I nodded to the agent, and we shook hands.

"...and Mark Marecki."

I turned to his partner, a short and stocky man with dark sunglasses. He was built more like a bricklayer than an FBI agent, and when we shook, his grip was firm.

"Jody?"

"Joseph," I said, thinking he had misheard the chief. "But everyone calls me Jody."

"It's Marcus."

Something in his voice, perhaps the way he said his name, was familiar, and we stood shaking far longer than necessary.

"Marecki?" I asked, confused.

"It used to be *Evans*."

My mouth dropped when I realized who he was.

"Marcus," I said, and my cool expression melted into a smile.

No one seemed surprised we knew each other—the FBI and Boston collaborated more than either organization wanted to. But my acquaintance with Marcus went beyond my job or even the war, back to my childhood over thirty years before. It was hard to reconcile that pug-nosed boy with the polished agent who stood before me, and in those few short seconds, I had a thousand questions. But I couldn't get out the first because the moment I went to speak, the chief interrupted.

"We got an ID on the car. Looks like the same group that hit the armory."

Marcus and his partner acknowledged the remark, but they were mostly just listening. Agents never said much around cops. Only three days before, the National Guard arsenal in Newburyport had been robbed, the culprits taking guns and ammunition and lighting the place on fire.

"How'd it go down?" I asked.

"They were parked in that alleyway," McNamara said, pointing to a narrow lane beside the bank. "When the officers showed up, Stapleton went in the front. Duggan went down the back to where the perps were parked. We don't have the logistics yet, but it looks like they fired on him as they were pulling out."

"They were leaving?"

"Already had the money," the precinct captain said, and one of the detectives added, "Almost sixty grand in cash. Biggest heist in years."

"Anyone else hurt?"

"No. The bank manager had just gotten there. He was opening the back door when someone with a mask came up from behind. Stuck a gun in his ribs."

"A lucky hit," I said.

"It wasn't luck," McNamara said. "This bank transfers cash every week. The days rotate and are confidential. The money was already sorted and packed, waiting for Brinks."

Someone called, and the chief looked over. Two plainclothes officers were at the corner with a group of reporters and news anchors, a pile of cameras mounted and ready. McNamara had to make a statement—he couldn't avoid it. He was good with the rank-and-file but awkward with the press, and public speaking wasn't his strength.

"If they had the money, why'd they shoot?" I asked.

"Because no one likes pigs."

It was harsh but true, and the past decade had been hard for law enforcement. With anti-war protests and student demonstrations, cops had gone from heroes to villains, the scapegoats for the problems of a society that was coming apart at the seams.

As the chief walked away, Marcus reached into his pocket and took out a card.

"Let's get lunch," he said, handing it to me. "We'll catch up."

I glanced down: *Marcus B. Marecki, U.S. Department of Justice, Federal Bureau of Investigation*. I didn't know what surprised me more, that I had run into him after all these years, or that the FBI issued business cards.

"I'd like that."

"Good to see you, Jody," he said.

He nodded goodbye to Harrigan and then hurried to catch up with the others. Squinting in the sun, I watched as he blended into the crowd of officials, reporters, and bystanders. Sometimes I envied the attention, although I never sought it, and it seemed some small validation for the stress of the job. But I was a lieutenant, too high in rank to avoid scrutiny and too low to deal with the public.

"An old friend?" Harrigan asked.

With my eyes still on the press conference, I said, "What?"

"Was that an old friend?"

"Just a guy I used to know—"

"Lieutenant!" someone shouted.

I looked across the street, and an officer was waving. When we walked over, his partner was leaning over a young woman sitting on the curb between two parked cars.

"She says she saw the suspects," the cop said.

"Why wasn't she interviewed?"

He looked at his partner, who just shrugged his shoulders.

"Don't know. We were looking for shell casings. She was just sitting here."

They moved away, and I knelt beside the girl. She was hysterical, her head in her arms and sobbing.

"Miss?" I said.

When she looked up, her eyes were swollen, her cheeks covered in streaks of mascara. Still, she was pretty, with full lips and a petite nose. Wearing a fur-collared coat, she looked more dressed for a night out dancing than a day of work or school.

"What did you see?"

Moving closer, I looked straight at her. Those precious minutes after an incident were critical, first impressions always being the most reliable.

"It shouldn't have happened," she said, stumbling. "I...I was walking up the alleyway. There was someone in the car. It was running."

"Can you describe him?"

"It was a woman," she said, wiping her face. "A student—"

"How did you know she was a student, Miss?" Harrigan asked.

Something about his voice put people at ease, compelled them to cooperate.

"She had a red sweatshirt on, Boston University."

"What happened next?" I asked, pressing her.

"A man came out the door of the bank."

"Did you see what he looked like?"

"Long hair. A mustache, I think. The way they all look."

The way they all look. I grinned because it was a phrase I would have used.

"He got in the passenger seat," she went on. "A police officer came down the alley. He yelled for them to stop. I heard a loud pop, like a firecracker, and they drove away. I didn't know what happened until people started screaming."

Standing up, I looked around. Over at the bank, some cops were running tape along the front, blocking it off until the area had been thoroughly vetted. Otherwise, things were returning to normal, people going into the subway station, students on their way to class. A couple of news trucks lingered at the intersection, but overall, the excitement was over. The quiet aftermath of a crime was as jarring as the crime itself.

"Miss," I said, turning back to her. "These officers are going to take you to the station to get a statement."

When she nodded, Harrigan held out his hand and helped her up.

"Thank you," I said.

She peered nervously at us, then the men escorted her over to the cruiser. In skintight jeans, she had a sexy figure, her hips swaying as she walked in high heels. Her short coat revealed the skin of her back, white and smooth, and I stared out of disapproval, not desire. I was no prude, but sometimes I couldn't believe how young women dressed.

"Rather unusual attire for a Thursday morning," Harrigan said.

"Who the hell would let their daughter go out like that?"

CHAPTER 2

THE DAYS WERE GETTING SHORTER, AND BY THE TIME I LEFT headquarters, it was already dark. I drove home along the Jamaica Way, a winding parkway that passed the mansions of Jamaica Plain and skirted some of the finer parts of Brookline. It was always a quiet ride home, and an opulence I wasn't used to because, for most of my career, I had lived in apartments. But three months earlier, Ruth and I had bought our first home in West Roxbury, the outermost section of Boston, a neighborhood of leafy side streets, baseball parks, and back-yards. The houses ranged from grand old Victorians to tidy post-war ranches, but it was mainly middle-class and only considered upscale by those who had less. Nevertheless, it was the closest thing to the suburbs, and because cops and public officials had to reside in the city, it was where many of them chose to live.

Aside from my time in Korea, I had never been around so many trees and flowers, and I awoke some mornings to a silence that was almost unsettling. I had spent my entire life in the inner boroughs of the city, places so dense that heat still emanated from the buildings and sidewalks long after summer was over, places so crowded you could reach out a window and shake the hand of your neighbor, places where laundry hung from all the back porches, giving the impression of a fleet of sailing tenements cast adrift in a sea of brick and cement. There was no denying I missed the grittiness. Something about poverty and squalor seemed to reflect the deprivation in my soul. But with a wife and an infant, I chose quiet over the hustle-bustle, safety over the excitement. After years of living on the edge, I finally accepted there was honor in just being ordinary.

As I pulled into the driveway, my headlights flashed across the small bungalow with white shutters that was our home. Someone next door peered through the curtain, but I couldn't see who it was—my eyesight was getting worse with age. It could have been Jim or his wife, Esther. He was a forty-something balding accountant who took the train each morning to his job in Copley Square; she was the stay-at-home mother of their two young daughters, a short brunette who wore day dresses and smoked Pall Malls. Like most of the neighbors, they were sensible and friendly, keeping their yards tidy and conversation light.

Turning off the car, I breathed deeply and tried to relax, never wanting to walk in agitated after a tough day. As I gripped the steering wheel, my hands were steady, but my body trembled, which I attributed to hunger or fatigue or the fact that I had run out of cigarettes and hadn't had one in over an hour. The truth was, however, that after all these years, the job was finally getting to me. Maybe I was getting old, I thought, or something about having a child made me especially attuned to the fragility of life. A dear friend had been shot, his condition uncertain, and even if I didn't know who the killers were, I wanted to blame a whole generation.

I saw them every day, young people with long hair and tie-dyed shirts, unclean and unshaven. They congregated on downtown streets, playing bongos and other peasant instruments, waving signs or selling flowers, smug in their self-righteousness. There had been a massive protest on Boston Common the year before where the department was so short-staffed that even Harrigan and I got called in to help. It was a large but mostly peaceful event, one-hundred-thousand strong, with long speeches about demolishing the power structure and remaking society, the rantings of middle-class kids who probably had never made their own lunch or folded their laundry.

Suddenly, the front lights went on.

I looked up, and Ruth was in the doorway, her hair in a bun and her nurse's uniform showing under her coat. I reached for my briefcase, empty except for a yellow pad of paper and a few pens. I had never been organized like Harrigan, who took careful notes of interviews, evidence, thoughts, and theories. I operated on instinct alone. But my new captain said that if I wanted to continue working the streets, a lieutenant's role was also administrative, and I had to at least look like I was more than just a beat cop.

I got out and went up the walkway, the silhouette of Ruth looming. "You're late again," she said.

"Sorry, there was—"

"This can't continue."

I skirted by her, defiant but in no mood to argue. When I walked into the foyer, I looked over and saw Nessie on the couch in her pink sleeper, staring at the television and laughing at the slapstick antics of *I Love Lucy*. The moment she saw me, her eyes beamed, and she cried, "Daddy!" I ran over, picked her up, and she reached for my nose.

"She's already had some carrots and chicken..." Ruth said.

I raised Nessie over my head, and she giggled.

"...If she's hungry before bed, give her some crackers, but nothing sweet..."

As Ruth spoke, I spun Nessie around and around.

"...Her nose is runny. I think it's hay fever. There's some Teldrin above the sink..."

I was starting to get dizzy, but she was so excited I couldn't stop.

"Dammit, Jody! Are you even listening?"

Stopping, I turned to Ruth, who stood by the door with her arms tight to her side, containing her anger. Her shift started at 6 p.m. and she was going to be late—again. Although I always tried to get home on time, my schedule was unpredictable, and no one ever knew when and where a crime was going to happen. I had asked her to leave her job to be a full-time mother. Like a lot of women now, she preferred the independence of a career and an income. It made our life more complicated, but I didn't resent her for it, and I even felt a mild shame because, with the high cost of living, it was hard to live on a lieutenant's salary alone.

I put Nessie back down on the couch, and although she tried to resist, I reassured her with a smile. I walked over to the foyer and faced Ruth, looking her in the eye.

"It was a crazy day."

"You can't just show up when you want to!" she said, speaking in a forceful whisper. For all our arguments and petty spats, we never shouted in front of Nessie. "You've been late twice this week already!"

I lowered my head like a repentant child, and I was truly sorry. As she stood waiting for me to reply, I leaned forward and tried to kiss her, hoping some affection might ease the tension. She just frowned and walked over to Nessie instead, kissing her on the forehead and rubbing her back. I stood by the door with my arms crossed, tired and feeling rejected. But even in my moment of bitterness, I couldn't help being touched by a mother's love for her child.

When headlights flashed over the lawn, I knew a car was coming. It was another sign that we were living in suburbia because I never would have noticed before. A Volkswagen stopped in front of our house, and it was Ruth's coworker Janice. Ruth grabbed her purse from the table. As she whisked by me, she gave me a smirk that was more playful than scolding, and I knew her anger had subsided. She would forgive me for being late, but it probably wouldn't be until morning.

Once she left, I went into the kitchen and reheated some chicken stew, knowing that Nessie would soon start getting drowsy. Loosening my tie, I sat beside her, shoveling the food into my mouth like it was coal for a dying fire. What I felt wasn't hunger, however, but more the vacant longing of a body that hadn't had nourishment in several hours. I was uncomfortably anxious, and the first moments of calm after a hectic day were always the worst. In many ways, I envied Ruth's job because, even though she had to experience the horrors of illness and death, she also got to see people get better. In crime, there were no happy endings, only the bleak and uncertain satisfaction of justice, and even that was a rare thing.

When Nessie giggled, I looked up. The TV cut to a special bulletin. All at once, I felt my blood pressure rise.

WE INTERRUPT *this program to report that the Boston Police officer shot today during a bank robbery in Kenmore Square has died.*

......

I FELT a soothing warmth along my entire back, against my shoulders. Under the haze of slumber, the sensation blended easily with my dreams, and I could have continued sleeping. But when I smelled perfume, felt the delicate touch of fingers, I was startled awake.

"Shhh," I heard, and it was Ruth.

"Nessie..." I grumbled, my eyes still closed, my arms wrapped around the pillow.

"She's fine. Out cold, just like you."

Ruth ran her hands through my hair, her sweet breath tickling the side of my neck.

"I heard what happened," she said, a soft sadness in her voice. "Jody, I'm so sorry."

I responded with a nod, thinking about Jerry and the five broken-hearted kids who would be in the receiving line at the funeral. Of all the horrors I had seen, both in Korea and on the streets, I could think of nothing worse.

"Did you know him well?"

"Well enough," I said, staring out at the darkness, the vague form of the dresser, the outline of the closet.

"Were you two friends?"

Again, I just nodded. How could I explain the vast web of relationships I had made growing up? It was a city where everyone knew everyone, from the days of playing stickball to joining the military to eventually returning home and getting a government job. Boston was one giant, extended family, chaotic and fractured in its loyalties. Ruth had had two best friends her whole life, a girl from her childhood in California and her college roommate, who now gave skiing lessons in Vermont and raised alpacas.

"We were friends," I said.

"I'm so, so sorry."

"These things happen."

She paused for a moment, her mouth just inches from my ear.

"Do you have your appointment this week?" she whispered.

"Yeah."

With her lying behind me, I couldn't see her face, but somehow I knew she was smiling. She snuggled even closer, her breasts pressed into my back. Then I felt her hand slide around my stomach and down. In an instant, I was aroused. I craned my neck and our lips met, and only then did I realize she had on a negligée. It had all been planned. If it didn't make up for the argument earlier, it was a good move toward reconciliation.

I rolled over in the bed, and we embraced, her muffled moans sending me into quiet ecstasy. I had just started to slip her gown up over her head when we heard something and stopped. Our eyes met in the shadowy light, a look of mutual frustration. But it was a tender disappointment and one I could accept. The murmur in the distance soon turned to crying, and I watched with a smile as Ruth clumsily pulled herself together and went to tend to Nessie.

CHAPTER 3

SOME DAYS IT FELT LIKE IT WASN'T MY CITY ANYMORE—SOME DAYS I felt like I was living on another planet. In less than two decades, Boston had gone from a small seaport to a shiny metropolis. The tenement blocks of the old West End had all been torn down, its poor and elderly residents evicted to make room for high-rises. Scollay Square, that seedy district of tattoo parlors, strip clubs, and gambling dens had been obliterated, replaced by the airy plaza of the new city hall. In Back Bay, the Prudential Tower rose from where the rail yards once were, now the tallest building in the world outside New York City. Everywhere around me, the old was being replaced by the new.

It wasn't just physical transformations because society was changing too. Throughout the Sixties, Boston had escaped some of the worst violence and upheaval. Unlike places like Newark or Detroit, the closest we had to a race riot was when a rally by some angry welfare mothers led to two nights of looting. A few people were injured, and no one was killed. But it left longtime residents with the feeling that the walls had been breached, the castle overcome. In the quiet safety of the city's ancient neighborhoods, people were starting to realize they weren't immune from the problems of the wider world.

As I drove up Beacon Street, I reached for my cigarettes on the dash. I had only taken my eyes off the road for a split second, but in the crowded mayhem of the morning rush, it was too long. I punched the brakes and screeched to a stop.

Standing at my bumper were two young women and a man, all dressed in faded jeans and suede coats, their hair long and straggly. They didn't seem concerned, plodding by and holding up traffic with smug indifference. When I beeped the horn, one of the girls looked back, and I threw up my hands. She took a drag on her cigarette and blew smoke rings at me.

"Fucking hippies," I said.

I cut the wheel and went around them. The incident left me fuming, and it often seemed like there were more students than people in Boston. I sped to headquarters and rushed inside, stopping at the bubbler before going to see the captain. I knocked once at the door and went in.

"Detective," he said, looking up from his desk. "You okay?"

"Traffic."

"Speaking of. The getaway car was found in Cambridge this morning. '66 Ford Impala. White."

"Any leads?" I asked.

"Just the ones on the battery," he said. "It was hot-wired, stolen from a house in Dorchester."

Even if the timing had been appropriate, the joke wasn't funny. But Captain Paul Egersheim wasn't known for his tact or his humor. Short and awkward, he had a thick mustache and a wisp of hair at the top of his head, giving him the impression of a younger Groucho Marx. He came to homicide after Captain Jackson died two years earlier, replacing a man who had led the department for thirty years. Rumors were that he had once hoped to be a great horse trainer, which explained why he had spent the previous decade in charge of the mounted unit. He smoked in the office, his ashtray always overflowing with butts. Considering Jackson hated cigarettes, it was almost a sacrilege.

"What do you know about SDS?" he asked.

"*Students for a Democratic Society*? Just what I hear in the news. Anti-war activists."

"They're more than activists. They're revolutionaries."

"So much for peace and love."

"The organization split last year."

"At that convention in Chicago, I read about it," I said, unable to contain my contempt. "Radicals vs. the super radicals."

"Leninists vs. Maoists, but you're basically right."

Even if I didn't understand the difference, I was glad to know idealists couldn't get along.

"It's the same car that was used in The National Guard armory robbery last Sunday," he went on. He reached for the report, a single hand-typed sheet of paper, scribbled with notes. "Objects found inside included a pack of Kent cigarettes, two empty coffee cups, and..." He extended the word *and*, building up the suspense. "...a small booklet, *Manual for Marxists*..."

After fifteen years on the force, I thought I had seen everything, but I didn't know much about political crimes.

The door opened, and I craned my neck to see Harrigan. As usual, he was impeccably dressed, his suit ironed and his tie-knot a perfect triangle. When he sat down next to me, he seemed flustered, and I knew it wasn't from rushing to get to work. After years of being single, he was finally dating someone, and that gleam on his forehead, that sparkle in his eyes, told me he might even be in love.

"We were just discussing the Shawmut Bank," the captain said. "We believe it was radicals. Same group that hit the armory."

"A strange target for people who hate capitalism," I snickered.

"Everyone needs funding, even traitors," Egersheim said, the word *traitors* harsh but accurate. "They wanna wreak havoc on society. Look what they did in Greenwich Village."

An explosion the previous March had not only destroyed a town-house, but it had also shocked the nation, making people see how dangerous the more militant radicals were. The Weather Underground had been building bombs intended for government targets, and the fact that one went off prematurely, killing three members was, to many, cosmic justice.

"The chief has ordered a task force," the captain said. "It will include us, of course. The State Police..."

As he read, my mind drifted, and fatigue was always worse when I was sitting. I hadn't slept well since Nessie came into our lives, the protective instinct of a parent, always watchful and always worried.

"Lieutenant? Are you listening?"

I snapped out of the daydream and sat up.

"Yes, sir."

"...Two agents from the FBI," Egersheim continued, squinting to read the memo. "Paul Shine and Mark Marecki—"

"Marcus," I said.

He looked up, seeming almost irritated.

"What?"

"It's Marcus," I said.

"You've worked together?"

"We knew each other as kids."

The captain responded with an awkward smile. I knew he wasn't surprised, but sometimes I got the feeling he was jealous, remarking more than once that I *seemed to know everybody*. He had grown up in Newton, a wealthy suburb that was close to the city by distance but far in mindset. Like everyone, he had started as a patrolman, but after a brief detour in forensics, he ended up with the mounties, supervising a unit that now was used mostly for parades. For much of his career, Egersheim had chosen to stay out of the fray, and we suspected the only reason he got the captain job was because his sister-in-law was married to the nephew of the chief. Either way, I was never convinced his heart was in it.

"There's gonna be another Vietnam protest on the Boston Common in three weeks. Every troublemaker from Berkeley to Brandeis will be there. Chief wants these jerks nabbed before then. We don't want them hiding in plain sight."

Finally, he closed the case folder. The meeting was over. I glanced over at Harrigan, and we got up. As we made our way to the door, the captain called, and we both turned.

"I'm sorry about Donlan," he said, and I felt the blood leave my face. "Really, I am."

If it hadn't sounded so sincere, I would have been more insulted than I was. But the truth was, Jerry, or 'Giraffe' as his friends called him, had always kept a low profile. All the rank and file knew him, but among the senior staff, he was just another sergeant. With almost fifteen hundred cops, the department had more Duggans and Donlans than anyone could count. Still, the remark made the captain look like a fool.

"Thanks," I said. "And it's Duggan. Gerald Duggan."

CHAPTER 4

Harrigan and I drove down Dorchester Avenue, a wide road that started by the abandoned docks of Fort Point Channel and ended at the Baker Chocolate Factory, just yards from the border of suburban Milton. Along the way, it passed dozens of communities, separate and unique in their own ways, endless blocks of three-decker homes and mom-and-pop shops, Irish taverns, and restaurants that served everything from Jamaican patties to Portuguese Bacalhau. It was a microcosm of the city, a cross-section of every immigrant group, and had a claustrophobic charm. Somewhere on that stretch, wedged between the highway and the industrial no-man's-land of South Bay, was a small neighborhood. Because of its unique shape and the people who settled there, it was known as The Polish Triangle.

We turned onto Locust Street, a tiny dead-end that once went straight through before the expressway was built. On it were a few scattered houses, rundown and weather-beaten, but the block was mostly commercial, with a warehouse, a junkyard, and vacant lots between.

I pulled over and got out, stepping over some broken glass. The street was quiet, the only sound the constant rush of cars on the highway and some seagulls squawking above. A bank robbery with the suspects on the run was going to take more than a survey of where the getaway car was stolen. But I had learned from Jackson the best place to start with any investigation was at the beginning.

Lighting a cigarette, I stared over at the house that had reported the theft, a small gray A-frame with cracked shingles and peeling paint. One side abutted a brick building; the other had a narrow yard cluttered with things; a rusted mower, a sawhorse, trash barrels.

"Strange place to steal a getaway car," Harrigan said.

"You know a better one?"

The side of his lips curled in what I knew to be a restrained smirk.

"But if it was hippies, they certainly went out of their way," I added, flicking my cigarette. When it landed near some trash, I went to stamp it out, and Harrigan mumbled something.

"What?" I asked, glancing back.

"Students," he said, gazing across the roof of the car. "Not hippies."

"Aren't they the same?—"

Suddenly, something creaked. We looked over, and the front door of the house opened. In the shadow of the vestibule, I saw an old woman, her hair in curlers. I waved to Harrigan, and we walked over, stopping at the fence.

"Ma'am," I said, and she blinked like she suddenly realized we were there. "We understand your car was stolen last Saturday?"

She looked confused, her fat jowls tense, her eyes suspicious. After staring at us for close to a minute, she turned her head and shouted something in a foreign language. Moments later, a young man appeared in the doorway. He was tall and thin, with dark curly hair and a goatee, reminding me of Carlos Santana. His shirt was unbuttoned, revealing a bony chest and a cross around his neck.

"Are you Stanislaw Sokol?"

"Yeah? Whaddya want?" he asked, and as I reached for my badge, he added, "Don't bother, I know who you guys are."

I paused, glancing at Harrigan.

"A car was reported stolen from this address," I said.

"I know. It was mine. I reported it."

"Did you know it was involved in a bank robbery yesterday?"

"I heard. And I'm sorry about your brother officer."

The remark caught me off guard, and considering how cold he was, I appreciated it even more.

"Any idea who might have taken it?" I asked.

I knew it sounded naïve, but I had to ask.

"Beats me. Shit gets ripped off all the time around here," he said, an honest answer because the area had so much crime.

"Thank you," I said.

I looked at the old woman, who stood crouched next to him, and smiled. The man put his arm around her and guided her back inside, glaring at us before slamming the door.

Harrigan and I walked back and got in the car.

"Find out who that guy was," I said. "See if he has a record."

"What makes you think he has a record?"

"Everyone around here does."

We drove to the end of the street and turned onto Dorchester Avenue. The road was a dense stretch of three-decker homes, flat-roofed monstrosities that made up for in utility what they lacked in elegance. The ground floors all had shops, their colorful signs giving the impression of an Eastern European village—Café Krakow, Pokarowski's Deli, Zaborski's shoe repair. Outside a deli, the red and white of the Polish flag flew beside the American flag.

When we reached the next light, I watched a man walk out of a corner store, a paper bag in his arms. The moment I realized who it was, I turned the wheel and sped across the street, cutting off oncoming traffic. Car horns honked, drivers raised their fists, and pedestrians looked over.

"Lieutenant?"

Harrigan braced himself, but by now he was used to my crazy driving.

I pulled to the corner and rolled down my window.

"Marcus!" I yelled out.

He looked back and then started walking toward the car, an amused grin on his face.

"Jody?" he said, "For chrissakes, you trying to cause a pileup?"

"The only way around traffic is through it."

He shifted the bag in his arms and stooped a little, nodding to Harrigan.

"What're you doing around here?" he asked.

"I was gonna ask you the same thing."

"Visiting my mother. She don't get out like she used to."

"In Dorchester?"

"I grew up on Bellflower Street."

I sat surprised, my hand on the steering wheel and peering up. In the harsh afternoon light, he smiled, and I saw the dimples I remembered as a kid.

"I figured you ended up in Martha's Vineyard," I joked.

"Not even close."

He smiled but said no more. It was obvious he didn't want to talk about the past on a busy street corner.

"What's your take on the robbery?" I asked.

Stepping closer, he leaned in as much as he could with the bag.

"Student radicals," he said. "You hear what they found in the car?"

"I did. I'm more interested in where they got the car," I said, nodding toward Locust Street. "A bit out of the way. No?"

When our eyes locked, I couldn't tell if he agreed or not. The bureau was good with the technical aspects of crime-solving, but agents weren't known for their dazzling intuition.

"Who knows? Maybe they came off the highway? Stole the first jalopy they could find?"

An elderly couple passed by holding hands, the man in a shabby suit and his wife wearing a traditional dress. They said something to Marcus, and he replied in Polish.

"Listen, Jody, I gotta go," he said. "Give me a call."

"We're both on the task force."

"Then you have no choice."

He flashed a tense smile and walked away. I backed out into the street and made a U-turn in traffic, almost causing another scene. At the next light, I reached for a cigarette and Harrigan looked at me.

"That man. How do you know him?"

"You met him," I said. "He's with the bureau."

"But how do you *know him?*"

The light turned green, and I hit the gas, fumbling with my lighter.

"It's a long story."

CHAPTER 5

"A<small>RE YOU UPSET YOU NEVER STAYED IN TOUCH?</small>"

I lay slumped in the stiff leather chair, my hands clasped and fidgety.

"There was no way to stay in touch back then," I said.

The room was dim but not dark, the window shade drawn almost to the bottom, revealing just a sliver of light from outside. Dr. Sandra Kaplan sat across from me, one leg crossed over the other, a notebook on her lap. Her hair was pulled back in a tidy bun; her glasses hung loosely on her nose. She wore a white blouse with a navy skirt, her body lean and her curves unusually defined for a fifty-year-old woman.

I sometimes forgot about her handicap, the two missing fingers on her right hand. She had lost them to hypothermia as a girl when her family fled to the woods after the Nazis invaded their small Hungarian town. By some miracle, they survived the winter of '44 and the war, arriving in America two years later and settling among the hordes of Jewish refugees in Washington Heights, New York. She never told me her story outright, but I gleaned it in small pieces over our weekly meetings. Something about her past made my own childhood seem less unfortunate, and that was why I trusted her. I was as interested in her life as she was in mine, which strained the professional boundaries she was obliged to uphold.

"What was he like?"

I shrugged my shoulders.

"Always in trouble," I said, recalling the time Marcus stole a cake from the kitchen and dropped it out a third-floor window. "But we all were."

I had been seeing her since the spring after Ruth threatened to leave the house and take Nessie with her. It wasn't so much that we argued, although we did, but my temper was getting worse and not better. I would fly into a rage over things as simple as burning toast or losing my car keys. There were other incidents too, the restless nights when, in a fit of insomnia, I would get up and wander the neighborhood with my handgun tucked into my waistband. She worried I was sleepwalking and maybe I was, although I felt conscious. But movement was the only thing that would calm my mind and my soul. Whether it was my youth, the war, or my job, I didn't know, but the demons of my past were starting to resurface. And running into Marcus after all these years only encouraged them.

"Was he there for your whole childhood?"

The farther back I went, the more uneasy I got.

"Yeah, I guess. Until he left," I said, and she smirked at the sarcasm.

Marcus and I had spent the first ten years of our lives together, two children among two hundred in a giant brick orphanage called the *Roxbury Home for Stray Boys*. On the backstreets of Roxbury, it was a harsh institution with an impossible goal, and even the name suggested the desperation of its charges. I arrived as a baby, having no memories of my birth parents, and he showed up at three, taken from his home after his father smashed his head with an iron ice clamp. It didn't kill him, but it left him with a permanent bump that was most obvious when the barbers came to shave our heads each month. Together, we played relievio in the yard, ate dinner on the cold benches of the basement cafeteria, and attended the nearby elementary school.

"Do you plan to see him again?"

"Yeah. We're on the same case."

Smiling warmly, she averted her eyes. Somehow, she understood without having to ask.

"I read about the officer who was killed. I'm very sorry. Did you know him?"

I chuckled. It was a question only a civilian could ask.

"Yes," was all I said.

"Do you want to talk about it?"

"No."

She raised her eyes and scribbled something on her notepad. For all the private shame of getting professional help, I enjoyed my time with her. She was easy to talk to, and in my line of work, there weren't many conversations that didn't involve some kind of competition, posturing, or evasion. In the small room, between the dropped ceiling and white walls, I experienced a level of honesty I couldn't get anywhere else, except with Ruth. And even though I told myself I was doing it for her and for our marriage, I couldn't deny I enjoyed the sessions.

"How are things at home?" she asked.

My thoughts came back to the present.

"Better."

"Better?"

"Good."

"Have you been going out together?"

It would have been easier to say yes—she had been suggesting it for weeks—but I hadn't lied to her yet. With our staggered work schedules, Ruth and I were like passing ships. All it took was one or two overtime shifts from either of us and a week could go by without us talking about more than bills and Nessie's nap schedule.

"Not...not really," I said. "Still haven't found a sitter."

She sighed, but it sounded more out of sympathy than disappointment. I was glad when the alarm rang, signaling our time was over. I could only deal with so many problems at once.

"Try to make some time together," she said, and we both got up.

"I will."

After we shook, I reached into my pocket and handed her a check. It was strange giving someone money after being so personal with them, almost like paying a prostitute. Psychotherapy wasn't something I was familiar with. Before I had gone, I would have scoffed at the idea, having been raised in a world where sentimentality was scorned and weakness reviled. When someone hurt you, you hurt them back, regardless of whether the pain was physical or emotional. What was hard to accept was the fact I was seeing a shrink, something so farfetched that whenever I thought about it, I would laugh. But I always felt good afterward, a goodness that was only rivaled by the fear I had that someone might find out. Of all my mistakes, disappointments, and regrets, it was my biggest secret.

I took a rickety elevator down, squeezing out the narrow doors and into the lobby. The building had a faded splendor, with marble walls and gilded plaster-leaf cornice, a relic from the turn of the century when architecture was as much about elegance as it was about function. It had once been a prestigious address, but as the city's financial district drifted eastward, so did all the law firms and investment companies. Now it was mostly psychiatrists' and psychologists' offices and was so well-known for mental health treatment that people called it *Headcase Hotel*.

I walked out into Downtown Crossing, a 10-block pedestrian zone of restaurants, department stores, jewelers, and pawnshops. The air was crisp, the smell of the ocean wafting from the harbor beyond. Across the street, a dozen students were near the entrance to Jordan Marsh, dressed in sloppy clothing and faded jeans, their shirts untucked. They were chanting anti-war slogans, handing out leaflets, and one held a sign that said: NO PEACE FOR NIXON. Most people ignored them, but one or two stopped to listen. Some cops stood nearby, making sure their public demonstration didn't rise to the level of harassment. If I had learned anything in the past few years, it was that protests couldn't be stopped, but they could be contained.

When one of the officers looked over, I got a creeping panic. I didn't know if he recognized me, but I didn't want to be seen coming out of that building. So I turned and quickly went in the other direction.

·······

I BARRELED into the driveway like it was the end of a road race. The sun was setting, but it still wasn't dark, and I had finally made it home on time. I left my briefcase in the car—I never used it anyway—and got out. As I hurried up the walkway, Esther next door was getting the mail. In her jumper and green turtleneck, she didn't look half bad; all the young wives in the neighborhood had a certain seductive charm. When she smiled, I waved and went up the stairs.

I opened the door and the moment I stepped in, I stopped.

"Hello?"

Sitting on the couch was a woman, probably in her mid-sixties, with a stout body and gray shoulder-length hair. She grinned and stood up, smoothing out her dress. Before I could say anything, Ruth walked in from the kitchen carrying Nessie, who had on a bib and was still chewing her dinner.

"Jody," she said, out of breath. "This is Nadia."

"Nadia?"

"She's going to be helping us with Nessie. A few hours a day. So you don't have to rush home."

Inside, I fumed. I told myself it was because we hadn't agreed to hire a caretaker, but the truth was, I didn't trust anyone watching my daughter. When Nessie reached toward me, Ruth handed her over, and I held her protectively.

"Nice to meet you," I said, and the woman just nodded.

Nessie grabbed my face, her hands covered in mashed potatoes, and all my anger subsided.

A car stopped out front, and I glanced over at the clock on the mantel, cringing when I saw it was 5:40—I wasn't as early as I had thought. Ruth kissed Nessie on the cheek, grabbed her coat and purse, and was gone. It all happened so fast that I stood frozen in the hallway, the woman looking over with a nervous smile.

She had the sturdiness of a hausfrau, with thick forearms and legs, her ankles swollen under her nylons, either from arthritis or high blood pressure. She reminded me of all the foreign grandmothers I had known growing up. She was too fair to be Greek, and her face was too round for an Italian. Either way, I could tell by the way she grunted that she was hesitant to speak English, and I wished Ruth had warned me.

I put Nessie down on the couch, and she didn't fuss. Her eyes went straight to the television, the pacifier of the new age. I walked upstairs to the bedroom, and put my wallet on the dresser, my .38 in the drawer. Coming back down, I heard activity in the kitchen and saw Nadia cleaning up.

"Are you from the area?" I asked.

She turned around, a broom in her hand.

"Dorchester," she said, rolling the r's.

"I grew up next door...Roxbury."

She made a wide grin but didn't answer. We stood facing each other for a few awkward seconds until I smiled and walked away. When I came into the living room, Nessie was holding a bottle in both hands, her little fingers gripping the glass. She giggled when she saw me, and I always loved that children could laugh for no reason. The nightly news was on, Walter Cronkite recounting the day's events, the death of President Nasser in Egypt, Nixon's visit to the Vatican. After a commercial break, it flashed to the story of two police officers shot in Cleveland, one killed and the other wounded, victims of a radical gunman from the Black Panthers.

I ran over and changed the channel, not wanting her exposed to the horrors of the world. But she probably didn't see it anyway, her eyes drowsy and head bobbing. Sitting down, I put my arm around her, overcome by a similar exhaustion. As I sank into the couch, I put my head back and closed my eyes.

Sometime later, I awoke. My arm was in the same position, but Nessie was gone. I jumped off the couch and ran upstairs, bursting into her bedroom like I was executing a search warrant. In the dim glow of the nightlight, I saw her snuggled under the blanket, asleep. My panic went away, but I was still worked up, my heart pounding and body tense. As I went back downstairs, I saw that Nadia's coat was gone. I was grateful for her help but horrified that Nessie could be taken from my arms and brought to bed without me noticing.

The moment I reached the bottom step, the front door opened.

"Jody?"

"I was just checking on her," I said before she could ask.

"Are you okay? You're as white as a sheet."

I nodded, my lip twitching and slightly dizzy.

"Yeah. I'm fine."

CHAPTER 6

I STOOD IN THE PEW, SHOULDER TO SHOULDER, THE CHURCH SO PACKED with grieving friends and relatives that the combined smell of cologne and perfume made me nauseous. I hated tight places, a hang-up from my years in the Army. I had almost forgotten Jerry Duggan was in the military until I saw the two soldiers in the front, sitting with their backs straight, their white caps pointed. Beside them were Jack's widow and his five children, three girls in white dresses, two boys in plaid suits. The youngest of them all, a four-year-old with blonde braids, was leaning against her mother, sobbing quietly. Just the sight of it got me choked up, the thought of my daughter in the same situation. Before Nessie, I had never considered the risks of the job, or if I did, I assumed Ruth could always find another man. But no one could replace a father.

The organ thundered, echoing through the vaulted ceiling of Mission Church, the ancient cathedral. People started to rustle, shifting in their benches, and moments later, a dozen pallbearers came up the aisle, Duggan's body resting for eternity in the pillowed comfort of the shiny black casket. While women wept openly, men had that contorted look of restrained grief, their faces red and nostrils flared. I knew the feeling because I had it, the overwhelming urge to break down but the absolute determination not to. I would never cry in public, or in private. I had been taught young that any outward emotion that didn't involve either fear or rage was a sign of weakness.

After the pallbearers exited, people filed out. At the back, I noticed Harrigan, his towering figure standing alone, one of only a handful of black faces in the crowd. As the procession gradually moved, I met him by the doors, and we walked out together.

The receiving line was mobbed, so I avoided it, knowing I would have time to give my condolences at the cemetery. I had met Jack's wife over the years, but we were never close, and once he got married, he kept his personal and professional lives apart. But I was with him on his first date, something we always joked about, the night I found myself in the same row as him and Susan at the opening of *East of Eden*. The coincidence was something neither of us ever forgot, although I could never remember the girl I had gone with.

Over on the sidewalk, Captain Egersheim was standing with some police officials in dark coats and gray hats. They ranged from captains to superintendents, all the top brass, and there might have been a chief or two from other towns. Harrigan and I were close enough to say hello, but they were talking, and I didn't want to interrupt. Even in the civilian confines of a funeral, hierarchy and rank were respected, and I never liked to be too chummy with the higher-ups.

We stepped aside and stood on the grass, watching as hundreds of people poured out. In the receiving line, there were officers from across the state, dramatic in their dress uniforms, shoes gleaming. Aside from whispered condolences and the tapping of feet, there was a poignant silence that only added to the solemness of the service. It was hard not to feel some tragic pride in being a cop.

The crowd around the family was a sea of blue, broken only by the fleeting image of Jack's wife, shaking hands with a fragile smile. Considering all the tragedy I had witnessed over the years, I had to admire her grace and dignity, not sure I would have been so composed. As I stood watching, some bodies parted and, for a moment, I saw one of Jack's daughters, her head up and looking around with a timid wonder.

"Detective," I heard.

The captain walked over, his hands clasped, and gave us both a warm smile. He had on a long coat, a dark tie, and a gold clip that said something about honor and sacrifice in Latin. I knew he hadn't been in the military, so I assumed it was from the Fraternal Order of Police.

"Holding it together?" he asked, patting my shoulder.

For all my doubts about the man, he was remarkably sympathetic when he had to be.

"Yes, thanks."

By now, he knew Duggan and I had been close. But I wasn't the only one, and Giraffe was the type of guy who had decided early on that he would rather have a hundred casual friends than a few good ones. Almost everyone on the force knew him, and those who didn't were either rookies or men in specialized units like the harbor patrol or internal investigations.

"We're going to Mulcahy's after the burial," Egersheim said. "I hope you gentlemen will join us."

I glanced over at Harrigan, who looked back with a silent dread. Despite our differences, we both hated barrooms, and neither of us drank; Harrigan because he didn't like the taste and me because I liked it too much. But standing outside the church in the presence of so many fellow officers, neither of us was in a position to say no.

"Of course," I said. "We'll be there."

......

THE DRIVE from Mt. Calvary Cemetery to downtown was almost as somber as the burial itself. I wasn't surprised when it started to sprinkle—it always seemed to rain on funeral days. Harrigan hadn't said a word since we left. He sat leaning toward the half-opened window, waving his hand while I had one cigarette after another. Like Captain Jackson, he disapproved of my smoking, something he let me know the first day we worked together. It was my one last vice, but after two bronchial infections the winter before, I was considering giving it up.

"You could have just said no."

I looked over with a smirk.

"Pardon?"

"The bar. You could have just said *no*."

"You don't have to go," I said.

"I meant for you."

While I appreciated the concern, I was long past the point of being bothered by booze. And if anyone should have been apprehensive, it was him. A bar full of rowdy white cops, many of them senior officers, was no place for a black detective.

"We'll stay a half an hour, pay our respects," I said.

"I believe we just did that."

"To the brass. We'll just make an appearance."

Soon we reached the South End, a vast stretch of brick rowhouses that was a poor cousin to the fancy Back Bay on its western border. What had once been a genteel neighborhood for the city's professional class was now rundown. Tremont Street, the main thoroughfare, was lined with liquor stores, jazz joints, dime stores, and laundromats. Homeless men congregated on the street corners and in the parks. Occasionally, a prostitute would appear from the shadow of an alleyway.

We turned down East Berkeley Street, where the area became less residential and more industrial, and there, in the shadow of the elevated railway, was Mulcahy's. The bar was famous or infamous, depending on who you talked to and had been a hangout for cops for half a century. It was the type of place where the windows were gray with cigarette smoke and your feet stuck to the floor from beer spilled the night before. The walls were exposed brick, and old beams ran the length of the ceiling, as thick and sturdy as the masts of a schooner. The building had originally been a horse stable, and the rumor was that whenever it rained, you could still smell manure. I spent many nights there in my rookie years, but I hadn't been back in a decade and was sure nothing had changed.

Knowing we wouldn't be long, I parked in front of a hydrant, and we got out. As we walked toward the door, I opened it for Harrigan, but he insisted I go first. Inside was packed. If the capacity was sixty, there was probably twice that number. Men—and it was all men— were huddled around tables, and squeezed into corners, many still with their coats on. It had been chilly at the cemetery, but the room was heating up fast, and already I was feeling claustrophobic.

I started to walk and Harrigan followed me. I said hello to people I knew, nodded to those I didn't, and I had the feeling that everyone was watching. Some men had cocktails, but most were drinking beer and hard liquor. I knew it would only be an hour or so before things got sloppy, and there was no better excuse to get drunk than a funeral.

"Brae?!"

I turned and saw Egersheim waving from the bar. Standing beside him was Chief McNamara, his gut protruding from his starched white shirt. There were other officials too, a couple of men from the Bureau of Criminal Investigations, a lieutenant from the K-9 unit.

"Gentlemen," the captain said as we walked up.

His face was splotchy like he had just come in from a snowstorm, and I could tell he had already had a few drinks.

"Detectives," the chief said, breaking from his conversation to greet us. "What can I get you?"

He leaned against the bar, and the bartender came right over.

"Just soda water," I said, then I looked at Harrigan.

"The same, please."

McNamara frowned, but I could tell he was only joking.

"Sorry about Duggan," he said, handing me my drink. "I know you two were tight."

I accepted his sympathies with a humble smile, and we toasted.

"We've got some info—" Egersheim said before McNamara interrupted him.

"There's a group that's been stirring up trouble. They call themselves the United Labor Front."

"Unions?" I asked.

"Hardly," he said with a chuckle. "They're a faction of SDS. Hardcore communists. They wanna use violence to overthrow the government."

The captain nodded in agreement, adding, "We believe they were the ones who hit the armory."

"Don't believe," McNamara said, and the captain got flustered. "We *know*."

Where Captain Jackson and the chief had always spoken as equals, Egersheim acted like a fawning sidekick.

"They were probably the ones who organized the takeover of University Hall at Harvard last year too," the chief went on.

"And the Black Panthers march last spring."

With all the noise, the back and forth was hard to follow, and a barroom after a funeral was no place for a refresher on political movements. When I felt a splash on my neck, I turned around. Someone had spilled a beer. The crowd was starting to annoy me, and when I looked at Harrigan, I could tell he wanted to go. We had only been there twenty minutes, but it was long enough. Now that we had a caretaker, Ruth didn't have to wait for me. But Nadia still had to get home, so it was a good excuse to leave.

"I've gotta go relieve the babysitter," I said.

The chief and Egersheim looked disappointed, but they didn't argue. I was sure they remembered what it was like to have young kids.

"Get some rest, Brae," the chief said, and Egersheim just smiled.

We headed toward the door and just in time because someone started singing *Johnny We Hardly Knew Ye*. Soon the whole room joined in, a chorus of half-drunk voices, slobbering and out of tune.

When we burst out onto the sidewalk, I felt like I had just come up for air. The temperature had dropped, and the sun was almost set. Walking over to the car, I noticed an orange ticket on the windshield. It was a bitter end to a tough day, and even Harrigan grinned at the irony. I pulled the citation out from under the wiper, crumpled it in a ball, and tossed it, knowing I would have it fixed later.

We got in, and I made a wide U-turn. As we passed under the elevated tracks, a train rattled by overhead and sent a sheet of water down over my windshield and hood. We reached the intersection at Tremont Street, and I was just about to go left toward Roxbury when Harrigan stopped me.

"Sorry, can you drop me off in Kenmore Square?"

"Kenmore Square?" I asked.

"610 Beacon Street. I'm going to see Delilah."

I hit the gas and continued straight down Massachusetts Avenue, the lights of the Citgo Sign glowing in the distance.

In all our time working together, he had never had a girlfriend, and at times I suspected he was queer. He lived in an apartment across from Franklin Park with his mother, an aging Caribbean woman with a gentle island lilt and a talent for making stews. Her husband had died when Harrigan was young, drowned after the Coast Guard ship he was on sank in a hurricane in '44. She never remarried and had lived alone until Harrigan moved in a couple of years before. He said it was to save money, but I knew it was to help her. As an only child, he had always been a doting son.

I pulled up and stopped at the address, a nine-story brick building.

"When do I get to meet this girl?" I asked.

"In due time, Lieutenant."

Before he got out, we shook hands, something we didn't usually do. But after a long and emotional day, we were all reaffirming our friendships and loyalties.

He shut the door, and I watched as his towering figure walked up to the entrance. In some ways I was envious, remembering those early days of romance, all the excitement and uncertainty. But it wasn't lost completely because Ruth—and womanhood in general—was as mysterious to me now as it was then.

I drove through Kenmore Square, the sidewalks crowded with students going in and out of the dingy bars and diners. Music was blaring from a nearby dorm, Curtis Mayfield or maybe Stevie Wonder. In front of a record shop, I saw a group of hippies, young men with long hair and barefoot girls in faded blue jeans.

Waiting at the light, I looked over to the Shawmut Bank, thinking how only three days before, it was where Jerry Duggan lost his life.

For many of us, time had come to a standstill that day, and now everything was back to normal.

I was so lost in thought that I didn't realize the light had turned. When someone behind me beeped, I hit the horn and glared back at them. I almost got out but stopped myself just in time, punching the gas and speeding through the intersection.

My temper was so sudden, so violent, that it often left me shaken and confused. I always said it was from the war, but the truth was I was angry long before Korea. And although I had learned to live with it, I always feared the day I could no longer control it.

CHAPTER 7

Victoria's Diner was one of the last of the old-time haunts, built after the Second World War by a Greek wise guy who needed a place to hide the money he made from bookmaking and other schemes. Situated on a lonely block of Massachusetts Avenue, it was at the junction of four neighborhoods—Dorchester, South Boston, Roxbury, and the South End—and therefore was not part of any. The area was technically called the *market district*, but anyone expecting the bustle of a Turkish bazaar would have been disappointed to find an industrial backwater of warehouses, truck stops, and commercial fisheries.

The restaurant had wide booths and dark paneled walls. By the back wall, a jukebox flashed, creating the illusion of a Buck Rogers robot in the low and smokey light. It shut down for a couple of hours each night, but it was never really closed, and you could get Salisbury steak at sunrise and pancakes after midnight.

"You've done well, Jody."

I stirred my coffee and looked up at Marcus.

"I'd say you've done better."

I said it as a compliment, not because I believed it. But on the petty scale of public sector achievement, someone who made the FBI had higher status than a city cop.

"Let's just say we've both done well," he said with a warm smile.

"Well, we made it out, if that's what you mean."

As I lit a cigarette, I noticed that his knuckles were swollen, either from recent damage or years of abuse. Thinking about Dr. Kaplan's injury, I realized that everything I needed to know about a person's past or personality, I could tell by their hands.

"A case in Springfield," he said before I could ask.

"Must have been a tough arrest."

"Some thugs were trying to extort a judge. One of them thought I was the judge."

"You weren't flattered?"

"All us Polacks look the same."

I laughed, but it was an odd remark from someone who, as an orphan, didn't know his family history.

"Marecki?" I asked, curiously.

I had always known him as *Evans*, but I wasn't surprised it had changed. In the tumultuous world of foster care and institutions, last names were as impermanent as everything else.

"My adopted parents are from Poland."

"Explains why I saw you on Dorchester Ave."

"I try to get back as much as I can," he said. "But I live in Humarock now—"

"Away from the hustle?"

He looked down with a guilty grin. While it was only a friendly dig, the subject of fleeing the city for the suburbs was always uncomfortable.

"I won't lie. I like the peace and quiet."

"I'm sure you get plenty of it."

"I live at the end of a spit, beside an old Army tower. The most trouble I have is when the local kids go inside it and raise hell."

"Married?"

Leaning back in the booth, he crossed his arms with a long, simmering smile that brought out his dimples.

"As single as a pringle," he said. "How about you?"

"Three years now. Her name is Ruth."

"I bet she's a lovely girl. Any kids?"

"A daughter, Nessie."

"Nessie? Like the Loch Ness monster?" he asked, and I laughed.

"Ernestine, actually. She's named after my old captain, Ernest Jackson. He died two years ago."

"Sorry to hear. Were you two close?"

"Yeah...yeah," I said, stumbling. At certain times and in certain settings, Jackson's early death still shook me up. "We were close."

The waitress walked over, a thin blonde with faded bell-bottoms, her hair feathered back. She asked if I wanted more coffee, and I said no, Marecki glancing back to check her out as she walked away. We hadn't talked about everything, but we had covered a lot, and the past was always a slog.

"What's your take on the case?" I asked.

"Pretty obvious, I think. Student radicals. SDS. The United Labor Front, maybe. We've been monitoring them since they formed in '69. "

"Don't you think it's strange they left that book in the car?"

Shrugging his shoulders, he reached for his coffee, which had sat untouched since we finished eating.

"We're not dealing with the Dillinger gang here," he said. "These are dumb kids. They probably used it for directions."

"Why hasn't there been an arrest?"

We locked eyes. His expression sharpened. It was a bit of a taunt, but anytime we worked with the bureau, there was a competitive tension. While they had more resources and more prestige, we had a better ground game, and the truth was, in crimes that violated local and federal law, both agencies needed each other.

"Maybe I should be asking you?" he said, finally, and I smirked as if to say *touché*.

The waitress came back, dropped the check on the table, and I grabbed it. I could have stayed longer, but even after the coffee, I felt tired, and I knew Nadia had to leave by eight o'clock.

"You should probably get on the road," I said.

"No rush. I'm staying at my mother's place."

"Good son."

"I do it a couple of nights a week. Keep her company."

I stopped the waitress as she passed, handing her the cash for the bill plus a few extra dollars. We got up and headed toward the front, people looking up as we passed.

"I gotta hit the head," I said.

"Go on, Jody. We'll talk soon. Thanks again for dinner."

We shook hands, and I went to the bathroom, loosening my tie with one hand while I peed into the urinal with the other. When my eyes adjusted, I saw scratched into the tile in front of me *Fuck Pigs*. The diner was far from the revolutionary fervor of places like Cambridge or Kenmore Square, but the dissatisfactions of the young and self-righteous were everywhere.

As I came out, I noticed a young black woman in the corner booth. She glanced up from her strawberry shortcake, and I smiled.

"Lieutenant?"

Turning, I was surprised to see Harrigan with her. He wiped his mouth with a napkin and went to stand, stopping only when he realized the space was too tight.

"This is Delilah," he said.

I held out my hand and we shook, her fingers soft and delicate.

"Jody Brae. Pleased to meet you."

"Likewise," she said.

She was younger than him, something I could tell not only by her appearance but by the way she dressed. She wore snug jeans and a flowered blouse with a wide collar. Giant hoop earrings hung from under her big afro; purple eyeliner accentuated her dark and sensuous eyes.

"What brings you out, Lieutenant?"

I looked around. Even in the dark anonymity of the backstreet diner, I didn't want anyone to know I was a cop.

"Just…a quick bite," I said, not wanting to explain. "And you?"

"I wanted to give her a taste of the real Boston."

"You're not from around here?" I asked her.

"Cleveland, originally," she said, peering up, her lashes fluttering. "I moved here for graduate school."

She had a soft, neutral accent, not devoid of its blackness but more refined than the jive and twang of the ghetto.

"Really? What are you studying?"

"Political science."

I cringed. Of all the majors, it was the one I dreaded the most, and I wished she had said *psychology* or *English literature.* B.U. was a hotbed of social activism, and it always seemed to come out of the political science department. But I was too tired to start making assumptions about my partner's new girlfriend. Not all college students were troublemakers.

"Well, I should get home," I said, bowing to her. "A pleasure."

"The pleasure was mine."

CHAPTER 8

HARRIGAN WALKED IN A MINUTE BEFORE NINE O'CLOCK, BUT IT DIDN'T matter because Captain Egersheim had gone down to the evidence department. As usual, he was clean-shaven and sharply dressed, his suits a steady rotation of black, gray, and navy. But he also seemed agitated, his jacket slightly ruffled, his collar uneven.

"Have fun last night?" I asked.

He took the chair beside me and put down his briefcase, glancing over with a wary frown.

"What's that supposed to mean?"

"*Did you enjoy your date*, that's all."

"It was delightful," he said, crossing one leg over the other and staring straight ahead.

I grinned to myself. He was easy to get riled up. Harrigan had an old-fashioned modesty that many found charming, but I knew masked some deeper insecurities. Even with his dark skin, I could tell when he was blushing. The subjects of romance or sex always made him fret, although he was hardly a prude. All the girls in headquarters were crazy about him, but it was mostly empty flirtation because, in a city where the taboos of interracial mingling were quietly but steadfastly enforced, none would ever dare to date him.

Moments later, Egersheim scurried in with his head down like a distracted professor. His shirt was untucked in the back, his pants wrinkled, and he had on boat shoes with no socks. As casual as Captain Jackson had been—he never wore suits or ties—his clothes were always pressed and perfect.

"We got some composites in," Egersheim said.

As he spread them across the desk, Harrigan and I leaned over to see. They were two charcoal sketches, a man and a woman, about as detailed as stick figures. Artist renderings of suspects were always bad, expressionless faces with beady eyes and undersized mouths, somewhere between the *greys* of UFO lore and a Betty Boop cartoon. The only distinguishing characteristic was that the man had long hair, which wasn't much help in an era where every young person did.

"I think I saw them playing guitar on Boston Common," I said.

The captain made a sour smile.

"Not a Picasso," he said, and it was the wrong analogy. "The depictions aren't great…they're from a milkman. But they're the best we got."

"What about the girl?"

He narrowed his eyes.

"Girl?"

"A young woman who saw the perpetrators. She walked right by the car."

Egersheim looked back at the report.

"We…we don't have…" he said, flipping through the pages. "A woman. Three tourists from Belgium—they were across the street. Several dozen people heard the gunfire, saw the car speeding down Beacon Street. A woman from Brookline saw Officer Duggan on the sidewalk and pulled over."

"There was a girl," I said.

"A young woman," Harrigan corrected.

"She's not on the witness brief. Did you interview her?"

"Not really. We talked to her. She left with two detectives from D4."

"I'll double-check downstairs," he said. "Regardless, we're focusing on Boston University. There's gonna be a meeting Friday night at B.U. *Students for a Democratic Society.*" He hesitated just long enough to frown, a sentiment we all shared. "The word is that the United Labor Front will be there. They've been trying to take over SDS for months. Like the chief said, we're pretty sure they were behind what happened in Harvard Square last April."

The incident had caught the City of Cambridge and Boston by surprise. What started as a peaceful protest had turned into a full-on riot, with windows smashed and businesses set on fire. Students fought in the streets with police, who had to use teargas, and there were rumors that armed Black Panthers were on their way. It was the most violent outburst so far in the local anti-war movement.

"How do we tell the difference between SDS and the Union Front?" I asked, realizing that I was confusing the names.

"We don't. They all look like tramps if you ask me. But there are two in particular…"

Reaching into the folder, he took out some photographs. One was of a man with long hair and thick eyebrows, dressed in a white linen shirt, leaning against a fence with a smug smile. The other was a thin woman with big sunglasses and a bandana, surrounded by people at an outdoor event.

"The man is Neil Kagan," he continued. "Born in 1946 in New York. The woman is Leslie Lavoie. She's from California."

"A lovely couple."

The captain grinned.

"They've been involved in radical politics since at least '65. She was arrested at a sit-in in Berkeley last year."

"Do we think they killed Jerry?" I asked.

"A pretty good match to the sketches, don't you think?"

Not sure if he was joking, I raised my eyebrows.

"Either way," he said. "I want you to go to the meeting at B.U. Sniff around."

"Both of us?" I asked.

The implication was clear, if uncomfortable. Even at a time when race relations were improving, it was still uncommon to see a black and white man together unless they were coworkers. The students might believe it—there was more integration in universities–but two guys over thirty walking into a meeting of radicals was bound to look suspicious.

"You can wait outside," he said to Harrigan. "In case anything goes awry."

It was a clever way of avoiding a sensitive subject, and Harrigan took the order with aplomb.

"Am I supposed to make an identification with these?" I asked.

Looking at the sketches, Egersheim frowned like he realized how useless they were.

"Not really. But you can see what this group is all about, gauge their zeal. Are they revolutionaries or just kids with too much time on their hands?"

"The bureau has been monitoring them," I said.

His expression changed.

"Where'd you hear that?"

I always gave the captain the respect his rank deserved, but I had more friends and contacts than him, and I knew he didn't like it.

"I…I had dinner with Marecki on Monday," I said.

"Then you know more than me."

Egersheim tilted his head with a bemused grin that I knew he was using to hide his jealousy or frustration. I reached for my briefcase, and Harrigan and I got up to go.

"Keep these," he said, handing me the drawings. "They're copies."

"Thanks."

As I went to leave, he said, "Oh," and I turned around. "Make sure to dress the part."

I looked down at my suit coat and pleated pants. It might have been the first time I was ever ashamed to be well-dressed. I hadn't shaved in two days, so I already had the beginnings of a beard, but it was going to take a lot more to look like a scruffy college student.

"Think they'd catch on?" I joked.

"You look like Spiro Agnew, for chrissakes."

I hadn't gone undercover in a couple of years, the last time at a carnival in Franklin Park where the carnies were selling heroin. The bust was easy, a hundred pounds of *China White*, but the prosecution never happened. The culprits made bail, and like any traveling community, they soon skipped town and were never seen again.

"I'm sure I can find some old jeans and a t-shirt," I said.

Harrigan and I left and headed toward the lobby. I had my own office, but it was in the other direction, and I never used it. For the longest time, all our administrative work, all our investigative brain-storming, was done with Jackson. Since he died, we were left with a void in our collaborative soul. Or maybe I just didn't like to be alone at my desk.

We walked outside and stopped on the steps.

"I've got a meeting," I said. "See what you can find out about that girl—"

"The young woman."

I gave him a sharp look. I was used to his excessive politeness, his insistence on proper terms, but his constant corrections were getting annoying. I had grown up in a time when *girl* also meant *woman*, when *kid* could also mean *man*, as long as the person was younger than you.

"The witness," I said, finally, and it seemed something we could both agree on.

......

I SAT in the chair in the low light, my eyes drooping and so relaxed I could have dozed. I liked the office of Dr. Kaplan, or *Sandra*. She always insisted I call her by her first name, something I still couldn't get used to. Even in an era of relaxed customs and declining manners, it seemed rude to address a doctor like a casual acquaintance. Although she was older by a decade, she had a youthful optimism and a modern outlook about living that made me ashamed to be a cynic. Her husband had died from a heart attack while skiing when they were in their thirties so she had never had children, something that explained her nice figure. They had gone to the Alps, she told me, her first and only time back to Europe since the war. I was amazed that anyone who had lived through the Holocaust would ever return to that cursed continent.

"So Marcus was hotheaded?"

"We all were," I said, looking up at the ceiling.

Something about the angle made my mind roam, and I saw and remembered things I hadn't thought about in years. Marcus and I used to leave our rooms after *lights out*, meeting by the stairwell, those cold winter nights when we could hear the mice running on the overhead pipes, the whistle of drafty windows. Lots of kids snuck out and, considering each floor had only one lavatory, the staff usually overlooked any midnight wanderers.

"We got into trouble a few times."

"Acting out?"

"We used to go down to the kitchen at night…"

She nodded as I spoke, and I liked that she was interested. But when Ruth insisted I get treatment, I assumed my problems had something to do with the war or maybe Jackson's death. My early life at the *Home* was a vague and distant memory, almost like a dream, and in no way related to the regrets that came later.

"One time," I said, recalling a harrowing event, "…we were probably about eight years old. The staff had made cookies for Christmas. There were hundreds of them., stacked on the tables along the walls on metal sheets, cooling. Marcus wanted some."

"Wouldn't any child?"

I chuckled to myself.

"We snuck out. He used a screwdriver to pick the lock on the kitchen door…"

Even though I was smiling, my memories from that time were always a hazy mix of nostalgia and terror. The institution was as strict as a prison, but I never blamed the staff or administration. Had I been in their position, I probably would have demanded the same discipline. Raising so many neglected and troubled kids was like trying to tame a herd of wild broncos.

"As we were leaving," I continued, "we got caught by one of the night watchmen. A real brute. Cyclops, we called him. He was missing an eye. He came out of the shadows and grabbed Marcus by the collar..."

Realizing I was twiddling my thumbs, I stopped.

"He tried to grab me too, but I got away and ran up the stairwell. Then I heard the man scream, and I stopped. I wanted to run back—"

"But you didn't?"

"I was...too scared."

Even in the safe confines of her office, it was still something I found hard to admit.

"What happened?" she asked.

"Marcus had stabbed him with the screwdriver, right in the throat."

She kept a straight face, but I could tell she was shocked.

"Did he get in trouble?"

"They didn't catch him. The man could barely see. He had no idea who it was."

"Do you think you should have told somebody?"

The question startled me, and I shifted in the chair. I knew it wasn't an accusation, but some part of me felt like it was.

"No," I scoffed. "He was a friend...I would never."

She scribbled something on the notepad, and I always wondered what she wrote. Things I thought were important she would ignore while things that seemed trivial, she would record in detail. I had been seeing her for almost two months, and we still hadn't gotten past my childhood.

"This stuff," I said, and she looked up. "It's so long ago. What does it have to do with...?"

"Your anger?"

I looked down, slightly embarrassed. It wasn't the word I would have chosen, but it was accurate.

"Yeah. That."

"Often we can trace our negative emotions to childhood."

"Not the war?"

"That too, of course. We're the culmination of all our experiences. But when we're young, we're especially vulnerable. That trauma can affect us all our lives."

I liked that she always said *we* and *us* instead of *you* because it made me feel less unique.

"So my childhood was traumatic?"

"What do you think?"

"Yes."

She gave a wide, warm smile like we had achieved some sort of therapeutic breakthrough. The timer rang, a poignant end to the session. As I got up, I noticed a diploma on the wall, the words *Universitas Bostoniensis* on parchment paper, faint but elegant.

"I didn't know you went to B.U."

"My Alma Mater," she said, looking up at it.

"Were you one of those hippies?"

She laughed out loud.

"That's kind of you. I'm a lot older."

"Then a beatnik?" I asked, remembering the word Jackson always used for artists, free spirits, or anyone else who didn't fit the norms of traditional society.

"My family was more concerned with not going bankrupt," she said. "I'm afraid I was a square."

"Nothing wrong with that."

When we got to the door, she stopped and turned to me.

"I think every generation needs its rebels. If not, the world would never change."

CHAPTER 9

HARRIGAN AND I WALKED INTO JOE & NEMO, A SMALL DINER WEDGED between a record shop and an arcade on a narrow lane off the Boston Common. It was busy for lunch, workers cramped into vinyl booths, standing around the counter, lined up at the register. The place was famous for its hotdogs, the foot-long giants in a buttered roll, but there were other things on the menu too, grilled cheese and Reubens, baked beans and coleslaw.

I hadn't been there in a couple of years, and it brought back memories. The obligations of fatherhood left me with little time for going out to gritty restaurants after work, and I usually ate at home. But it hadn't changed. The walls were still covered with old-style floral wallpaper that was stained from cigarette smoke, faded by time. All around were photographs of Boston icons, Babe Ruth and Ted Williams hanging in mismatched frames, all uneven like the pictures at a barn sale.

Seeing the two detectives from D4, I nodded to Harrigan, and we walked over.

"Gentlemen," I said, and they both moved so we could sit.

They were younger than us, and I would have called them rookies except they probably had been on the force for ten years. The officer beside Harrigan was chubby with thinning red hair, and the one next to me was tall and skinny with a protruding Adam's apple that moved as he spoke. They were still having lunch, their plates covered with half-eaten hotdogs, french fries, and splotches of mustard. We all shook hands, and they reminded me of their names, which I soon forgot.

"How goes the investigation?" the tall one asked.

"We're looking at B.U.—radicals."

"Boston University?"

When I noticed a man in the next booth look up, I leaned in and lowered my voice. I didn't think he was listening, but I couldn't be sure, and what we were discussing was confidential.

"There was some…let's say…salacious material found in the getaway car."

"Salacious?" the other officer asked, like he didn't know what the word meant.

"The robbery might've been political."

"Fucking hippies," the tall one said, shaking his head.

I chuckled.

"Listen," I said. "I need to know what the girl said."

"The girl?"

"The witness. The girl you found crying on the sidewalk."

The men looked at each other.

"Oh, you mean the prostitute?"

"Prostitute?"

"The girl with the dark hair?" the redhead asked. "Sure looked like one. The pumps, the earrings, the halter, the makeup."

"Where'd she go?"

"We handed her off."

I felt my blood pressure rise.

"Whaddya mean you *handed her off?*"

"A couple guys from the bureau took her," the tall one said.

"They said they would do the interview," his partner added.

I glanced across to Harrigan, his expression blank but his eyes somehow reflecting the same suspicions I had. I wanted to berate the officers, but it technically wasn't bad police work because we always collaborated with the FBI.

"What'd they look like?" I asked.

"Suits. The usual. One guy was thickset, probably 5' 8." The other a little taller."

I knew immediately that it was Marcus and his partner.

"Did you see them take her to a car?" I asked.

They looked at each other again. The aftermath of any incident, especially a shooting, was chaotic, and it was hard to remember what and when things happened.

"Nope," the redhead said. "They walked away. We continued looking for shell frags."

The news was unusual, but it wasn't entirely outside protocol, and I would ask Marcus about it later. I put my hands down on the table, looking at them both.

"Thanks for your help," I said.

"Anytime, Lieutenant."

I shimmied out of the booth, and Harrigan did the same. As we all stood, the taller officer said, "Did she see something?"

"We don't know. There's no statement from her in the witness report."

I could see the curiosity on their faces, but it was the most I was going to reveal. With the case assigned to our unit, they had no involvement, and anything we said would have just been gossip.

The diner had gotten busier since we arrived, and Harrigan and I had to push through the crowd to get to the door. As we went to leave, he stopped and looked at me.

"What?" I asked.

"I haven't eaten."

The remark surprised me because I was the one who was always hungry.

"I thought love was supposed to make you lose your appetite," I joked, but he didn't seem amused.

"Would you like something?"

"No. I'll meet you out front."

He got in line, and I walked out. I lit a cigarette and stood against the wall while people rushed by on the narrow, crooked sidewalk. Hearing music, I looked across to see a guy in a head bandana strumming a guitar. Around him were three or four young women, all dressed in torn jeans, t-shirts, and baggy coats, the style of the new generation. One of the girls was calling to pedestrians as they passed by. At first, I thought she was asking for money—there were always lots of panhandlers downtown. But when she handed a woman a flier, I knew it was something political, the draft, the war, women's rights.

"See something interesting, Lieutenant?"

Startled, I turned and Harrigan was next to me. He held a hotdog in both hands, sliding it into his mouth, his fingers covered in ketchup and relish.

"How 'bout a bite?" I asked.

"Not a chance."

CHAPTER 10

I PULLED INTO THE DRIVEWAY, AND THE LAWN WAS COVERED WITH leaves. Through the curtain, I could see Ruth standing in the living room with Nessie in her arms, twirling her around. I imagined that the radio was on, but Ruth didn't need music to dance. Turning off the engine, I watched them for a couple of minutes, the image of all that was good, nearly everything I lived for.

I walked up the front path and went inside, putting down the briefcase and loosening my tie. The house smelled of something rich, the warmth of home cooking. Ruth smiled and swooped over with Nessie, who giggled and held out her arms. I took her and cuddled her against my shoulder, breathing in her soft warmth, the scent of her hair.

I followed Ruth into the dining room, and over the table was a white linen cloth, plates and silverware, bowls of hot food, a high-chair for Nessie. Ruth rarely set the table, since we usually ate in the kitchen. With overlapping shifts, our meals together happened quickly, if at all. But she had the night off, something I knew because I had arranged it. I didn't do overtime like I used to, but when I did, I had a friend in administration at City Hospital who would alter her schedule. I never said anything, one of the few secrets I kept from her, although she did mention the coincidence once or twice.

"Ruth, I have to go in tonight," I said, and her face dropped.

"But I made Shepherd's pie."

I looked at her with a long and sentimental smile, remembering how she had cooked it on our third date. After I mentioned I was Irish, she assumed it was my favorite meal, and I never told her otherwise.

"Why?" she asked.

"We've gotta check out some students at B.U."

She nodded, and I appreciated her understanding. The Shawmut Bank robbery was personal.

"Undercover?"

"Yeah," I said, not wanting to get into details.

"Is it dangerous?"

I gave her a sharp look.

"It's just a meeting."

"When do you have to leave?"

"I've got twenty minutes."

She pressed her lips together, a look of quiet disappointment. Taking Nessie from my arms, she put her in the seat. We sat down and filled our plates, eating in silence until she said, "Did you hear an officer was killed in New Jersey last night?"

"Um, yeah."

It wasn't true because I had stopped keeping track. While Vietnam made most of the headlines, there was a war raging across the country too. The Black Panthers and other militant groups had already killed dozens of cops that year, wounding many more.

"Another one in Cleveland on Monday," she added.

Holding my fork to my mouth, I peered up.

"I know," I said.

She nodded with a trembling smile and stared down at her food, which she had hardly touched.

"Let's all go to the Boston Common this weekend," she said, and I was glad for the change in subject. "The foliage should be lovely."

I looked over at Nessie, whose face was now covered in mashed potatoes. Just her smile was enough to make me forget all the madness in the world.

"That sounds nice," I said.

CHAPTER 11

Harrigan and I got to Boston University just after 8 p.m. George Sherman Union Hall was an ugly building, slabs of cement with sections of brick. If someone had told me it was a former military bunker, I wouldn't have been surprised. A mile west of Kenmore Square, it sat between Commonwealth Avenue and the onramp to Storrow Drive on a stretch of road that was the heart of the campus. During the day, the area was busy, but at night it was quiet, with scattered groups of students, the clang of the Green Line trolley.

I turned down a side street and into the rear parking lot where, in the distance, I saw the lights of Cambridge on the far side of the Charles River. The wind was low, the sky clear, and it was a perfect autumn night. I couldn't help thinking it was usually the time I put Nessie to bed, and some part of me resented the job for taking me away from her.

I pulled into the last spot beside a college van and turned off the car. It was hardly a stakeout, but I hadn't done surveillance in a while, and I even found myself a little nervous. I could deal with street criminals because I understood, sometimes even respected, their motives. Political agitators were a mystery.

"If you hear shooting, start the engine," I said.

Harrigan responded with a low chuckle.

"Don't get brainwashed, Lieutenant."

"Gimme an hour or so. Go get a coffee."

"Too late for coffee," he said.

It sounded like a contradiction—I could drink coffee a minute before bed and sleep like a baby. But he had always been moderate in his habits, a quality I admired and often wished I had.

"Then go visit your girlfriend," I said, handing him the keys.

"She's got class tonight."

I got out and walked across the lot. Used to wearing suits, I felt uncomfortable in my jeans, sneakers, and the beige parka Ruth had bought me in NYC a few years before. It was the most casual and the most modern I had dressed in years. Still, I probably looked more like an unemployed accountant than a campus radical.

A side door was open, so I entered and walked up a stairwell to the second floor. Following a long hallway, I kept my head down, not making eye contact as I passed some students. The walls were lined with notices and posters. While some were for university activities, most were calls to action, words of righteous rage: STOP THE DRAFT, WOMEN OF THE WORLD UNITE, AVENGE KENT STATE! For most of the Sixties, I had stayed out of politics, preferring the familiar turmoil of homicide and other gang activity. I didn't know the difference between a *hippie* and a *yippie*, but I couldn't help feeling that I was in unfriendly territory.

I got to the lobby and saw some young men standing around the entrance. They were all students, something that was less obvious by their age than by their rolled-up jeans and plaid shirts. As I went toward the doors, they all turned.

"Hey, man. What's up?" one of them said.

"I'm here for the meeting."

They stared me up and down. I kept a straight face, but inside I was fuming.

"A little old to be into SDS, aren't you, man?"

The one who said it was the smallest guy, which wasn't a surprise because they always had the biggest mouths.

"I thought the United Labor Front was here."

"What's your interest with the Front?" the big guy asked.

His tone was disrespectful, but I couldn't push back, and it was one of the hardest parts about going undercover.

"I've been outta work," I replied. "I like what they have to say."

"Yeah, what work is that?"

"I'm an ironworker. Local 7."

Just the mention of a labor union changed their attitude. Like a lot of students, they idolized jobs they would never have to do, if only because it flattered their sense of outrage toward the world. And they took the bait like fish.

"Alright, my man. Welcome."

While two of them got the doors, another guy extended his hand, and I reluctantly shook it. Inside, the auditorium was packed, people crammed into rows of folding chairs, lined up against the walls. The crowd was mostly white, middle-class suburban kids with long hair.

I stood beside a young girl with a braided bag over her shoulder, a flower in her hair. When she smiled, I smiled back. A few people looked over, but most were focused on the speaker at the front. He had a high, almost whiney voice that didn't seem to match his height and angular face. He wore faded jeans and a western shirt, open to reveal some necklace or chain. As my eyes adjusted, I realized it was Neil Kagan.

"No more cooperation! No more collaboration! Now is the time for action!"

The reaction from the audience was odd, almost like the call and response of a Baptist service. But not everyone who replied agreed, and little arguments broke out among the groups. They bickered, squabbled, and shouted each other down.

"Cool out, friends," Kagan said. "We have our differences, but we're all in the same struggle!"

As everyone pleaded for calm, a woman walked over to the mic, and I knew it was Leslie Lavoie.

"This is what the pigs want!" she shouted, and the remark stung.

"They want us to fight among ourselves so they can continue to serve the interests of the capitalists..."

Her voice was piercing, her manner much more defiant than his, and it seemed to unify the audience.

"They protect a banking system that's financing the war in Nam while the workers of the world suffer!"

It was all clichés, the same tired slogans and rallying cries, and I had expected more from student intellectuals.

"Fuck the pigs!" Kagan said, leaning over his girlfriend, raising his fist.

He turned his ear, and the crowd began to yell it back.

"Fuck the pigs! Fuck the pigs! Fuck the pigs!"

As they continued to chant, I became self-conscious. Over at another doorway, I saw a single black guard, but otherwise, there wasn't much security. They could have torn it apart if they wanted to.

"Hoover's rats are everywhere," Lavoie shouted. "Probably in this room!"

The words sent a shiver through me; I hadn't expected a witch hunt. Whether it was real or for dramatic effect, everyone started to look around. I glanced at the young girl, but this time she didn't smile, and I got a strange feeling she knew. The second she looked away, I sidestepped to the door with my back to the wall, trying not to draw attention. Then I turned and ran out.

"Pardon..."

I froze. Standing in front of me was Harrigan's girlfriend.

"Delilah?" I asked.

She peered up with a hesitant smile, somewhere between shock and dread.

"What are *you* doing here?" she asked.

The men who had been watching the door came over and circled us.

"Hey Dee, how do you know this dude?" one of them asked.

She and I locked eyes. Any misstep and she could have blown my cover. But I was more frustrated than worried. If any of them got hostile, I would just take out my badge; if any of them got violent, I would whip out my gun.

"We've met before," she said, still staring at me. "…at meetings."

All at once, the tension went away. I was relieved by her clever answer, but it also told me she was involved in student activism.

"Cool, man," one guy said, and they all walked away.

Dalilah and I lingered for a moment in uncomfortable silence. Then, with a quick wave, she turned and went into the auditorium.

The encounter left me stunned, but I couldn't tell Harrigan—I would have to let her do that. I felt as bad for myself as I did for him. It was never easy knowing your partner was associating with the enemy. Or was she the enemy? Students had always been rebellious, always trying to upset the status quo. I hadn't gone to college, but I knew it was the one place where young people could explore new ideas, consider different ways of living. While I hated the hippies for their arrogance and self-display, some part of me respected, maybe even envied, their courage. I had grown up in a time when no one questioned or challenged anything.

I followed the corridor out to the back, and when I reached the parking lot, the temperature had dropped. I got in the car and Harrigan was still seated in the same position, his hands resting on his lap. It was almost like he hadn't moved.

"How'd it go?" he asked.

"I saw Kagan and the woman."

"And?"

"A whole lotta nothing," I said. "Lots of shouting and cheers."

"Any threats of violence?"

I started the car and turned to him.

"Nothing specific. We're gonna need better evidence than two students who want to overturn society."

Even as I said it, I knew it sounded ironic.

"And that's not enough?" Harrigan asked.

"Above our pay grade…*fortunately*."

I hit the gas, and we sped away.

CHAPTER 12

I DROVE SOUTH DOWN DORCHESTER AVENUE, THE CITY BEHIND ME IN the rearview. I passed Our Lady of Czestochowa, a small white church nestled between the giant triple-deckers, so inconspicuous it could have been mistaken for a house. Situated on the boundary between South Boston and Dorchester, it was the gateway to The Polish Triangle and the spiritual heart of the community. I followed the bridge over the expressway, and the language of the shop signs began to change, Polish flags draped in windows and doorways. The neighborhood had a quaint intimacy, like some Pomeranian hamlet in the middle of the city.

Turning onto Bellflower Street, I took the first spot I could find. With the homes so close together, there were no driveways, and the road was lined with parked cars. Luckily, the address was only a few doors away, a towering three-family with aluminum siding and a statue of the Virgin Mary in the tiny front yard. I got out and walked up the steps, the treads splintered and warped, the white paint peeling. I looked at the names beside the bell: Kowalczyk, Zielinski, and finally, Marecki. I rang it once and waited.

When I called Marcus, he had agreed to meet only after I said it was urgent. He had worked the night before and was tired, reminding me that the Shawmut robbery wasn't their only case. He told me to come by his mother's place where he stayed a couple of days a week, and I appreciated his cooperation.

The buzzer rang, and I went into the vestibule, climbing up a narrow staircase to the third floor. When I reached the top, the door opened, and Marcus was standing in a white t-shirt and sweats, a cup of coffee in his hand. He greeted me with a wide smile that accentuated his dimples, but also the creases of age. Somehow he looked older without a suit, his paunch showing through, his shoulders slightly hunched.

"Jody," he said, and we shook. "Can I get you coffee? Tea?"

"I'm fine. Thanks."

The apartment was bigger than I expected, with a long hallway that ran the length of the house. It had a nostalgic charm, gold wallpaper and ornate furniture, pieces that some immigrant worker would have saved a lifetime for but were now considered old-fashioned, even tacky.

We walked into the living room, where he invited me to sit on a velvet camelback sofa and then took a chair across from me.

"Will your mother be surprised to meet someone from the *Home?*" I asked.

"No, I told her all about you. Unfortunately, she's at church."

"On a Thursday morning?"

"The life of a babushka," he said, reaching for a pack of Kent's on the table. "Mind if I smoke?"

"I'll join you."

He gave me a light, and I leaned back on the cushion, savoring the cigarette because I could never smoke at home.

"Ever since my father died," he continued, "she's been wedded to Jesus."

"I'm sorry to hear. How long ago was that?"

"'53."

I raised my eyes—seventeen years was a long time.

"He must've been a young man."

"Too young," he said, taking a deep drag. "With the war over, they wanted to see Poland again. We took a steamship to Gdańsk, a train to Ostroda, a horse cart to my mother's village…"

As he spoke, I followed his gaze to a black-and-white photo on the mantel. In it, he was standing between his parents, his father a stocky man with a thin mustache, his mother plain but dignified.

"My father's brother, Mariusz. He never came to America. He fought the Germans in a partisan unit."

"A worthy cause."

"Ha," he said with a snicker. "Stalin despised the resistance. He saw them as a threat to the Soviet regime in Poland. The NKVD arrested him after the war. He was tried and executed."

"And your father?"

"They came for him that summer, four men in a car. I was playing in a wheat field with my cousins. They said he was being investigated for *previous associations with hostile elements*. Can you believe it? The man hadn't been to Poland in twenty years."

"And what happened?"

Marcus stopped and turned, his face strained, his eyes cold.

"I never saw my *tata* again."

There was an uncomfortable pause.

"Sorry," I said, averting my eyes.

"The same is happening in this country right now. SDS, the Weather Underground, the Panthers. These kids have no idea what they have…"

Reaching to the glass ashtray, he stamped out his cigarette with particular force.

"We're gonna get those little punks who killed your friend."

I shared his resentment, but not his rage. Either way, it was a perfect segue to the investigation.

"Which is what I came to talk about," I said. "We're missing a report."

He narrowed his eyes and reached for another cigarette.

"A report?" he said.

"Witness report from the girl. Or woman. A young woman. Dark hair—"

He thought for a moment.

"Oh, right. The junkie."

"Junkie?"

"She was useless. High as a kite."

"But she said she saw the perps."

"She was all over the place, kept changing her story. Then she asked my partner for ten bucks. You know what crime scenes are like. You gotta weed out the crazies."

"You can't just let a—"

"Look, Jody," he said, his voice firm. "We don't tell BPD how to do its job..."

He stopped midsentence, which I took as a sign that he didn't want to argue. I trusted his judgment, both as an old friend and as a professional, but it still seemed like sloppy work.

"Besides, we know who did it."

"Yeah? Who?"

"Neil Kagan. We sent all the intel to BPD."

"I know," I said, ashamed for trying to call his bluff. "I went to see him speak last night at B.U."

"He's some sort of hippie guru. A communist—"

"United Labor Front," I said.

"Whatever they call themselves, they're dangerous people."

"And you think they rob banks?"

"We're pretty sure they hit a bank in Philadelphia last month based on witness reports. They need the funding, and they preach violence."

It seemed like a stretch. Kagan had talked generally about overthrowing the system, but he never said anything about specific methods or targets. Young people always had more bark than bite, and I didn't think for a second that he was someone capable of starting a revolution.

I heard the rattle of a lock. When the door opened, a woman walked in carrying a plastic bag, so large that at first, I couldn't see her face.

"Mamusia!" Marcus cried, jumping up to help her.

His mother was younger than I expected, probably in her early sixties, and far less matronly than the word *babushka* would suggest. She wore a frilled blouse and plain skirt, her gray speckled hair in a bun. He took the bag and put his arm around her, escorting her into the living room.

"Meet Jody," he said.

Out of breath from the stairs, she just looked at me with a flustered smile and bowed. Then she put her pocketbook down on the table, said something to him in Polish, and walked away. I would have said *nice to meet you*, but I got the sense she didn't know much English.

"Clothes," Marcus said, holding the bag up proudly. "They take a collection at church, then we send it back to Poland."

"For the poor?"

"For the people."

I gave him a curious look, wondering what the distinction was. The only thing I knew about the country was that they ate pierogies and danced the polka.

"Things are bad over there, Jody. People wait in lines for bread. The government cracks down on anyone who speaks out. Soviet bastards."

I shook my head in sympathy. The FBI hated communists more than the CIA did, and I was old enough to remember the red scare of the fifties. But I hadn't come to talk politics, and when his mother called from the kitchen, it was a good excuse for me to leave.

"Well, I should get going," I said.

"I'll keep you posted."

"And I'll do the same."

He walked me to the door, and we shook hands again. As I started down the stairs, he called to me, and I looked back.

"We're gonna get these hippies who shot your friend."

CHAPTER 13

EGERSHEIM STOOD BY THE WINDOW, HIS ARMS CROSSED AND STARING out. With his golf clubs in the corner, I knew he had an afternoon tee time, and he never worked late on Fridays. Harrigan sat beside me with a forced patience, and the fact that he was going to see the *Jackson Five* at the Boston Garden with his girlfriend that night told me he also wanted to wrap up the day. I didn't blame them; it had been a long week.

"Per your request, I've contacted D4 about the girl," the captain said, turning around. "They're gonna keep an eye out for her."

I couldn't remember much about her except that she was pretty and upset. She had been dressed seductively too, but then all young girls were, and everyone her age looked the same.

"A needle in a haystack," I said.

"If the bureau cleared her, she probably wasn't much use. We've got other witnesses."

"None who saw their faces."

He looked up, and I felt a sudden tension. Captain Jackson used to encourage debate, but Egersheim always seemed threatened by it.

"Doesn't matter," he said coldly. "We've got a witness from the armory robbery."

"What if it's a different gang?"

"Unlikely. It was the same car. The hits were two days apart."

Even if the connection was strong, it didn't mean it was conclusive. I hadn't yet read the report from the state police, and the only information we had gotten so far from the bureau was verbal. As a federal crime, bank robberies always involved several government agencies, most of which didn't get along. In some ways, it was like playing poker with people you knew.

"Once we get the prints back," the captain went on, "we'll go to the DA. If we've got a positive ID, we'll make an arrest."

"But we need a match."

"The feds got one. They've been watching Kagan for months."

"Couldn't we go on probable cause?" I asked, a last-ditch try.

He shook his head. I could tell he was getting annoyed.

"Enjoy the weekend, gentlemen," he said, and the meeting was over.

As Harrigan and I walked out, I was seized by a gut-wrenching frustration, a feeling of stalled progress. The investigation seemed to be going nowhere fast, or maybe I was just too eager. Many solid cases had been bungled by overzealousness, and with an officer dead, the department had to be extra careful. I hadn't gone to see Duggan's widow because I wanted to wait until we had someone in custody. It felt like a coward's excuse, but I couldn't face her or the children knowing his killer was still on the loose.

We left headquarters and got into the car, pulling out of the lot and into midday traffic. We drove back to Roxbury in silence, but it wasn't awkward or even unusual. Harrigan could go hours without speaking, and I didn't mind. It gave me time to think, and Delilah was at the top of my mind. He wasn't to blame for his girlfriend's associations, but I wondered if he knew. If he did and didn't tell me, I would have been furious; if he didn't and I told him, he might have been just as angry because I hadn't mentioned it earlier. It was a dilemma I couldn't avoid.

Coming down Seaver Street, I stopped in front of a brick apartment building overlooking Franklin Park. When I was young, the area had been a melting pot of ethnic groups, mostly Jewish but with a smattering of Irish and Italians. Now it was all black. And everywhere were the signs of deep neglect born by a community that had to fight for everything it had. Many of the homes were boarded up; the small corner shops and bodegas had bars on the windows.

As Harrigan opened the door, I said, "Tell Delilah I said hello."

"I will, Lieutenant."

"By the way, what's she studying?"

With one leg out of the car, he stopped and turned to me. The question was abrupt.

"Political science. I believe she told you."

"Right. But what's she planning to do?"

"We haven't gotten to that yet," he said, and I grinned.

"Have fun at the concert."

Not quite a smirk, he responded with a similar disdain, and I understood why. Neither of us liked rock 'n' roll, preferring the popular melodies and big band sounds of our generation.

"I'll try," he said.

As I drove away, I glanced down the side streets, hoping to catch a glimpse of the *Roxbury Home for Stray Boys*. A once-thriving institution, it was now just an abandoned shell, closed when the funding dried up in the '40s. After the war, the government had been too busy trying to care for the millions of returning veterans, and the state's social services were taken over by newer public facilities. Still, it held a special place in my heart. It was where I met Marcus, my first best friend, two boys cast into the world without a family and without a past.

Like everything about my early life, those years were marked by bitter impermanence, and I never expected anything to last. I was ten when Marcus got adopted, and it happened so fast that we didn't have time to say goodbye. It was the dead of winter, the sky a dull gray, the paved yard covered in ice and snow. I had gone down to the cafeteria like I did each morning before school, only to find his seat at the table empty. At first, I thought he had been expelled because of a fight a few weeks earlier. Noticing my dismay, a staff member put her hand on my shoulder and kindly whispered that he *had been placed*. And that was it. Marcus was torn from my life, like a death without a funeral, a memory that I clung to as it faded over time. Considering all the friends I lost later in the Korean War, it was no wonder I had a problem with anger.

......

NEWBURYPORT WAS a small coastal community on the North Shore. Nestled at the mouth of the Merrimack River between the highway and the ocean, it was a quaint stretch of 18th and 19th-century structures, from grand ship captains' homes to modest workers' cottages. Like many old New England towns, its commercial center was rundown, a mix of mom-and-pop shops and barrooms. As a rookie, my coworkers and I rented a place for several summers on Plum Island down the road. There we would drink all night under the stars, lighting bonfires on the beach, an escape from the crime and congestion of the city. One Fourth of July, a couple of the guys fired their service weapons, provoking a panicked response from the local police. But they were no match for a dozen hardened street cops, and all they did was ask us to dispose of the shells.

I left early enough that rush hour hadn't started, and I made the trip in under an hour, which was a record. Driving down Water Street, I could see the river between the brick buildings, the masts of sailboats and a couple of barges. I turned at a warehouse and went up a narrow lane, stopping at a yellow clapboard house. Reaching for the report file, I confirmed the address and got out.

I opened the gate and walked up to a small front porch where I saw the name *Kozlowski* taped to the mailbox. I couldn't find a bell, so I swung a brass lobster knocker and waited. The door creaked open, and a middle-aged woman with glasses peered out.

"May I help you?" she asked with an accent.

"I'm looking for Margaret Marie."

She hesitated, then said, "Wait."

Moments later, a young woman came to the door. She was tall and thin, with dark eyes and dark hair pulled back in a ponytail. I hadn't expected such a pretty witness.

"Hello," I said.

"Can I help you?"

"Are you Margaret Marie?" I asked, taking out my badge.

"Yes. Margaret Marie *Kozlowski*."

Her last name made more sense, and I wondered why the report had it simply as *Marie*.

"Mind if I ask some questions about the armory robbery?"

"Sure," she replied, but her tone wasn't convincing.

"Did you see the car?"

"Yes. I already told the men everything."

"Which men, Miss?"

"Marcus, and the other one," she said, rubbing her lip. "Shine, I think his name was."

Something about her was distracting, and it wasn't just her beauty. As she spoke, her eyes darted, and her body squirmed. I couldn't tell if it was nerves, impatience, or something else.

"Why were you driving by at 6 a.m.?"

"I work in Boston. I always leave early."

"Do you work Sundays?"

"Sometimes."

"You reported the plate number. Wasn't it dark out?"

"Sunrise is before six. 5:49 a.m. that morning, to be exact."

"You know a lot about sunrises?" I asked, and finally, she smiled.

"My father was a fisherman. I used to go on the boat with him when I was little. I got to know the tides…and the sun."

My expression softened. I hadn't done anything so memorable with Nessie yet, but when I did, I hoped she would speak as fondly about it.

The subject of sunlight reminded me it was getting late. Having Nadia around took some of the pressure off the race to get home, but I knew the traffic would be heavy.

"Thank you for your time," I said.

"You're welcome."

I turned to go and then stopped.

"Have you always lived here?" I asked.

She hesitated.

"We moved here three years ago after my father died."

"I'm sorry."

Whether he had died at sea or some other way, I didn't know. But the life of a fisherman was as hard and dangerous as a cop's, and I sympathized with her loss.

"Thank you," she said.

"And where did you live before here?"

"Dorchester."

CHAPTER 14

I T WAS A CRISP FALL MORNING, THE SKY A SHEET OF PASTEL BLUE AS Ruth, Nessie, and I drove into town. Fall was in full bloom, and the trees along Beacon Street were a patchwork of red, yellow, and orange brilliance. When a leaf fell on the windshield and I used the wipers to clear it, Nessie laughed. She liked the foliage as much as I did, and whenever I took her out to the backyard, she would sit among the dead leaves and toss them into the air. Ruth loved the colors, but she didn't seem to have the same nostalgic wonder for the sounds and smells of autumn, which I assumed was because she had been raised in California.

We parked on Arlington Street, and it was early enough in the day that all the good spots hadn't been taken. While Ruth took Nessie out of the car seat, I got the stroller from the trunk. We went into the Public Garden, following winding paths where a statue of some famous historical person or event was around every bend. Nessie walked with us, but when we got to the Boston Common, she reached for the stroller, and Ruth put her in it.

We continued up a shallow hill, the walkways wide and paved, and in the distance, I could see the gold dome of the State House.

At the junction of several footpaths was an open area with a twirling carousel. When Nessie saw it, she pointed and screamed, "Horses!" I glanced at Ruth, and we both smiled. At the ticket booth, an older black man sat in a red coat and striped hat, the theme of the ride or the company that owned it. I bought three tickets and walked over to the attendant, who unhooked the cordoned rope. With the tourist season over, there was no wait, and we were on in seconds.

I lifted Nessie onto a silver horse with a serpent's tail until she decided she wanted the pink one. Ruth sat on a gilded goat, and I stood between them. The carousel began to move, creaking slowly and then picking up speed, the lights blinking and organ music playing. We were the only ones on the ride, a cavalry of empty horses going up and down on shining poles.

"Make sure you have her," Ruth said, and I gave her a reassuring nod.

I managed to keep steady, but it was mostly through stubborn determination. My balance hadn't been the same since the war, something my doctor attributed to hearing damage from artillery blasts. But it wasn't just the motion, it was the sounds too, and I couldn't tolerate excitement like I used to. When the carousel finally slowed down, I was relieved because I was getting dizzy.

I helped Nessie off, and we walked down the ramp. Ruth got the stroller, but Nessie preferred to walk, and the moment she saw a cotton candy cart, she ran straight for it. I went after her, Ruth trailing behind yelling, "That's too much sugar!"

"I'll eat some."

I bought a bag, and we continued to stroll through the park. I was glad we had come into town, something we never did anymore because, between working full-time and taking care of Nessie, it was just easier to stay home. But Boston was beautiful, I thought, something that after fifteen years on the force—five of them in homicide—I needed to be reminded of. I spent so much time in bad neighborhoods that I sometimes forgot there were good ones.

Lost in a daydream, I heard a megaphone and looked up to see a crowd. Some people had signs, STOP THE WAR and PEACE NOW, but any dignity in their message was ruined by what they were chanting:

"1...2...3...4...we don't need no fucking war!"

Ruth stopped first, then me. In an instant, my mood changed, and I stared ahead, resentful that they were disturbing the quiet of the morning. But I wasn't surprised. Protests against the war had been going on across the city since at least '68. There were other demonstrations too, and every political movement, from anti-nukes to Puerto Rican independence, seemed to have merged into one big revolt against an ordered society. The department had been struggling to curb or control them without violating anyone's civil rights, and not out of some noble sense of constitutional duty. Most cops hated the student activists. But with the American public divided, the chief didn't want any bad press or, even worse, a lawsuit from the ACLU.

Ruth turned the stroller around, and we were just about to go another way when I heard more shouting and realized there were counter-protesters too. The young men wore leather jackets, the women bell-bottom jeans, and they looked more like working-class kids than hippies. They stood in front of the demonstrators, heckling them.

"Jody?" Ruth said.

I held up my finger and went toward them. But I understood her concern because the situation was escalating. When two of the girls started arguing, people stopped to watch.

"The American government kills!"

"Communism kills!"

I grinned to myself; I had never seen anyone stand up to protesters. I didn't have time to gloat, however, because when someone grabbed one of their signs, all hell broke loose. The groups charged each other, the men throwing wild punches, the women shrieking at each other.

I ran into the fray with my badge out, but no one seemed to notice or care. If I had learned anything about melees, it was that they took on a life of their own. So I ducked and sidestepped, doing my best to avoid getting hit. When I broke free from the scuffle, I stood dazed beside a trash barrel. I looked around for Ruth and Nessie and saw that they were safe on the grass in the distance.

Suddenly, two police horses appeared. They neighed and whinnied, kicking their front legs while the officers struggled to control them. They charged into the brawl, and instantly the groups separated. More cops approached on foot, and the counter-protesters seemed to get nervous. They walked off in the opposite direction, but not before I recognized the guy whose car was stolen for the bank robbery. For a split second, we locked eyes, and although I was tempted to stop him, I didn't have a good reason to.

With the agitators gone, the police started telling the protesters to disperse. It was an action I agreed with, but I wasn't sure it was legal.

"Lieutenant? You okay?"

I turned around and saw an officer from headquarters.

"Yeah," I said, still out of breath.

His sergeant walked over too and asked, "You see who started this?"

If they had pressed me, I would have said the group with the signs. I was sick of self-righteous students. But the truth was, I didn't know, and it would have been like trying to assign blame in a war.

"No idea," I said. "I was just—"

I felt a tug on my arm, and it was Ruth. I could tell she was upset. Nessie stood beside the stroller a few feet away, her bottom lip quivering, watching with a confused look that made me ashamed for having intervened.

"C'mon. Let's go," Ruth said. "Nessie wants to see the Frog Pond."

I nodded to the officers, and they understood. The last thing anyone wanted to do off-duty was get involved in a civil disturbance. Ruth took my hand, her fingers warm and tense, and we walked away.

CHAPTER 15

ANOTHER COP KILLING HAD MADE THE NEWS. THIS TIME THE CULPRITS were the Black Panthers, who ambushed two officers during a traffic stop in Portland, Oregon. Violence against the established order was coming from all sides, from idealistic student activists to hardcore revolutionaries, and not a week went by without some terrible incident. The previous month, the Weather Underground and other radical groups had bombed two police stations, a bank, an army recruiting center, and a courthouse. No one had been killed, but it left people with the feeling that society was crumbling. In the early years of the war and the civil rights movement, guys in the department would grumble about politics, longing for the stable days of the fifties. But the country had changed so much and so fast that no one talked about it anymore, as if silence would somehow stall the momentum.

Walking toward headquarters, I saw Harrigan coming across the parking lot. It was the first time we had arrived at the same time in weeks, possibly months. Before he lived with his mother, he had his own apartment, the reverse of how most men's lives unfolded. I would pick him up each morning and we would drive in together, talking about the latest investigation or the Red Sox. I missed those simpler days when Ruth and I were dating and I still clung to the freedoms of my youth. Now I was married with a child and a home, and Harrigan had a girlfriend. Only five years younger than me, he was finally growing up, and we had both long outlived our adolescence. I wanted him to be happy, and maybe that was why I didn't mention I had seen Delilah at the SDS meeting.

"Good morning, Lieutenant," he said.

"How was the Jackson Five?"

"Loud and smokey."

I chuckled. We walked up the steps and went into the building. As we approached the captain's door, I heard voices and knew he wasn't alone. I knocked first, something I never usually did, and then opened it. Chief McNamara was standing next to Egersheim's desk, hands on his hips, his underarms damp with sweat. His assistant, a younger man with big ears and a pock-marked face, was sitting in one of our chairs, and I was almost offended. Everyone turned as we entered, and I felt like I was interrupting.

"Come in," Egersheim said, and I could tell he was distracted. "The prints are back. We've got a partial on Kagan."

"Partial?"

"It's good enough," the chief said. "I've already talked with the DA."

I smiled, but inside I felt a mix of relief and doubt. A partial match could have meant anything from an undeniable likeness to a vague similarity, and I had seen defendants walk based on evidence from the latter. But the entire department, and much of the public, was waiting for an arrest. Even if the case still wasn't airtight, I knew the chief wanted to get someone into custody and quick.

"I want you boys to move on him ASAP," he said.

If the word *boys* felt condescending to me, I wondered what it was like for Harrigan. But I didn't begrudge McNamara. He was gruff but fair, and even if he lacked social graces, his instincts were good and that was what mattered.

"We'll get on it," I said.

He nodded to his underling, who then rose from the chair like an obedient dog. They walked out, leaving us with a stumped silence. I didn't know if Harrigan and I were expected to stay or run out the door to get Kagan.

"This is gonna be tricky," Egersheim said.

When I sat down, Harrigan did the same.

"We have his last known address," I said. "Not sure if he's still there."

"Kagan shouldn't be hard to find. But I want it done when he's alone."

"Who's to say he'll be alone?"

"What I mean is *not in a crowd*, not with all his cohorts around. These nutjobs are looking for a reason to have it out with the cops. I don't wanna put your lives at risk…"

I appreciated the precaution. For all his bad qualities, I never doubted he cared about his detectives.

"Case him tonight. See if he's still living there. I'll call over to Area B and make sure you have backup."

The captain looked at each of us separately, raising his eyes as if to ensure we were all in agreement. We had a plan, or so it seemed. More than anyone, I wanted to catch Duggan's killer, and I had every reason to be gung ho. But something about the investigation, whether it was the flimsy evidence, the missing witness, or the convenience of the theory, made me uneasy. I had a gnawing skepticism that wouldn't go away.

As we got up to leave, Egersheim called to me. I glanced over at Harrigan, who took the hint and walked out, closing the door behind him.

"Captain?" I said.

"What's this about you going to Newburyport to harass a witness?"

"Harass?"

"I was told you showed up at her door. Grilled her about the armory suspects."

"Who said that?—"

"Doesn't matter!"

Both his tone and the accusation caught me off guard, and I thought carefully before responding.

"I didn't grill anyone," I said. "I asked her a few questions."

"She said she was scared, that you didn't identify yourself."

"That's a lie."

"It's your word against hers if she files a complaint. That's why you never question a witness alone..."

I nodded and looked down.

"Her statement was already obtained...*by the bureau*. You know how petty they are."

There were times when he had to assert his authority, and in this instance, I couldn't blame him. FBI agents were as guarded as they were stubborn, and they clashed with local departments all the time. The task force had come together so fast we hadn't had time to agree on jurisdiction or evidence handling, and Marcus didn't mention it.

"Look, Lieutenant," Egersheim said, lowering his voice. "I know things were done differently under Jackson..."

The mere mention of my old captain gave me a bitter chill. It wasn't the first time he had made a comparison between then and now. Despite getting scolded, it didn't hurt my pride. Although I liked Egersheim, he was just a bureaucrat and had none of the qualities of a mentor. In short, I didn't respect him enough to feel ashamed.

"I understand," I said.

"Now let's go get Kagan."

......

WHEN I PULLED into the driveway, the lights of the living room, dining room, and kitchen were on, a soft glow coming through the curtains. I worried about the electric bill—I always worried about money. But the beauty of the vision was worth it, and I hadn't felt the warmth of a real home in ages, if ever. The apartments I rented were always plain and cold, like military barracks with some décor. Ruth had brought the house to life, and a woman's influence always made a place more welcoming.

I walked up to the door, and it swung open so fast I flinched. There stood Ruth, her coat buttoned to the top, her purse over her shoulder.

"I thought you were off," I said.

"I got called in. Nadia is feeding Nessie. Janice will be here any minute—"

"Ruth, I have to work tonight."

She sighed in frustration.

"Why didn't you tell me?" she asked.

"I didn't know until today."

She hesitated for a moment and then strutted into the kitchen. I was surprised when I heard her speaking to Nadia, who responded in broken English. I had always communicated with the woman using hand signals and facial expressions, never realizing she could understand me.

Ruth came back into the foyer and said, "Nadia can stay. I'm only working until midnight."

"I'll be home before that."

"But you have to give her a ride home."

As I nodded, a car pulled up in front and stopped. Ruth leaned forward, and I thought she was going to whisper something, instructions for Nadia or Nessie's bedtime. But instead, she kissed me. Our schedules were so erratic that we went days, even weeks, without physical contact, and just that small peck got me aroused.

"Bye!" she said.

Standing with a vague smile, I watched her get into the car and drive away. I took off my coat and walked into the kitchen to see Nessie at the table. Ruth and I always used a highchair, but Nadia insisted on a regular chair, and we trusted her matronly wisdom about such things.

While Nessie finished her dinner, Nadia offered me some stew by holding up a spoon and pointing at a plate. I declined with a smile. Harrigan and I had had a late lunch, Reuben sandwiches from Sam LaGrassa's, a deli around the corner from headquarters. Even if we hadn't, I never ate before an operation, as much from nerves as because I didn't want to feel weighed down.

I carried Nessie into the living room and sat beside her on the couch where she asked me questions, clapped her hands, and tried to take off her socks. Much like Nadia, she spoke in single words and fractured sentences, but it was enough that we could have a conversation. When the news came on, I got up and changed it, not wanting to hear any more about war or politics. We watched *Flipper* instead, one of Nessie's favorites, and the sunshine, ocean, and dolphin were a lighthearted distraction. She was getting tired, her eyelids sagging, and it was only six-thirty. I kept my arm around her, holding her close but not tight, the warmth of her small body a comfort to my soul.

Once the show was over, I got up. Nessie held out her arms and moaned, and Nadia came in to help. I had to get ready, and there was nothing worse than coming home and then having to leave again. I went upstairs and washed up and put on casual clothes. I wasn't trying to look like a hippie or grungy college student, but arrests could get rowdy, and I didn't want to be out in a suit.

I thanked Nadia and kissed Nessie on the head. Before walking out, I glanced over to the couch, where they sat close, Nessie sipping apple juice with a straw. Having to leave my daughter to go back into the cold night made me bitter. I couldn't blame it on the job, so I blamed it on the culprits, and if we found Kagan, he was going to get an extra whack for my troubles.

CHAPTER 16

Harrigan and I drove into Kenmore Square, the neon signs of diners, bars, and record shops lighting up the area like a carnival. With the weather still mild, it was bustling. Young people congregated on the sidewalks and in front of stores, smoking cigarettes and talking, the smell of marijuana in the air. Above a diner, music was blaring from a second-floor window, and I could see a party. Outside a pharmacy, a homeless man was reaching into a barrel, and on the corner, a beatnik in a leather coat was playing the sax. Like any place with college students, it was a strange mix of seediness and sophistication.

As we crossed the intersection, I glanced over to the Shawmut Bank, hidden in the shadows, another anonymous block of glass, cement, and asphalt. But for anyone on the force, it was where Giraffe Duggan had died. Whether it would be memorialized, I didn't know—they couldn't honor every cop, fireman, or soldier killed in the line of duty, or the city would be covered in plaques. Still, that spot would always be sacred, some hidden shrine in the plainness of day, remembered only by those who had known and loved Duggan.

We went down a side street and turned onto Bay State Road, a small neighborhood of brick rowhouses. The homes had once all been private residences, but now were mostly dorms, fraternities, and administrative offices for Boston University. I stopped before the address and parked, shutting off the headlights but keeping the car running.

"What time is it?" I asked.

Harrigan pulled up the sleeve of his coat.

"9:18."

I was impressed that he could see in the darkness—my vision was terrible at night.

"I want you to stay here," I said.

He glanced over, but he didn't argue. He was never interested in being at the center of the action, although he never hesitated to get involved.

Moments later, a black car pulled behind us, and I knew it was Marcus. I put on gloves, even though it wasn't cold out. If things got chaotic, I didn't want my prints interfering with the forensics. Taking out my .38, I checked the safety and put it back in my shoulder holster, hidden under my coat along with my handcuffs.

As I reached for the door handle, Harrigan said, "Good luck."

I turned to him with a sarcastic smirk.

"You think I need it?"

I waited until he smiled and then got out. Marcus and his partner were walking toward me, dressed in long trench coats, their collars up.

"Lieutenant," Marcus said, his voice low but friendly. "You look like you should be at Woodstock."

I glanced down at my outfit, which consisted of a t-shirt, bomber jacket, and the denim jeans I had owned for years, faded and frayed at the seams.

"If we don't beat 'em, maybe I'll join 'em," I said, and they both chuckled.

"This is Paul Shine."

"We met," I said, but we shook hands anyway.

"We got support?"

"They should be here any minute."

As if on cue, I saw headlights, and two police cars approached. I stepped off the curb and waved for them to stop, worried that if they got any closer to the address, our suspect would see them and flee.

With the team now assembled, we had to move. Starting down the sidewalk, I squinted to see the house numbers. The street felt like one long dormitory, the Latin words of fraternities mounted above doorways. In one window I saw the Cuban flag and in another, a lava lamp on the sill between two naked figurines.

Finally, we reached number 133, a three-story brick townhouse. All the lights were on, music was blaring, and out front, some students were passing around a joint.

"If we don't get someone for murder, we'll get them for narcotics," Shine said, and I couldn't tell if he was joking.

But pot was the least of our concerns. Egersheim had planned the arrest at night because he thought Kagan would be alone, yet we were going into a full-on bash. I considered turning around, but short of unexpected danger or a change in the logistics, I didn't have the authority to call it off.

"Let's do this," I said.

We rushed up the walkway, and the students on the stoop all got up.

"Who the hell are you?" one of them asked.

I whipped out my badge and shoved it in his face.

"Does Neil Kagan live here?"

"I dunno," he said, recoiling in the doorway.

"Leave him alone, pig!" a girl shouted.

With her braided hair and a beaded necklace, she looked like an enraged pixie, and I just snickered in disgust. Another girl yelled more insults, but they were only trying to taunt us. We all knew the best way to deal with cop-hating kids was to ignore them.

I held the door for Marcus and his partner, and we walked inside. The front room was packed, people leaning against the walls, piled onto couches, beer cans and glasses everywhere. There was a stereo system in the corner, but otherwise, it was sparsely furnished, with a shag rug, a dart board, and a poster of Woody Guthrie. At first, no one noticed us, probably because they were too drunk or stoned. But when they did, the mood changed instantly.

"I need to speak to the owner," I said, holding out my badge.

"Cool out, man," someone said. "He's not here."

"Do you have a search warrant?"

I turned around and standing behind me was a short, scraggly-haired young man with glasses and a goatee. He had a wine glass in his hand, strangely pretentious for a college student. I could tell by looking at him he considered himself an intellectual, his nostrils flared and eyebrow raised, that expression of smug condescension.

"We have an arrest warrant for Neil Kagan," I said. "Is he here?"

"An arrest warrant isn't a search warrant."

As we spoke, I noticed Marcus wandering into the next room.

"The front door was open," I said, and although it didn't techni-cally justify our intrusion, it left some room for legal interpretation. "Where's the owner?"

"The owner lives in New York. I'm going to have to ask you to leave. Now."

I didn't like his attitude, but before I could respond, his eyes darted to the foyer.

"Sir, you have no right to go up there!"

When I turned, Shine was walking up the stairs as casually as if he was going to bed. The man went after him, but Shine didn't stop. I chuckled to myself, admiring the audacity of federal agents, who flouted some of the most basic constitutional principles. But it really wasn't funny because our department would suffer the consequences, an acquittal by way of procedure or, even worse, a lawsuit.

Suddenly, there was shouting.

I ran toward the back of the apartment, pushing through the crowd and almost knocking over a beer keg. I came into a small kitchen where some students were pacing anxiously, two hippie girls glaring at me from the corner. As more people came in, I started to get nervous. I never liked being the only cop in a hostile environment.

"Where's Marecki?" someone asked.

It took a second to remember that *Marecki* was Marcus, and I was relieved when Shine walked in. Everything had happened so fast that I didn't realize the back door was open until then. I flew out of it and came to an access road between the back of the buildings and Storrow Drive. Hearing sounds, I looked and saw two figures running in the distance. I quickly followed them, sprinting over litter and potholes, worried that, at any moment, I might trip and break my ankle.

As I came to the end of the block, I realized one of them was Marcus. He was slowing down, his shoes smacking against the asphalt, arms flailing in exhaustion. He had put on weight since we were kids, but none of us were in the condition to be chasing suspects on foot.

I was just about to call him when he raised one arm. In the darkness of the narrow lane, I saw the shimmer of steel in the moonlight and gasped. It was his gun.

"No!"

Springing forward, I knocked into him, and the gun went off. The bullet strayed, dinging off a street sign or drainpipe.

"What...the...hell!" I said, so winded I couldn't get the words out.

"Jesus, Jody!"

"Was that Kagan?"

As we both stood panting, he just stared at me and shoved his pistol back into the holster. In his face, I saw restrained fury, and I knew he would have berated me if we weren't friends.

He fixed his collar and started to walk away.

"What were you gonna do?" I asked. "Shoot the guy?"

"Fuck these hippies."

......

I DIDN'T LEAVE until after midnight. Any time an officer discharged his weapon, it became a crime scene. I didn't know if the statute applied to the FBI, but it did to us, and after everyone had been interviewed, we still had to wait for forensics to finish. If the incident had taken place on some quiet back street with no one around, we probably could have avoided it. The degree to which any of us adhered to the details of procedure depended on what happened and where. In the middle of the city and with a hundred students watching, the department had to cover its tracks.

Marcus had told investigators the suspect had pointed a gun, something I couldn't confirm or deny. The area was dark, and it had happened in a flash. I was glad they didn't press me on it because I didn't want to be in the position of contradicting a colleague or, even worse, lying on his behalf. But Marcus' behavior had been strange, something I couldn't ignore.

When we finally left, Harrigan decided to walk to Delilah's apartment, which was only a few blocks away. I didn't like the fact that I had run into her at B.U., but lots of students were involved with causes. Just because I saw her at one SDS meeting didn't mean she was a radical. Aside from that, the relationship was convenient because I was tired of driving him back to headquarters on days he drove in, or back to his mother's apartment when he took the subway.

When I got home, the only light on was in the kitchen. Nadia and Ruth were sitting at the table when I came in, Ruth still dressed in her nurse's uniform, Nadia with her coat on. They got up and met me in the foyer.

"Jody," Ruth said, whispering with a smile.

"How's Nessie?"

More than anything, I wanted to go up and see her, that loving angst of a parent. Of all the things about fatherhood, it was what surprised me the most. But I couldn't go into her room because if she woke up, Ruth would be left having to soothe her.

Nadia wanted to get home, so I walked her out to the car and got the door. A cigarette was still smoldering in the ashtray; the seat was still warm. We drove through the empty streets, the only other vehicles being an occasional car or delivery truck. She sat with her pocketbook on her lap, staring out at the darkness. I glanced down at her hands, sturdy but gnarled, and knew she had worked hard all her life. I admired her generation, the pride and resilience of people who had lived through two world wars and a depression. She was always humble, going about her duties with quiet persistence and never complaining. I wondered what she had done in Poland, whether she was a factory worker or the daughter of a farmer. Either way, it was obvious she was happy to be here, the eternal gratefulness of an immigrant, so different from the attitude of American kids. When Marcus had said *fuck these hippies*, I knew he wasn't talking just about people who wore suede vests and bell-bottom jeans, peasant dresses and sandals, folk jewelry and beads. He meant anyone young and self-righteous, and I couldn't disagree.

With almost every light green, we got to Dorchester in ten minutes. For the first time, Nadia spoke, giving me directions with words and half-phrases. As we passed through the intersection of Massachusetts Avenue, I could see the city lights over the industrial flatlands of South Bay. We continued onto Boston Street, the western border of The Polish Triangle, a winding road of massive three-decker homes interspersed with autobody shops, machinists, and other commercial businesses.

She pointed, and I turned down a dead-end street, driving slowly until she blurted, "this!" I looked over to her house, and the only light was a dim glow on the top floor. I thanked her, and she smiled, getting out and hobbling up to the front door. Once she was inside, I drove to the end, struggling to make a U-turn with so many parked cars.

Waiting at the stop sign, I looked to my right and noticed some young people in front of a building, smoking cigarettes and talking. I thought it was a bar or a diner until I saw the Polish flag and realized it was some kind of private club. As I rolled out onto the main road, I stared over. My eyesight was bad at night, but they were close enough that I recognized Stanislaw Sokol. And there beside him, I thought I saw the young woman from Newburyport who had witnessed the armory robbery. But I didn't have time to confirm it.

Suddenly, a horn. Lights came at me. I cut the wheel and hit the gas, swerving out of the way a second before a truck hit me. I pulled over, my heart racing, and looked in the rearview mirror, but they were gone.

CHAPTER 17

"Something's not adding up," I said.

"You're just realizing it now?"

Harrigan sat across from me at the table, sipping coffee and eating an orange. It was a strange combination, so acidic I was getting heartburn just watching him. We had come down to the basement cafeteria because Egersheim wasn't in yet. Times like these reminded me how different he was from Captain Jackson, who would never arrive to work late after an incident.

"Why? You know something I don't?" I asked.

Harrigan glanced around before speaking. Even in the safety of headquarters, we never talked openly about cases.

"The book they found in the car. I always thought it was a little convenient. Don't you?"

"Manual for Marxists," I snickered.

I had always stayed out of politics, more focused on the grind of day-to-day living than on big ideas and mass movements. But anything about communism struck me with particular disgust because I had fought in Korea.

"Do you really think they'd leave something like that behind?"

I shrugged and took a bite of my blueberry muffin.

"They got sloppy. This isn't the Dillinger gang," I said, borrowing a line from Marcus. "They fit the profile. Plus, we've got prints."

"Partial prints, Lieutenant."

"We got a witness—"

"Who was cleared by the feds as unreliable."

Even if he wasn't right, I was too tired to argue. I hadn't slept much the night before, and I blamed it on Marcus, who had turned an arrest attempt into an internal investigation.

"Look," I said. "SDS, United Labor Front, the Black Panthers... these groups are a big threat. They're trying to take this country down. Kagan and his girlfriend are..."

Harrigan listened, but I knew my reasoning was absurd, like saying *even if they didn't do it, they could have done it.*

"That still doesn't make Kagan guilty."

Whether it was from nerves or exhaustion, a surge of rage came over me.

"Fuck the hippies!"

A couple of patrolmen, just back from the overnight shift, looked over, and I was embarrassed by the outburst.

"Sorry," I said.

"Just don't let your prejudices cloud your judgment."

"Now you're starting to sound like Captain Jackson."

"I'll take that as a compliment," Harrigan quickly replied.

"Good, because I meant it that way."

When I smiled, he smiled back, and the tension went away. My anger was never aimed at him, but at the general state of the world, some deep and simmering rage of which specific crimes and cases were only a symptom. I hated losing my temper, something I had been seeing Dr. Kaplan for, because I knew it could destroy me.

"I saw the guy last night," I said.

"Which guy?"

"With the car."

"Which guy with the car, Lieutenant?" Harrigan asked, and I could tell he was getting frustrated.

"Sokol. From Locust Street. The Impala."

"Where?"

"Dorchester. I drove the babysitter home," I said.

The term didn't seem to fit Nadia, but *nursemaid* sounded pretentious and *domestic* even worse.

"That's not so unusual. He lives around there."

"Yeah, but I think he was with the Newburyport witness."

Harrigan's expression sharpened, and he leaned forward. The bit of orange stuck between his teeth did nothing to detract from his seriousness.

"You think or you know?" he asked.

It was a fair question, and I knew he was only trying to protect us both. The complexities of an investigation, especially one so personal, could torment even the most sensible cop, making him see people who weren't there, sense patterns that didn't exist.

"I can't be sure," I said, finally.

"Should we tell the captain?"

"Not yet."

......

WHEN WE WENT BACK to the captain's office, his light was on—he was in. I knocked once, and we entered. Unlike Jackson, who spent as much time at the window thinking as he did at his desk, Egersheim always seemed to be working. But I was never impressed, and there was no bigger sign of either self-doubt or incompetence than someone who was constantly busy.

"Detectives," he said, putting down his pen.

"Sir."

"What the hell was that about last night?"

I chuckled to myself—it was a blunt way to start the morning. He motioned for us to sit, and we did.

"Agent Marecki said the suspect had a gun," I said.

"Did you see a gun?"

"I didn't see a suspect," I said, and he looked puzzled. "There was a party, probably a hundred people. Marcus walked back into the kitch—"

"Did they let you enter?"

I stopped. I knew why he was asking.

"Technically, no. But the front door was open."

His mustache twitched, the closest we were going to get to an approval. I liked that he was lax with procedure because Jackson would have scolded me for entering without a search warrant.

"Kagan went out the back door," I continued. "Marcus ran after him. By the time I caught up, they were a block away."

"And you didn't see Kagan?"

"I...it was dark," I said, stumbling. "I saw somebody."

"Well," the captain said with a sigh. "Let's hope that doesn't become an issue."

He grabbed a newspaper off the desk and held it up. It was the Daily Free Press, the student paper of Boston University. Across the top was a headline in bold: BOSTON POLICE FIRE SHOTS AT DORM PARTY.

I just blinked, too stunned to even frown.

"Boston Police?" I asked.

"They saw cruisers out front. They don't know the difference."

"How is that our fault?"

"It's not our fault, but it's our problem," he said, and he was right.

"Could we not have *public affairs* clear it up?" Harrigan asked.

"Possibly. But the Free Press is run by the students. No friends of law enforcement. Even if they did retract it, the damage is done. Chief McNamara isn't happy. We've been trying to work with B.U. about the protests. This ain't gonna help."

Egersheim sat with his arms crossed, a bemused look on his face. Jackson never would have tolerated such a mix-up, and even though he was the first one to criticize bad police work, he was also the first one to stick up for the department. But I had to stop comparing the captain to him because it only made me bitter.

"Where do we go from here?" I asked.

"There's only one way to go."
"And where's that?"
"Find Neil Kagan."

CHAPTER 18

As with most college students in Boston, Neil Kagan was from somewhere else. Born in the Bronx, he was the son of a butcher from Vienna and a housewife from Queens. He had started at Columbia University before transferring to U.C. Berkeley, dropping out his senior year. Like a lot of aspiring radicals, he used college as a gateway into the world of left-wing politics and social activism. After a stint with SDS, he joined the United Labor Front, speaking at campuses and trying to attract recruits to the organization's more militant approach to social change. By all indications, however, he was heavier on talk than he was on action. In the twenty-page dossier the FBI had given us, there were hints at collaboration with the Weather Underground and other violent groups, but not a single piece of evidence.

Startled by a knock, I looked up and saw Marcus. I had been sitting in my car in the parking lot for almost an hour. It was late afternoon, but the sun was still out, the traffic heavy on the Southeast Expressway beyond. When I had called him earlier, he suggested we meet at the Howard Johnson Motor Lodge so he could get on the highway afterward.

"Did I wake you?" he asked as I got out.

"Trust me, it's not that easy."

He smiled, and we shook hands.

"Sorry to keep you waiting. Something came up at the office."

He leaned against his car, a blue '68 Dodge Charger, its lines sharp and chrome glistening. It was flashy for an agent, and not the kind of attention I would have wanted. But even as a child, Marcus liked nice things, and he could tell a Cadillac Coupe from a Phaeton when most kids at the *Home* had never been in an automobile.

Taking out a pack of cigarettes, he offered me one. But I said no because I didn't want to owe him anything. With the shooting incident and my doubts about Kagan, I knew it was going to be a hard conversation.

"Tough situation last night," I said, trying to feel out his mood.

"No hard feelings, Jody. You panicked."

I made a deep, defensive frown.

"I didn't panic. A dead suspect isn't a suspect."

"I don't agree," he said.

"Do you think Kagan had a gun?"

"Don't think. *Know.*"

"He was running away for chrissakes."

"Before he went around the corner, he turned and pointed it," Marcus said, blowing smoke out his nose. "How's your eyesight, Jody?"

I wanted to say *fine*, but it would have been a lie. And for all I knew, the bureau had my optometry records.

"I don't think Kagan robbed the bank," I said abruptly.

He stood up straight, his expression changing from casual to something more formal, even hostile.

"Yeah? And why is that?"

"Because I saw the guy whose car was stolen for it. He was with the armory witness."

"Where?"

"On Boston Street. Last night. Some kind of social club."

"You were in my neighborhood?" he asked.

"Not your neighborhood. You live in Humarock."

I could tell it stung, and it was payback for his remark about my eyesight. But I was tired of people moving to the suburbs and still claiming they were from the city.

"You're reading into things," he said.

"What about the girl who saw the shooter?"

He paused to think, but I could tell it was an act. He knew exactly who I was talking about.

"I told you. Just a junkie. She changed her story three times in five minutes."

"I still wanna talk to her."

"Then talk to her," he said, shrugging his shoulders. "Good luck finding her."

The conversation was getting tense. He puckered his lips and stared at the ground, his collar flapping in the breeze. It felt like some sort of reckoning, but I didn't expect an epiphany. If he was hiding something, it wouldn't have been unusual because the feds were never generous with their information. But this was different, deeper than the case itself, and I got an eerie feeling.

"Jody," he said, looking up with a sentimental smile. "Remember when we got new baseballs that time?"

"What?"

"At the *Home*. Someone donated new baseballs."

"Yeah," I said.

"We were playing in Franklin Park. You were in the outfield. Vecchio hit one beyond the tree line. We all watched it go over the fence, but you thought it went in the woods. So you went to find it and got lost."

"We never got anything new."

"You were in there for over an hour. They had to send the groundskeeper in to find you."

As he laughed, my smile turned sour. I thought it was a friendly reminiscence, but I realized it meant much more, and bringing up the past was a cheap shot.

"What's your point?"

"My point?" he said. "Kagan's the killer. Look for that girl if you want, but you're being stubborn. Wasting your time."

We stood facing each other in silence until, finally, he broke the stare. With a quick nod, he walked back to his car.

"Marcus," I said as he opened the door.

In the shadowy twilight, he looked over but didn't respond.

"I found that ball."

......

HARRIGAN and I got to the Polish American Club just after 9 p.m. With Ruth off, I had to take advantage of it, even though she didn't like me working nights. I learned it was better to do it consecutively than with days in between, so we could argue about it once and get it over with. Harrigan was also reaching an age where being home was worth more than the overtime. But he never complained, and the only thing he asked was that I drop him at Delilah's afterward.

The building was on Boston Street, across from a warehouse and just yards from the bridge over the highway to South Boston. With its yellow-brick construction and glass-block windows, it looked as sturdy as a fortress, and I wondered if the founders had intended it that way, a symbol of the resilience of the Polish people. Situated between Germany and Russia and with no natural boundaries, the country had always been vulnerable, its history a long struggle against invading armies.

As we walked toward the entrance, some part of me felt like I was encroaching on Marcus' territory because he had grown up there. But we shared the case, something Egersheim had reminded me, and any investigation involving the bureau was always a tug-of-war over jurisdiction.

Out front, two guys stood smoking by the door, dressed in flannels and work boots. One of them glanced up, but neither seemed interested in saying hello.

When we walked in, a dozen faces looked up from the bar. The interior was wide and open with a dance floor, stage, and a jukebox in the corner. With its folding chairs and dropped ceiling, it had the modest charm of a VFW post. But it wasn't just about American patriotism because the signs of ethnic pride were everywhere, the Polish flag, the coat of arms of Poland, a lithograph of Warsaw.

Harrigan and I stepped over to the bar, where a tall man stood mixing drinks with his back to us. When he turned around, our eyes met, and I was surprised.

"Stanislaw?"

He glanced at Harrigan, then back to me.

"I'm Alex," he said bluntly.

I frowned. With his high cheekbones and curly hair, he was no doubt the same man whose car was stolen for the robbery.

"Stan is my brother," he added, which explained the confusion.

"Mind if we ask you some questions?"

I took out my badge, and he nodded. When someone called for a drink, he held up his finger and went to get it. He had the same cold personality as his brother, which made me wonder if unfriendliness ran in families or if they both just didn't like cops.

As Harrigan and I stood waiting, I looked around the room. Behind the bar was a large poster with the silhouettes of some men against the sunset, words below it in Polish and English: *Fundraiser for The Dockworkers of Poland*. Beside that was a round sticker with the word communism crossed out in red. In the corner, there was a dartboard with the face of Leonid Brezhnev, the leader of the Soviet Union, his eyebrows thick and his expression grim. I didn't know much about Polish politics, but those three things were a quick lesson.

Finally, Alex came back.

"I take it you don't like communism?" I asked.

"Who does? The Russians butcher our people."

"What happened to *Workers of the World, Unite*?"

Even as I tried to goad him, I knew I was in over my head. My knowledge of Russian history was limited to one class in high school, and in the Army, communism was something we had all been taught to fear.

"What do you want, officers?" he asked.

"Were you here last night?"

"No."

Knowing now that he had a twin, I couldn't prove if he was lying or not.

"Do you know a Margaret Kozlowski?" I asked.

A couple of the older men looked over.

"Kozlowski is a very common Polish name."

"That's not what I asked," I said.

"Then the answer is no."

"Was that you or your brother I saw at the Boston Common last week?"

"The Boston Common?"

"At the protest."

"Ah," he said, smiling like he was proud. "That was Stan. I was working that day."

"So you heard about the scuffle?"

"It always happens when we go to heckle the protesters, the traitors."

Even if I didn't like his attitude, I couldn't deny I got some small satisfaction in knowing they taunted the activists.

"Traitors, are they?" I asked.

"Of course. They want to bring communism to America," he said, and the more he spoke, the more I noticed a slight accent. "They've no idea what freedom is. They read too many books."

I silently agreed. I never resented the students for wanting peace, but the anti-war movement had become about more than getting us out of Vietnam. Many wanted more radical change, socialism and even communism which, ironically, was what we were trying to stop in Southeast Asia.

"So, did you come here to talk politics or something else?" Alex asked, leaning on the bar, the veins of his forearms pulsating.

"Margaret Kozlowski was a witness to a robbery in Newburyport a couple of weeks ago. Are you familiar with it?"

"I don't pay attention to local news."

"They stole a bunch of weapons, lit the place on fire."

He stared at me, shaking his head.

"Can't help you, officers."

The jukebox came on. I heard the sound of an accordion followed by strings. Men at the bar rustled from their barstools, raising their glasses; people at the tables were similarly stirred. Soon everyone started to sing, some Polish anthem or a patriotic song. I knew it was time to go.

"Thanks," I said.

......

HARRIGAN and I drove down Massachusetts Avenue, which was lined with abandoned brick rowhouses, once elegant and now crumbling. A few of the old jazz bars remained open, but much of the area was derelict, the sidewalks covered in litter, homeless men on the street corners. When I was young, it was still a vibrant part of the city, bordering wealthy Back Bay and within walking distance of Symphony Hall and the Museum of Fine Arts. But after the war, with most of the older residents gone, the buildings were converted into apartments and flophouses for the thousands of blacks coming up from the south for jobs.

Harrigan yawned, something he seldom did. I assumed it was from too much sex because he hadn't been working a lot of overtime.

"How's Delilah?" I asked.

"She's well, Lieutenant," he replied, his emphasis on *lieutenant* telling me he didn't want to talk.

I turned onto Beacon Street and stopped at her building. As he reached back for his briefcase, I smiled, and he grinned, an almost boyish awkwardness about the fact that he was going to see his girl-friend. Harrigan wasn't shy, but he liked to keep his personal life private. And I knew that anything he wanted to say about her or their relationship, he would say when he was ready.

"I want you to pull the record on that guy," I said.

"I will."

"Alex Sokol."

Reaching for the handle, he looked at me.

"I know."

He shut the door, and I pulled away, watching in the rear view as he walked up to the front doors and waited to be buzzed in. I got some secret thrill that he was dating, and I missed those easy years of courtship. But Delilah worried me too, not personally but her circumstances, and after our encounter at the SDS meeting, I knew I should have talked to her. College students were the biggest enemies of law enforcement, and the only thing I could think was that her and Harrigan's connection as black people went deeper than politics.

I came into Kenmore Square, the lights shining in the crisp night air. The weather was changing fast, and people who would have worn t-shirts two weeks ago now had on fall coats and turtlenecks. As I went through the intersection, I glanced over at the Shawmut Bank, the spot where Jerry Duggan was killed. In moments like this, when I was tired and alone, his death hit me harder than the day it happened. For me, the pain of loss never came all at once but resurfaced in the months and years after like a stubborn ghost. Ruth was different, experiencing her grief in one inconsolable burst. When a young nurse on her floor died suddenly from a pulmonary embolism, she cried for two days straight and then never spoke of it again.

For the sake of Duggan's wife and kids, I wanted to get the killer, but the case seemed stalled, at least for me. I just couldn't accept that Kagan shot Duggan and that his girlfriend, Leslie, was the driver. The evidence was average at best and probably could have convinced a lazy jury. But it was also a bit too convenient, and I never trusted investigations that came together too easily. Harrigan had sensed it too, but he was smart enough to only imply his skepticism, not say it. As a junior detective, he had no reason to voice his theories and speculations, especially when they went against what everyone else in the department wanted to believe.

I rolled into the driveway, and the light was on in the living room. As I walked up the steps, the door opened and Ruth was standing in a nightgown, a glass of wine in her hand. For a second, we both hesitated like we were trying to assess each other's moods. With Nessie, our lives had become so frantic that I sometimes forgot whether we were fighting or on good terms, something I was sure she felt too. I wouldn't have traded the world for Nessie, but I wondered how couples with several kids did it, and it gave me a new respect for the staff at the *Home*.

As I stepped closer, I realized that her expression was more sad than serious.

"Everything alright?"

"There were three bombings," she said, her voice quivering. "In California. Two military places. A courthouse."

"That's far away."

I squeezed to get by, but she wouldn't move.

"I wanna leave," she said.

"And go where?"

"Anywhere. We could move to Ireland."

I put down my briefcase and loosened my tie, smiling nostalgically as I thought about our honeymoon there. I turned and faced her, looking down into her eyes. It wasn't the first time she had been shaken by world events. Bobby Kennedy, Martin Luther King, the My Lai Massacre, riots in the cities—the pace and intensity of the past few years were enough to give a yogi a nervous breakdown.

"You have to stop watching the news," I said. I didn't want to be dismissive, but I was too tired for drama. "How's Nessie?"

"She ate a whole bowl of mashed potatoes."

"I'm not surprised if you made them."

Ruth smiled and took a sip of wine. I went up the stairs to check on Nessie, and she followed me, tiptoeing on her bare feet. When I got to the top, I opened the door and peeked in to see her, face-up in the crib and breathing softly. If I didn't have to sleep, I could have watched her all night.

I walked to the end of the hallway, and when I turned into the bedroom, I stopped. Standing by the bureau was Ruth, completely naked and holding her wine, her expression somewhere between seductive and sassy.

"Can I just pee first?" I asked, and she chuckled.

When I returned from the bathroom, she was on the bed, her legs turned to one side. I unbuttoned my shirt, took off my pants, and lay down next to her, rubbing her shoulder, smelling her hair. In years past, I would have skipped foreplay altogether, but the urge to rush to sex was diminishing, and I didn't mind.

After we kissed, she rolled over, and I got on top. I had only been inside her for a couple of seconds when she stopped.

"The door," she said.

I glanced back; it was only slightly open.

"Nessie won't hear."

She raised her eyes and giggled. Soon the mattress began to creak, the only other sounds her quiet moans and the heaves of my exertion. It was over in an instant, hardly the lovemaking finesse of our younger years. As she lay curled up, her face flushed, I got up and went to the window for a cigarette. When we first started dating, she smoked too, but it was always more of a hobby than a habit, and I admired her discipline.

"Have you found the bank robbers?"

"Not yet," I said, flicking the ash.

At one time, she was interested in what I did, no surprise considering I met her while she was working at headquarters. She had lost her interest in crime and law enforcement, or maybe she never had it, going instead into a profession that better fit her personality. She had a natural compassion and a genuine concern for the welfare of others. It was something that fascinated me because I didn't have it.

"I know you loved him," she said.

I stared out at the backyard, the dead leaves rustling in the darkness. *Love* was a harsh word to describe the closeness and comradery between two friends, or maybe I was just too afraid to admit it. Nevertheless, I got choked up.

"Duggan was a good guy."

CHAPTER 19

HARRIGAN AND I GOT TO THE SHAWMUT BANK HALF AN HOUR BEFORE IT opened. The street looked different without all the cruisers and news trucks, a quiet block of buildings, mostly offices except for a Catholic Chapel. Beyond, Kenmore Square was starting to awaken, with commuters waiting at bus stops, students walking to class, the smell of bacon from a nearby diner. It was a beautiful fall morning, the sky a clear stretch of blue, much the same as on the day of the robbery.

Getting out, we walked over to the entrance, where I leaned toward the glass and looked in. From out of the shadows came a man, short and fat, with a gray suit and glasses. He pressed some numbers on a keypad and then opened the door with a key.

"Mr. Brae?" he asked, squinting. "I'm Herb Shepherd."

We shook hands, and I said, "This is Detective Harrigan."

He nodded with a smile and waved us in. As we walked through the bank, female tellers were getting ready for the workday, their skirts short and lipstick heavy. I never understood why they were always so primped in such a dull occupation, but they were second only to airline stewardesses in terms of sexiness.

"Mr. Brae," Shepherd said, and I realized I was gawking.

He led us into a small office with fluorescent lights and a carpeted floor, inviting us to sit before taking the chair behind his desk.

"Now," he said. "I've already told them everything at the last interview."

"We won't take up much of your time. Any idea why you were targeted?"

"Hard to say. We're a small branch. Typically, we don't have a high transaction volume. Except for September. That's when we receive an influx of deposits from the universities for tuitions."

"Boston University?" Harrigan asked, his notepad out and ready.

"And some of the smaller colleges; Bay State, Emerson, Emmanuel. At the end of the third quarter, we prepare the money for transfer."

"Prepare?"

"That's right. Counted, itemized, and bagged." With his elbows on the desk, he spoke like he was conducting a business meeting. "Brinks was scheduled to come that morning. Either the thieves knew the money was waiting, or they got lucky."

"No one gets lucky," I said.

"That's true. One of our tellers saw what was happening and hit the silent alarm."

"Any reason to believe it was politically motivated?"

"Political?"

"Like students...radicals."

Shepherd tilted his head, thinking.

"I didn't see him, of course. He had on a mask, came from behind as I was opening the side door. But no, he didn't sound educated."

"How did he sound?" Harrigan asked, beating me to the question.

"To be frank, like a local. A very thick Boston accent."

I glanced over to Harrigan, who was already looking back. In the background, I could hear voices and movement—the bank was opening. The conversation was brief, but we got what we needed.

"Thank you," I said.

"My pleasure."

We all got up and headed for the door.

"One more thing," I said, stopping. "Anyone with a Polish last name ever work here?"

Shepherd looked up, frowning like he was either confused or offended.

"Mr. Brae. We don't discriminate by nationality."

Even if it was true, it was the canned response of a midlevel manager. Prejudice was rampant in Boston, the most clannish of cities, where ethnicity was the first thing you knew about a person.

"Could you check your employee history? Let me know?"

As I groped to find my wallet, Harrigan handed the man his card, always one step ahead of me.

"If you think it will help," Shepherd said.

"I do."

......

I SAT NESTLED in the soft leather chair, the room so quiet I could hear my heartbeat. From the sixteenth floor, I could see the city through the window shades, but I felt far away. I liked my visits with Dr. Kaplan as much for the relaxation as for the therapy. I had never done meditation, which I saw as the practice of hippies and Hare Krishna devotees, but I imagined the experience was similar. With the low lights and her gentle voice, I felt safe from the threats of the world, even when the things we talked about were difficult.

"Don't you trust Marcus?"

"I don't know if I trust him," I said.

It was a delicate conversation, revealing things about an investigation that was not only active but involved the feds. She was bound by client confidentiality, something she had reminded me of twice already. But I still wasn't comfortable, and maybe it was my upbringing because I grew up at a time when secrecy was honored and squealing scorned.

"Does this relate to current circumstances?"

Circumstances. It was a code word for the bank robbery case, and I appreciated her tact. She didn't know any of the details, but she knew Duggan had been killed.

"Marcus is hiding something," I said. "I don't know what."

"Do you know why?"

I shook my head *no.*

"Could you maybe talk to him about it?" she added.

I raised my eyes; it sounded naïve. But we had been talking in circles. Without specifics, how could she know my suspicions about Marcus were criminal and not some petty squabble?

"It's bigger than that," I said.

When our eyes locked, I got the feeling she understood.

"Let me tell you a story," she said, putting her notebook down on the table. "When we came to this country after the war, my father opened a small shop in New York. My uncle, the husband of his sister, worked there. We all worked there. One winter, my sister and I discovered our uncle was stealing. He was taking sides of ham, blocks of cheese, hiding them in the alleyway to take home. We knew he was poor, and he wasn't right in the head—he had been in the camps. But we had to tell our father. You know why?"

She paused, and I waited in suspense.

"Because that shop was the lifeblood of the family. If it didn't survive, we didn't survive."

The story was like a parable, the lesson clear.

"What happened?" I asked.

"Pardon?"

"What happened to your uncle?"

"My father confronted him, told him he never wanted to see him again."

"I'm sorry," I said, although I knew her reason for telling me was for insight and not sympathy.

"We all make choices that are difficult but necessary."

"Now you sound like my wife," I said, remembering a similar phrase she always used.

The mention of Ruth was enough to make Dr. Kaplan move on to the subject of my marriage.

"How are you two?"

I made a hesitant smile. I almost preferred to keep talking about Marcus.

"She's good, I guess," I said. "She's frightened."

"Frightened?"

"With everything that's going on."

Dr. Kaplan nodded slowly, her gaze gentle yet penetrating. I didn't have to explain because, with the war and all the social turmoil, there wasn't a person alive who didn't feel at least some sense of doom.

"Is it your job?"

"She worries. There've been…a lot of incidents."

Again, we spoke in vague generalities, but everyone knew cops were under attack across the country. It was on the news every night.

"Have you assured her you don't take any unnecessary risks?"

I got a slight chill. I had never considered it. I always thought the best way to shield Ruth from the dangers of my job was to not talk about it.

"She worries more about Nessie," I said, avoiding the question.

She smiled warmly.

"A mother's prerogative."

The bell rang, and our time was up. When I rose from the chair, I got lightheaded, struggling for balance as I smoothed out my jacket and fixed my tie. Each time we parted, I didn't know whether to bow, shake her hand, or give her a hug, such was the emotional impact of our sessions.

"Be gentle with her," she said, and I didn't know if she meant Ruth or our daughter. "These are uncertain times."

"I will."

I left and went down the elevator with an almost euphoric calm. As I exited the building, I stopped in the doorway, looking to make sure no one I knew was around. The sessions always left me feeling better, if only because we discussed things I could never say openly. But in my line of work, psychotherapy was viewed as a sign of weakness or mental incapacity. The risks of being caught leaving *Headcase Hotel* ranged from gossip to ending my career, so I had to be careful.

When I got back to headquarters, I rushed through the lobby with my head down and went straight to see the captain. Knocking once, I opened the door and was repulsed by an awful stench. If I had known he was eating an egg salad sandwich, I would have waited. But it was too late, and when he waved me in, I had no choice but to enter and sit down.

"We've got a report," he said, his mouth full, mayonnaise on his mustache, "that Kagan is still in town."

"I guess he can't take a hint."

He stopped chewing, and his expression sharpened.

"He's a cop killer, Lieutenant, not a jilted lover."

The remark was harsh, almost insulting, especially considering I had been friends with Jerry Duggan, not him.

"Yes, sir."

"We believe he's staying at an apartment on Beacon Street," he continued, wiping his lips. He leaned forward and read something on the desk. "Number 610."

"B.U.," I mumbled, and he looked up.

"You know it?"

"It's a Boston University dorm. In Kenmore Square."

"Criminals never stray far from their crimes."

The proverb might have been true in the past, but it wasn't now. With most investigations I was involved in, the suspects were usually found miles from the scene, sometimes in other states, and often not at all.

Someone knocked on the door, and I glanced over to see Harrigan. I could tell he had just had lunch, that look of satisfied fullness, and it reminded me I was hungry.

"Detective," Egersheim said. "We've got a lead on Kagan. We're gonna move in."

"When, sir?"

"Immediately."

"Right now?" I asked.

"There's no time to lose. If he's armed, he's dangerous—"

He stopped short, staring both of us in the eyes. I could sense his urgency.

"I've arranged for two patrol cars," he added. "Will that be enough?"

"Should be. Does B.U. know we're coming?"

"The chief called the provost to let him know we'll be executing an arrest warrant."

I glanced up at Harrigan, who was still standing, then back to the captain.

"I'm ready," I said.

The meeting was quick and direct like they always were with Egersheim. Under Captain Jackson, discussions could last hours, and I missed that camaraderie almost as much as the man. I would have voiced my doubts about Kagan to Jackson, but with Egersheim and the chief so determined to put a name to the killer, I knew it wouldn't have changed anything for them.

"One more thing," the captain said as I got up. "Don't make a spectacle. We don't need any more bad press."

"Yes, sir."

CHAPTER 20

I<small>F THE WHOLE CITY WASN'T WAITING FOR AN ARREST, EVERYONE ON THE</small> force was. There was a time when the murder of a cop would have made it seem as if time had stopped, the public outrage and collective feeling of grief would have united residents. But Boston had lost the intimacy it once had, those years when it was like one giant, extended family, with all the bickering and spite that went along with it. Beyond that, America's youth didn't have the same respect for authority, and with the country in a crisis, most people were too distracted to care.

As we pulled up to the Beacon Street address, I got a creeping dread, and it wasn't because we were moving in on a suspect. It was where Delilah lived, the featureless brick building that, by now, had become Harrigan's second home. He didn't seem anxious or concerned, and with over seven hundred students, he probably saw no reason to be. But I wondered if he knew yet about her associations with SDS.

"Of all the places," he said.

"If we knew last night, you could've grabbed him yourself."

He made a sarcastic smile.

We waited for the backup, but I wasn't expecting a standoff, and I wouldn't have been surprised if Kagan wasn't even there. When ten minutes passed and they still hadn't arrived, I nodded to Harrigan, and we got out. We walked to the front doors, and I pressed a button, the building manager buzzing the door after I identified myself.

Right before we entered, I heard sirens. Not one or two, but dozens. Then, like in a scene from Dragnet, police cruisers appeared from every direction. They raced up to the building, stopping at different angles, officers jumping out.

"So much for secrecy," I said, shaking my head.

We walked in and took the first stairwell so we wouldn't alarm anybody. On the seventh floor, we came out to a long hallway where all I could smell was marijuana and cigarettes. A couple of girls sat cross-legged on the floor, and when I forced a smile, they just glared at us.

I counted off the numbers, one by one, until we got to the room. While Harrigan stood with his back to the wall, out of sight and ready to pounce, I stepped up to the door. Hearing voices inside, I knocked once. Seconds later, it swung open, and I froze. It was Delilah.

"Hello," I said, the most awkward greeting I ever had to make. "We're looking for Neil…"

Before I could finish, someone moved in the background. A face turned to me. It was him. Instantly, I reached for my gun and ran past her into the room.

"Hands up!" I shouted, and he obeyed.

There were three young women too, dressed in faded jeans and baggy shirts. One raised her hands, another jumped back against the wall, and the third got up off the bed.

"Leave him ALONE!"

"What are you doing, pig?!"

In the frantic confusion, my eyes followed them, worrying someone might try something stupid. But the moment Harrigan walked in, they all seemed to calm down. One of the benefits of having a black partner was that liberals saw them as allies, ironic considering he had voted for Nixon and Goldwater.

"Hands against the wall!" I said to Kagan.

I walked over, and did a quick search, groping his legs and arms, not expecting to find anything.

"You're under arrest for the murder of Sergeant Gerald Duggan."

My voice cracked as I said it, as much out of sadness as because I wasn't convinced it was true.

"A lie!" one of the girls shrieked.

Kagan dropped his head as I cuffed his hands behind his back. The fact that he didn't argue or resist somehow confirmed my doubts. The guilty were always the loudest at proclaiming their innocence.

"That's absurd, man," was all he said.

As we turned to leave, I heard footsteps in the hallway, and a dozen officers appeared at the door. The whole thing happened so fast that I realized they probably had only been a minute behind us. If their dramatic arrival on the street wasn't going to cause a public uproar, then entering the dormitory in force would. But even if Egersheim or the chief had told them not to, it was hard to expect any officer to show restraint in the apprehension of a cop killer.

"Need assistance, sir?" a sergeant asked.

I shook my head, still out of breath.

"Them too?" he added.

The three girls who had been so defiant before were now cowering in the corner. If I was going to arrest any one of them for harboring a fugitive, I would have had to arrest them all, including Delilah. And I couldn't do that to Harrigan.

"Naw," I said, finally. "They didn't know."

As I led Kagan out, the cops stepped back, lining the wall. I was sure some would have spit on him if they could have, but they maintained a cool, if bitter, professionalism. I looked around for Harrigan, but he and Delilah were gone. I took Kagan down the elevator, and when we got to the lobby, Harrigan came out from a stairwell.

"Wondered where you went," I said, but he didn't reply.

We walked out the front doors, and the news trucks were already there. I took Kagan over to the closest cruiser, where a cop stood holding the door open. A journalist tried to ask questions, but a patrolman got in his way and shoved him back. The relationship between the media and the BPD wasn't cordial at the best of times.

"Hey, officer!" someone called out.

I thought it was a colleague or a reporter, but when I turned, I saw three guys watching from the sidewalk. With casual clothes and baseball caps, they could have been students, and my first instinct with young people was always mistrust.

"Good work, man," one of them said, holding up his thumb.

I was so stunned by the comment that I stopped, but only for a second. Then I guided Kagan into the backseat with a little less force than I would have without the praise. It was comforting to know not everyone was against us.

"You got the wrong guy, man," he said.

"Take that up with your lawyer."

I pushed his leg in and slammed the door shut.

......

BY THE TIME Harrigan and I left headquarters, it was dark. With the media camped out front, we had to bring Kagan in the back when we arrived. And they were still there. A small crowd of supporters had gathered too, confronting officials and chanting for Kagan's release. I was surprised the chief hadn't ordered them removed, but with the political situation so delicate, he probably didn't want the attention.

Harrigan and I drove home in silence like we always did. This was a different kind of silence, however, more like a simmering tension than the absence of sound. He didn't seem upset, but he was always hard to read. There was a lot to discuss, and in some ways, the case was the least of my concerns. But like everything I dreaded or feared to say, I waited until the very last minute.

"I owe you an apology," I said as I pulled up to his building.

"You do?"

"I wanted to tell you before. I saw Delilah at the SDS meeting."

"You did?"

"I'll talk to her if you want."

As he reached for his briefcase, I could detect a subtle mischief in his voice.

"You will?"

We had worked together long enough that I knew something wasn't right, and I was confused. He opened the door and just before he stepped out, he turned to me.

"Who do you think told us Kagan was staying there?" he asked.

The relief I felt was only second to my humiliation—it was something I never could have predicted.

"Are you serious?"

He nodded.

"The captain doesn't know," he said.

"Son of a bitch."

He shut the door, leaving me stunned.

I drove off through the dark streets. Roxbury always felt foreign to me at night, the gangs of black youths on the corners, figures creeping in the shadows of alleyways, the neon of the endless liquor stores. Crime was so bad that the houses had bars on the windows, and I couldn't go a few blocks without hearing sirens. The slum I had grown up in was still a slum, only the people had changed.

I thought back to my childhood, those years at the *Home* when I never felt unwanted because I didn't know what it was like to be wanted. Growing up during the Depression was hard, and I remembered always feeling cold, even in summer. Marcus had come into my life at the age when I was starting to realize I was alone in the world. Under different circumstances, we probably never would have become friends. He was wild and always getting into trouble; I was quiet and obedient, something a lot of my friends now would have had a hard time believing. But within the bleak walls of the institution, everyone needed an ally. Marcus and I bonded from that first morning we sat together in the basement cafeteria, he in his ragged knickers and me in my overalls. Both of us liked comic books, as well as frogs, which we would search for in the dense weeds beside the schoolyard.

Our time together didn't last. Around the age of ten, he got into a fight with a boy who had stolen his ring, beating him to a pulp in the hallway while other kids cheered. When he disappeared not long afterward, we all thought he had gone to jail or juvie until one of the staff members told us he had been adopted. Thinking back about those times, I assumed he had now come back into my life for a reason, although I didn't know if it was God's or the Devil's.

By the time I got home, it was late, and I yearned to see Nessie before she went to bed. As I walked in, Ruth rushed down the stairs. I didn't notice the panicked look on her face until she came into the light of the foyer.

"Why aren't you at work?—"

"Nadia's daughter is missing," she blurted.

"Pardon?"

"Nadia. Her daughter has been missing since yesterday."

I didn't know much about the woman's life, other than that she was from Poland and lived in Dorchester.

"From school?"

Ruth shook her head, her hair bushy and wild.

"She's an adult. She's twenty-five. She didn't come home from work."

It was a relief to hear she was older because I dreaded nothing more than when kids or adolescents went missing. Putting down my briefcase, I looked up the stairs to the dark hallway.

"How's Ness?" I asked, always my first concern.

"Asleep. Can you talk to Nadia?"

I took Ruth around the waist and brought her into the living room, where I saw a glass of wine on the table beside a *Ladies' Home Journal* magazine. The television was on, casting shadows on the wall, but the volume was low. We sat together on the couch, my feet aching after a long day. When a picture of Neil Kagan flashed across the screen, I turned to distract her because I didn't want to talk about work. But it was too late.

"You were on TV."

"Bozo the Clown?" I joked.

She looked at me with a sentimental smile, our faces just inches apart. Her eyes were glassy, but I didn't know if it was the wine or if she had been crying.

"You got the killer," she said.

"We got someone."

Snuggling closer, she pushed my bangs aside.

"You don't sound so sure."

"I'm not sure about anything," I said.

"You're not sure about us?" she asked, her voice soft, sensual.

"That's not what I mean."

CHAPTER 21

"Brae, this has got to stop!"

I had come to work expecting a commendation but instead got a lashing. The FBI had called Egersheim to complain that we met with the manager of the Shawmut Bank, something they had already done. They said it was out of concern for the integrity of the investigation, but I knew it was pride. The bureau never liked having their work double-checked.

"We just…um…had more questions, sir," I said.

"Then you should've at least called Marecki or Shine as a courtesy. You know the terms—they handle anything under federal jurisdiction. We deal with the local stuff."

"Was firing at a suspect *federal jurisdiction?*"

He gave me a sharp look. It was a bold response, and I worried I had gone too far.

"Look, I agree," he said, and I was relieved. "That was unusual. You didn't see a gun. But I'm not about to contradict an agent. Besides, aren't you friends with the guy?"

"A long time ago," I mumbled.

For the first time, I found myself distancing myself from Marcus which, in some strange way, felt like a betrayal. I assumed it was a hang-up from my youth, that blind loyalty to friends and groups that had helped us all survive.

Egersheim put his hands on the desk and looked at the clock.

"There's a press conference at eleven. I've gotta see the chief beforehand."

He paused with a tight smile—the meeting was over.

"And Brae," he said, and I looked up. "Good work yesterday."

The compliment surprised me, if only because it was so late.

"Even with the twenty cruisers?"

He smirked, raising his eyes. The amount of backup at Kagan's arrest was excessive, and I knew it wouldn't help relations between the department and the university.

"That was a fuck up."

When I walked out, Harrigan was coming toward the door. I put out my hand to stop him, hoping to save him the aggravation of an admonishment by Egersheim for our bank visit. But the captain was never as hard on him as he was on me. I had only heard him raise his voice to Harrigan once, and that was for losing a case file that Egersheim had mislabeled.

"My office," I said.

"Lieutenant?"

He hesitated for a moment and then followed me down the hallway and around the corner. I unlocked the door, and we walked inside and sat down, me at the desk and him in the chair beside it.

"Why didn't the captain mention Delilah?" I asked.

"He doesn't know."

"Whaddya mean he doesn't know?"

"It was an anonymous tip."

Raising my chin, I gave him a sideways glance. I expected him to say more and when he didn't, I felt like he was being dishonest.

"Just come clean, dammit!"

"Delilah was with Neil Kagan and Leslie Lavoie the morning of the robbery."

Stunned, I shook my head.

"Unbelievable," I said.

"It was only a planning meeting…for a protest on Boston Common."

"Where our brothers get spit on? Called pigs?"

"She's in the anti-war movement, not a member of SDS or the United Labor Front—"

"That's what they all say!"

"I can assure you she's not a radical," he said, firmly but not yelling.

In all our time working together, Harrigan had never pleaded for anything. I didn't know what it was like to date an activist, but I knew what it was like to be young and in love. Even if I wasn't convinced Delilah was completely innocent, I believed he believed it, and I owed him my trust.

"I just wish you had told me," I said.

"I just did."

I nodded, knowing he was right. The shooting, the investigation, the arrest—everything had happened so fast the subtleties of the case had been lost in the fray.

"Okay."

"Lieutenant, my apologies."

I gazed out the window, downplaying it with a smile. No one felt worse about the argument than I did.

"Don't worry about it."

CHAPTER 22

Like most homes in The Polish Triangle, Nadia's had three floors and a flat roof, and the only ornamentation was some trim above the windows. The siding was gray, faded and peeling, and on one corner, I noticed a piece of wire holding the downspout in place. It reminded me of Marcus's mother's house, but then all the buildings here were weather-worn and shabby.

The dead-end street was tight, but there were fewer cars during the day, so I found a spot out front. Harrigan and I walked up to the door and rang the bell. He stood still with his hands in the pockets of his coat, and even with his sunglasses, I could tell he was looking around anxiously. With its narrow streets and ethnic shops, the neighborhood was as insular as an Eastern European ghetto, and I knew he didn't like being the only black face around.

The buzzer sounded, and we walked in, ascending a steep staircase, the steps creaking beneath our feet. When we reached the top, an older man was waiting for us at the door. He was short, with dark eyes and a chiseled face, tanned from either drinking or working outside. In his flat cap and wool trousers, he had the old-world appearance of an immigrant laborer.

"Is Nadia here?" I asked.

He smiled and turned his head, shouting something in Polish. He waved to us, and when we walked in, Nadia burst from the hallway.

"My God," she exclaimed. "My baby!"

"Nadia, what happened?"

"She gone!"

I looked at the man, and he nodded. Together, we escorted her over to the couch, and Harrigan shut the front door.

"Calm down, please," I said, sitting beside her. "Tell me what happened."

"She no come home."

"Come home from where?"

"She work—"

"Where?" I asked.

"A bar. In Boston."

"Does she have a boyfriend?"

Nadia hesitated, then shook her head.

"No. She good girl."

"Of course. What's her name?"

"Alina," she said, and I could barely understand it with her accent. "Alina Jankowski."

I looked over to Harrigan, who stood by the wall with his notepad out.

"Could she be staying with friends, perhaps?"

She gave me a confused look.

"Friends," I repeated, speaking louder like it would help. "Could she be staying with friends?"

Nadia looked at the man, and they spoke in Polish, the words quick and harsh-sounding. Then she turned back to me and said, "No friends."

I didn't know if she meant Alina had no friends or that her friends didn't know where she was. I was getting frustrated, thinking we should have brought an interpreter, if the department even had one. Nadia and I communicated fine at my house when our conversations were about Nessie's bed and bath time, the occasional foray into the weather, or the best kind of cabbage for soups.

"Do you have a picture?" Harrigan asked.

"Yes, a picture," I added.

"Picture? Alina picture?"

"Yes," I said, forcing a smile.

She got up and went into the dining room, where I watched her open a china cabinet. She came back with a framed photo, holding it against her breast with exaggerated longing. Or was it exaggerated? In the past, I would have scoffed, but now that I had a daughter, I understood.

She gave it to me like she was handing her baby over to a stranger. Taking it, I turned it around and was stunned. It was a teenage girl with dark shoulder-length hair and perfect bangs, smiling awkwardly for the camera. It could have been any senior year portrait, but I instantly recognized her as the witness from the bank robbery, the girl Marcus and Shine had let go.

"This is your daughter?" I asked, peering up.

Nadia nodded, her mouth quivering.

I looked at Harrigan, and when he came over to see, I could tell he was shocked too.

"May we take this?" I asked.

"Take?"

"For a missing person's report."

Nadia hesitated like she was translating the words in her mind. Even if she didn't understand what I said, she knew what I meant.

"Yes. Take," she said.

"Where does Alina work, exactly?"

When she replied, it took me a moment to realize she had said *Piccadilly Lounge*. I always prided myself on being indifferent to facts and circumstances, a cold professionalism that got me through the toughest investigations. But I knew Nadia, and she took care of Nessie, so learning that Alina worked at a strip club was especially disturbing. I wondered if Nadia knew, or if she thought her daughter was a waitress or barmaid.

"Thank you," I said, then I glanced over to the man, who had been standing quietly. "We'll open up a report today."

I still didn't know who he was, except that he had the concerned look of a husband, brother, or friend. I got up to go, and as they walked us to the door, I remembered something.

"Do you know a Margaret Marie?"

"Margaret Marie *Kozlowski*," Harrigan added.

Nadia looked at the man and, again, they had a quick exchange of words.

"She work at club."

"Club?"

"Polish American Club," the man said. "Boston Street."

"Thank you."

Harrigan and I walked out, down the stairway and into the afternoon sun. Some boys were playing street hockey, their sticks as worn and ragged as their clothes. As we got into the car, they stopped and stared at us. If they didn't know we were cops, they definitely knew we weren't from around there.

"Piccadilly Lounge," Harrigan said as we got in. "That's in Kenmore Square, is it not?"

"Stop pretending you don't know."

"Pardon?" he asked, looking offended.

"It's a strip joint."

We made a U-turn and drove away, the boys watching us until we reached the end of the street. Turning right, I pulled over, and the Polish American Club was so close we should have walked.

When we entered, a couple of men looked over from the bar, and in the corner, some women were knitting. The bartender was a middle-aged lady with frosted hair and a collared shirt. As I approached, I took out my badge, showing it discreetly so I didn't draw any attention.

"Afternoon," I said.

"How can I help you?"

It was a much friendlier reception than the first visit, but I wasn't surprised. For the most part, people in blue-collar neighborhoods appreciated the police; our biggest enemies were always college students and liberal suburbanites.

"Where's Alex?"

"He's off today. He's working."

I was confused until I realized he was probably just part-time. Without the money for permanent staffing, a lot of social organizations were run by volunteers.

"And where is that?"

"At the docks."

"Do you know Margaret Kozlowski?" I asked, and when she hesitated, I wanted to give her a chance not to lie. "I was told she works here."

"She does, but not today."

"Can you tell me when she'll be in next?"

She walked over to the wall, where she squinted to read a small calendar.

"Next Friday," she said.

Beside the rows of liquor bottles was the poster I saw the last time: *Fundraiser for The Dockworkers of Poland.*

"For the event?"

"Yes."

"What's the fundraiser for?"

She gave me a funny look—the title was obvious.

"To help the workers in Poland."

"And why do they need help?"

Seated at the bar was an older man, a newspaper and a pint of beer in front of him. I had sensed he was listening, but I didn't expect him to chime in.

"Because the communists are bastards," he said, then he raised his glass. "The Soviets raise prices, and our people starve."

I responded with a cold nod. Although I respected his loyalty to his homeland, it wasn't my fight.

"Do you know Alina Jankowski?" I asked the waitress.

"Of course."

"Have you seen her?" I asked.

"She lives around the corner—"

"I know."

I gave her a kind but deliberate stare. I could have said Alina was missing, but word traveled fast in such a close community. If anything had happened to her, I didn't want to alert the culprits that we were investigating.

"To be honest, I haven't seen her in a while," she said.

"Do you know where she works?"

She sighed, smirking like she was aware that I knew.

"She does what she has to. We all do."

CHAPTER 23

WHEN EGERSHEIM FINALLY GOT TO WORK, HARRIGAN AND I HAD BEEN waiting for half an hour. Dressed in casual pants and a cardigan sweater, I knew the captain had an afternoon tee time, and he played golf almost every Friday. I didn't mind that he had hobbies, something I wished I had more of, but it was a level of professional moderation I wasn't used to. In thirty years, Captain Jackson had never missed a day of work. His only interests were trout fishing at his cottage in Maine, where he went twice a year, and a daily walk in Boston Common.

"Detectives," Egersheim said. "The State Police arrested Leslie Lavoie yesterday near Smith College."

"Smith College?"

"Northampton," Harrigan said.

"Ah, out west."

They both grinned. I didn't mean to be sarcastic, but to me, any part of the state past Greater Boston was the frontier.

"She's at Charles Street Jail. The female wing," he said.

"What do we have her on?"

"Accessory."

"Just accessory?"

"Even if the feds push for felony murder, she probably won't do much time. You know how judges are…"

The remark was cynical but accurate. While women had made a lot of gains since I was a kid, they were still coddled in many areas of society, often to their advantage.

"If you could pull all your case notes together," he added. "Get them over to Marcus and Shine."

"Everything?"

"Everything. The case is going to federal court. We're done, boys."

He wiped his hands as if to emphasize it. I hadn't seen him so excited since he was asked to speak at the Patrolman's Association dinner. Kagan's arrest was a relief for everyone, and I understood why Chief McNamara was eager to see a quick conviction. But there were too many inconsistencies, too many unanswered questions. Harrigan and I may not have been the only ones with doubts, but we were the only ones in a position to make them known.

"Sir," I said, hesitantly. "We've got a possible missing person."

He was organizing his files, face down and only half-listening.

"Um, send it down to the second floor."

I glanced over to Harrigan for encouragement, and he nodded.

"It's the witness," I said. "The girl."

Egersheim looked up. I knew I had his attention.

"What girl? There are dozens of witnesses."

It wasn't really true. Dozens of people were questioned, but they were mostly pedestrians who had heard the shot or seen the car speed away.

"The girl who saw the suspects. She was questioned by the feds, but they let her go."

"Then they must have had good reason."

"I don't believe so, sir," I said.

The room filled with a quiet tension. When his brow furrowed in thought, I couldn't tell if it was out of genuine interest or an attempt to appease me. But even if he, like the administration, wanted to close the investigation, it was a coincidence that couldn't be ignored.

"Who reported this?" he asked.

"The girl's mother. She's our babysitter."

Crossing his arms, he leaned back in the chair.

"You think it might be related?"

I could have talked about my gut, my instincts, and all the other intangibles that came with almost twenty years on the force. But holding up the prosecution would require facts, not feelings. Delilah was our one wildcard, someone who could vouch for the alibi of Kagan and Lavoie and prove they didn't rob the bank. But I didn't want to bring her into it unless we couldn't find evidence for who did.

"I think it's suspicious," I said, finally.

"Okay, okay. See what you can find out. I've got a meeting. I'll be out the rest of the afternoon..."

I laughed to myself, knowing it was a stretch.

Harrigan and I left the office, walking in silence until we got to the parking lot. As we went to get into the Valiant, he stopped and faced me across the hood. I knew what he was going to ask.

"Should we have told him?"

"Told him what?" I asked.

"About Delilah."

"Not yet."

"Why, Lieutenant?"

"You finally got a girlfriend. I'm not about to ruin it."

......

WE PULLED into the lot for Charles Street Jail, the oldest municipal prison in the city. Situated along Storrow Drive, it looked out of place next to Mass General Hospital and the lavish brownstones of Beacon Hill. Constructed of solid granite, it had tall arched windows with bars and a central rotunda with four wings that, ironically, gave it the shape of a cross. Over the years, it had housed everyone from vagrants to German POWs, and the guards had a reputation for being tough.

The main doors opened to a dingy lobby, the floors scuffed up, folding chairs and pedestal ashtrays along the wall. At the counter, an overweight guard sat behind a sheet of plexiglass. When we showed him our badges, he waved us through with a yawn. I didn't envy their job, the endless hours of boredom.

At the end of the hallway, two guards were sitting by an entry gate, their hats tipped and batons at their sides. I knew one of them was a lieutenant by his white shirt, and as we approached, he said, "Detective Brae."

Although he looked familiar, he could have just recognized me from the news. Kagan's arrest had gotten a lot of attention.

"We're here to see Neil Kagan."

"The cop killer," he snickered as he got up.

"Is he trouble?"

"He's no Charles Manson. Just a punk."

He told us to follow, and we took a staircase to the third floor, coming out to a long walkway of cells that overlooked the unit. Halfway down, he stopped and unlocked a steel door, pushing it open with a creak. When I peered in, Kagan was standing at the window with his back to me. In his t-shirt and jeans, he was thinner than I remembered, and I wondered if he had lost weight.

"Neil?" I said, and he turned around.

"What?"

He took a drag on his cigarette and put it out in a small metal sink.

"Detective Jody Brae," I said. "And this is Detective Harrigan."

He frowned and shrugged his shoulders.

"Whaddya want?"

"Just to talk."

"Where's Leslie?"

"Here," I said, and his eyes widened. "The women's wing."

"When can I see her?"

I knew *I don't know* wasn't a good answer—he could have easily refused to speak with us. So I made a promise I wasn't sure I could keep.

"Answer some questions, and I'll arrange it."

"Fire away," he said, grinning at the irony.

I glanced back to make sure the guard was gone. The prison staff was a gossipy bunch, and I didn't want him to overhear.

"Were you at the Shawmut Bank on the morning of September 24th at 8:45 a.m.?"

He looked at me pointedly and said, "No."

"Where were you?"

"I dunno, man. Some dorm. We were meeting with some chick about some stuff."

Meeting with some chick about some stuff. Sometimes I felt like my generation spoke a different language than his. But it matched what Harrigan had said about Delilah, and that was all the proof I needed.

"Do you know a Margaret Kozlowski?" I asked.

Kagan shook his head, curled his lips.

"Nope. Who is she?"

I ignored the question—witness names were confidential. But I had to keep pressing, knowing that most suspects were only cooperative until they realized they were cooperating.

"How about an *Alina*?" I asked.

This time his expression changed, and he stood thinking.

"Yeah, man," he said, finally. "I knew a chick named Alina. She called herself Lena. Hot little babe, dark hair—"

"How do you know her?"

"She dances at a place in Kenmore Square."

"The Piccadilly Lounge?"

"So you've been?"

My response was somewhere between a smile and a frown. I could always appreciate sarcasm.

"Do you know why you're in here?" I asked.

The question was vague, and I intended it that way. I didn't want to give him any indication that we had doubts about his guilt.

"The feds wanna pin this shit on me. They've been up my ass forever."

"Why is that?" Harrigan asked.

"Who knows? Maybe 'cause I make waves, man. I expose the truth about capitalism."

"Then you're familiar with a book called *Manual for Marxists*?"

"Sure. But it's pure crap," he said, and I was so surprised I thought I had misheard him. "Marxism is for Western elites. Maoism is about the people."

For anyone raised with the bread-and-butter simplicity of pre-war America, the sixties were a confusing mash of social theories and political ideology. I knew enough about the Soviet Union to fear it, but the distinctions between Marx and Mao were like splitting hairs on a bald man. The young could fret over big ideas, I just wanted the protests and riots to stop.

"Thanks for your time," I said.

As Harrigan and I turned to leave, Kagan said, "Hey, cop," and I stopped.

"I may be a communist, but I'm not a murderer."

We locked eyes, and I thought he had more to say. But when several seconds passed, and he didn't, I looked at Harrigan, and we walked out. The guard was standing a few cells away, chatting with another inmate through the bars.

"Get what you need?" he asked as we approached.

"We did, but he didn't."

"You mean a beating?"

He laughed out loud, the darkness of jail humor. I waited until we turned into the stairwell then asked, "Any chance you could get him a visit with his girlfriend?"

"That piece of sh...?"

He stopped when he realized I was serious. But a favor asked was a favor owed.

"Let me see what I can do."

......

THE PICCADILLY LOUNGE was on a small lane that ran between the Mass Turnpike and the backside of Commonwealth Avenue. The building looked more like a warehouse than a business, which made sense because the two upper floors were a tool and die shop. It had started as a speakeasy during Prohibition before becoming a jazz club. In the late fifties, there was so much controversy around urban renewal that the owner was able to get an adult entertainment license without drawing much attention. For all the watchdog organizations intent on keeping the city's seedier establishments confined to the Combat Zone, it was a slap in the face. But the location was just hidden enough that people forgot about it.

The only sign was a white placard, small and faded, that said *Piccadilly Lounge, Gentleman's Establishment*. When I opened the heavy black door, Harrigan gave me a distasteful look, and we walked inside. The lights were low, the air smokey, and Creedence Clearwater Revival was playing. It was only midday and there were a couple of dozen patrons, huddled around a stage while a scrawny blonde, nude and tattoo-covered, danced to the music. Half of them looked like college students, with long hair and untucked shirts, and the others looked like married men. It was a creepy scene, the girl on display like a wild animal, and it made me ashamed for having once been so young and lustful.

I walked over to the bar, where a big guy with a beard stood wiping down a glass.

"Afternoon," I said.

"What can I get you guys?"

"Does Alina work here?"

Stiffening up, he looked at Harrigan, then me.

"Who's asking?"

I had hoped to get out of there without flashing my badge, which was always risky. While some people were intimidated by the presence of a cop, others could get obnoxious, even hostile. But I was too tired to waste any time, so I took it out, and he didn't seem to mind.

"Lena hasn't been in for a few nights," he said.

"Yeah, I know."

"You do?"

"She's missing."

"I only work Fridays and Saturdays."

It was a familiar reaction. Anytime I questioned someone, the first thing they did was give me an alibi.

"Do you know if she has a boyfriend?" I asked. "Maybe someone we could talk to?"

"She has a lot of boyfriends," he said with a wink.

I responded with a sour grin, not knowing if he meant she was easy or that she sold sex. Whatever the insinuation, it was hard to hear. Fatherhood had given me a new sympathy for troubled young women.

Suddenly, there was cheering. I turned, and the dancer was fully bent over at the edge of the stage. With her face between her legs, she smiled while a man placed a bill in her mouth.

"There is someone," the bartender said.

"I'm listening."

"He used to come in to see her."

"Used to?"

"He hasn't been in in a few weeks. An older guy."

"What'd he look like?"

"Short, dark hair. Stocky."

"Did he wear a suit?"

"Yeah, I'd say he looked more like a professional."

As I stood thinking, I heard more voices, applause. Now the girl was flat on her back, her ankles on the shoulders of another guy, rocking her hips as his friends tossed her bills. I glanced over at Harrigan, who looked appalled but didn't turn away.

"Tell me, what time do you close?" I asked the bartender, and he laughed.

"Close? We never close."

"So, do the girls work all night?"

"A lot do."

"Thanks."

I nodded to Harrigan, and we turned to go.

"Hey," the bartender called, and I stopped. "Is Lena alright?"

"We don't know yet."

When we walked out, two homeless men were standing by the fence, dressed in dark coats, passing a bottle between them. Rush hour had started, a steady hum of traffic on the highway below. As we crossed the street, I could see between the buildings the narrow alleyway beside the Shawmut Bank. It was only a thirty-second walk from the club and the route Alina would have taken the morning of the robbery.

"Glad to be outta there," I said as we got in the car.

"You think it's Agent Marecki?"

I started the engine and looked at Harrigan.

"Who?"

"The guy who comes in to see her."

"Short with dark hair? That could be a million people."

"Stocky."

If Harrigan didn't always know what I was thinking, he at least knew what I suspected. Or maybe our minds just worked the same way. But he was right, and something the bartender said struck me. People used words like heavyset, chunky, or squat, but no one ever said *stocky* unless they meant it. And of all the words I could have picked to describe Marcus, it was the most accurate.

"I do."

CHAPTER 24

I SAT RESTLESSLY IN THE CHAIR, FIDGETING WITH MY FINGERS AND looking around. Our sessions were always at the same time, but the room was darker, a sign of the ever-shortening days. Whether it was her training or personality, Dr. Kaplan never spoke until I did, our conversations a perfectly balanced exchange of thoughts, ideas, and observations about life. Usually, it flowed, but today it didn't. For most of the hour, I jumped from topic to topic, my thoughts scattered. But as we got close to the end, I could no longer avoid what I dreaded to say.

"I think Marcus was involved with the bank robbery."

She nodded slowly as if absorbing the news, her gaze so strong I blushed. Under almost any other circumstances, I wouldn't have told her because it was a violation of confidentiality, and I didn't want to betray a friend. I was tormented by the investigation, however, the rush to judgment and the questionable evidence. I was sure that, even in normal times, the case against Kagan and Leslie wouldn't have made it to trial. But these weren't normal times. With an officer dead and the country divided, the department was looking for an easy scapegoat. And where better to find one than from a generation that didn't respect order?

"Do you think? Or do you know?" she asked.

"That's the problem. I think, but I don't know."

"You have a hunch?"

I always appreciated her delicacy, never pushing for details, letting me reveal things on my own terms.

"I don't get what the motive is. He has a good job."

"People do things for all sorts of reasons," she said.

"Maybe he's a crook."

"Maybe he always has been. You said he was unruly?"

"We were just kids," I scoffed, looking away.

"If you were certain he had something to do with it, would you feel obligated not to say anything?"

I smiled. She had summed up my dilemma in one sentence.

"It...it was different then," I said, drifting back to my boyhood, my one refuge in times of confusion or distress. "You didn't rat on friends."

"Even if they were wrong?"

"Never."

"Do you think that's an honorable way to live? Or was it maybe something you had to do to survive at the *Home*?"

If I had discovered anything about our sessions, it was that whenever I felt defensive, it meant she was right. When I looked up, our eyes met, and I was forced to give an honest answer, both for her and for myself.

"It was what we had to do," I said.

All at once, I felt a great relief, as if admitting it somehow absolved me from my past mistakes. I was never a bad kid, but my early life made me hard, and I learned to suppress fear and anxiety like I was flexing a muscle. Toughness was a useful skill—it made me a good soldier in Korea—but wars didn't last forever. Ruth always said she couldn't get through to me, and I had never understood what she meant.

When the timer rang, I felt like I was awoken from a trance. The room wasn't hot, but I was sweating, the same sensation as when a fever breaks.

Putting down the notebook, she gave me a warm, sympathetic smile that was almost motherly.

"I can't advise you about protocol in this area," she said, and I nodded. "But you need to talk to him."

It was the first time she had given me an order, not a suggestion.

"I will."

. . . . . .

THE FBI FIELD office was on the 3rd floor of the John F. Kennedy Federal Building, only a block from city hall. The complex of two white towers was built soon after the president's assassination, a glistening testament to the boy from Boston.

As I walked in, I showed my badge to the guards. With the rash of attacks on police stations, courthouses, and other government buildings, security was high, so I had to pass through a metal detector and get patted down. It was one reason I left Harrigan in the car because, although easygoing, he hated anything intrusive, whether a hug, a physical exam, or a frisk.

I took the elevator up, a large binder under my arm. It opened to a lobby with faux leather couches, ashtrays, and some abstract paintings that looked more suited to a chic hotel. Maybe I expected a door with a peephole, but it was remarkably modern for such a secretive organization, and I wondered if they were trying to improve their image. Throughout my career, I had collaborated with the FBI dozens of times, from the red scare in the fifties to the Irish gang wars more recently, which left bodies scattered across the city. But I had never been to the office, always consulting with agents by phone or at some inconspicuous diner or pizzeria.

Behind the desk, a secretary was filing her nails, her blonde hair in a beehive style. As I walked over, Marcus came barreling around the corner as if late for a meeting, a wide grin on his face, an expression I now found insincere.

"Jody," he said, and we shook hands. "Great work last week. Follow me."

When I called him earlier to talk, he wavered. For the first time since the start of the investigation, he was too busy to meet. But I had to deliver the case files, a convenient excuse, and I was glad he agreed because I would have come anyway. If I owed him anything for our years of friendship, it was one final conversation.

We walked into a small conference room, where arrows and shapes were scribbled on a whiteboard, a tactical blueprint for some plan or investigation.

I dropped the binder on the table.

"Everything's in there," I said.

"Thanks. Want some coffee? Water?"

"I'm fine. This won't take long."

Once we sat, he lit a cigarette and offered me one, but I declined.

"So? What's up?" he asked, holding his smile like he was holding his breath.

"Marcus, I don't think Kagan and his girlfriend robbed the bank."

His face dropped; his cheery expression vanished.

"Ridiculous," he said.

That feeling of kinship, something we always had, was gone, replaced by a cold suspicion that bordered on hostility. Maybe it had always been there, I thought, buried under the layers of nostalgia. Despite all its hardships and letdowns, my childhood was something I cherished. Those early years together were like another time, and now I felt like I was dealing with an adversary rather than a friend.

He took a quick drag on his cigarette and blew out the smoke.

"Brae," he said, and he never called me by my last name, "we've got these bastards dead to rights. Fingerprints—"

"Partials."

"Subversive literature—"

"A book you can get in any college bookstore!"

"Witnesses—"

With each exchange, the conversation got more heated, and

although we weren't shouting, our words had all the bitterness of an argument.

"One witness!" I said. "From the armory robbery. You let the other girl go."

"You're still hung up on that junkie?"

"She's missing."

All at once, the room went silent. We sat facing each other in a wordless standoff that felt like some moment of truth. He looked mad, but he also looked worried.

"How do you know that?" he asked.

That single question validated all my suspicions—he never could have expected she was the daughter of our babysitter.

"A little bird told me."

He had to grin. It was the phrase the warden at the *Home* always used whenever we were brought into her office for some mischief or infraction.

"Get her name. I'll look into it."

"We're already on it."

Leaning forward, he softened his tone.

"Jody, how long have we known each other?"

"What's it matter?"

I knew agents were trained in psychological techniques but seducing me with old memories and lost sentiments wasn't going to work.

"You gotta trust me on this," he said. "You're chasing windmills."

Chasing windmills. He said it all the time when we were young, a phrase he had fallen in love with after we saw the film Don Quixote at the local library one summer. Back then, I never understood what it meant and knew he didn't either. But the implication now was clear.

"I know what I see."

He stood up, looming over me with his hands on the table.

"Let us do our job. Let this case go!"

He stared into my eyes, his nostrils flaring, trying to intimidate me. But I wasn't afraid of him now and never had been. So I calmly got up and headed for the door.

"Brae," he called, and I turned around.
"Just curious. Why are you seeing a shrink?"
With our eyes locked, I shook my head in disgust.
"Go to hell."

CHAPTER 25

I DROVE HOME UNDER THE WEIGHT OF A NEW DESPAIR, KNOWING THAT IF the charges against Kagan weren't a setup, they were at least a diversion. If it was only our department handling the investigation, I would have had no problem expressing my doubts. It was easy to stand up for justice when the stakes were low. But with Duggan dead and the FBI on the case, I didn't want to seem like a turncoat.

As I came up the front steps, I saw Ruth and Nessie through the window, seated on the couch and playing Pattycake. I stopped and watched, captivated by their intimate time together, knowing the mood would change once I walked in. And my instincts were right because the moment I opened the door, Ruth rushed over from the couch, leaving Nessie with a confused pout.

"Any news on Alina?" she asked.

I put down my briefcase and unbuttoned my coat.

"I submitted a report."

"Well? Are they looking for her?"

I walked into the living room, and Nessie held out her arms. Nothing was more tender than the feeling of being wanted by a child.

"It doesn't work like that," I said to Ruth as I picked up Nessie. "There're hundreds of active missing persons' cases."

"Jody, you gotta find her. Nadia is beside herself."

"I know, I know," I said, spinning Nessie around just enough to make her giggle without getting dizzy. "I went by her house today."

Ruth crossed her arms and stood with a restrained anxiousness. She was beautiful when she was worried, her face flushed and her cleavage showing through her satin blouse. When I found myself getting aroused, I turned away and took Nessie to the window. I never liked mixing the pleasures of marriage with the pleasures of fatherhood, ironic considering the first led to the second.

"Do you think they'll find her?" Ruth asked.

"Who knows? Maybe she left town with a boyfriend for a few days. She's a young woman, an adult."

"She's never done anything like this. She's very close with her mother."

"Who was the man at her house? Her father?"

"No. She never knew her father. He died in Poland after the war."

Nessie pointed outside to my car, asking me why I had chosen green, if it was faster than other colors. Between her questions and Ruth's, I was torn between two worlds, the magical innocence of childhood and the brutality of life. Twenty-five years later, I was still hearing about the consequences of the Second World War.

"It hasn't even been 48 hours. We gotta give it time, see if she calls or comes home."

With Nessie getting heavy in my arms, I put her down, realizing she was growing fast. She scrambled over to her box of toys, and I turned to Ruth, who stood waiting for my reassurance.

"I wouldn't panic yet," I said, slightly winded. "I don't think it's suspicious."

The first point would have been enough; the second put me in the position of having to lie because I did think it was suspicious.

"You promise?"

"Daddy?!"

When I looked down, Nessie had her toy phone, red and blue with a face on the front. She wanted to play a game where she would talk to me on it while I used the real phone.

"I promise," I said.

Ruth was satisfied enough that she smiled. She looked over at Nessie, then at me, and for a moment, I thought we might embrace.

"I'll go get dinner ready."

......

AFTER WE ATE, Ruth and I sat on the couch with Nessie and watched *I Love Lucy*, her favorite show. That precious time between dinner and bedtime was always too short, while my hours at work seemed to drag. When I felt Ruth's fingers touch my shoulder, I looked over, and she smiled. She nodded to Nessie, who was asleep with her head on her chest. Ruth picked her up, and we took her upstairs, placing her in the bed and pulling up the covers. In the nightlight's shadow, we stood gazing down at our daughter, a moment of near-perfect bliss between the chaos of days.

Ruth closed the door, and I went into the bedroom, where I took off my suit jacket and hung it in the closet. Even though I was tired, it was too early for bed, and we always stayed up later on nights she was off. I had just gotten my sweater on when I heard a forced cough and turned around. Standing by the dresser was Ruth, her shirt opened to reveal her bra and stomach. She had a seductive gaze, her eyes low and hips tilted, and I was always amazed at how she had gotten sexier over time.

We walked toward each other and met at the bed. When I put my arms around her, she pressed her lips against mine, and we kissed passionately. I was so aroused that I picked her up, and she giggled when I plopped her on the mattress. In the passion of the moment, neither of us had time to fully undress. So I pulled my pants down to my knees, and she lifted her skirt, as frantic and clumsy as two teenagers.

Sometime later, I was startled awake. In the darkness, my heart pounded, seized by panic. For years I had nightmares about Korea, some winter firefight where the blood ran red in the snow of the mountains. I had seen more death and mutilation in the war than in all my time as a cop. But this was different, more a sense of urgency than doom. I knew it was the investigation.

Beside me, Ruth lay on her side, the only sounds her breathing and muffled snores. With work and Nessie, we were always exhausted, but she seemed to need sleep more. I got dressed and tiptoed downstairs, grabbing my coat and keys. As I walked out, I double-checked the lock, a habit from my years living in rougher areas. I got into the Valiant, turning the key slowly as if it would lessen the jolt of starting a car at midnight.

As I drove away, I didn't have to think about where I was going. Whether by some force or instinct, I was drawn to the one place where all the tangled threads and loose ends of the bank case seemed to lead. The Polish Triangle.

The neighborhood looked different at night, the narrow streets quiet and empty, almost tranquil. Even the homes, those box-like giants with splintered shingles and leaky gutters, had a humble grandeur that was absent by day. I went past Marcus's mother's apartment, glancing up at the top floor, wondering if he was staying over. Next, I drove by Nadia's house, the tiny dead-end road in the shadow of the expressway. Noticing a faint light in the back, I imagined her sitting in the kitchen, fretting away the early hours with tea, too heartbroken to sleep.

I always found it difficult to have compassion for people I didn't know well, and Ruth complained I was cold. Dr. Kaplan called it a "coping mechanism," some emotional defense I had developed as a consequence of my upbringing and the war. So I was surprised to find myself worried about Nadia and Alina. Maybe it was a sign that, after all these years, I was getting better.

I rolled up to the corner and looked over to the Polish American Club, looming like a giant shadow on the sidewalk. As I smoked a cigarette, I watched two men come out the front doors and get into a car. They could have just finished closing the bar, but I was curious enough that when they pulled out, I followed them.

Keeping a safe distance, I continued over the bridge into South Boston, past a brick housing project and streets of derelict rowhouses. After the residential area, I came out to the seaport, an industrial no-man's-land of warehouses and factories, many of them abandoned. I kept my eyes on the taillights of the car while it turned onto Northern Avenue and headed toward the water. The road was pitch dark, the shapes of trawlers and other commercial vessels visible in the distance. Even with the windows up, I could smell the stench from all the fish processing plants.

Suddenly, the car turned down one of the wharves. I pulled over and parked, reaching into my glove compartment for my Beretta .32, which sat hidden under my registration papers and some napkins. Harrigan had been warning me for months to secure it, but I always felt safer with a spare gun around.

I got out and walked toward the pier, the only sound the echo of my footsteps. The sky was clear, the breeze soft, and I sometimes forgot how beautiful the harbor was at night. As I came around one of the buildings, I heard voices and stopped. With my back to the wall, I peered around the corner and saw two men leaning against the car smoking, their leather jackets shining in the moonlight. One was either Stan Sokol or his brother Alex—dealing with twins made a mockery of any investigation. The other person I didn't recognize.

I stepped back, and when I looked again, there was someone else. With his back to me, I couldn't see his face. Whatever they were doing, it looked shady; no one met on a dock after midnight to talk sports or politics. I looked around, noting the location so I could investigate the company. As I did, the man turned, and I gasped when I realized it was Marcus.

My heart sank, and my temper flared, but it only confirmed what I already knew. Still, a part of me had held out hope I would be wrong, that some new details or overlooked evidence would shatter my suspicions and make me ashamed for ever having had them. Now that I saw it in person, all doubt was gone, and there was no going back.

I sped all the way home, slowing down only when I got to my street, where I shut off the headlights and rolled into the driveway.

Tip-toeing up the steps, I put the key in the lock, my hand still trembling from what I had seen. When I crept into the dark foyer, I saw a figure on the stairs and flinched.

"Ruth?

"Are you seeing someone?"

"No—"

"I heard the car! Where the hell were you?!"

With Nessie asleep, she didn't shout, but her whisper had all the intensity of it. Yet she sounded more worried than mad, and I understood why. There was a time when my nerves were so frayed I couldn't sleep, and I would go walking at night, sometimes with my gun. I had made so much progress with Dr. Kaplan that just the appearance of going back to those days made it feel like a setback. So my first impulse was to be completely honest.

"Marcus planned the bank robbery," I said.

Her mouth dropped open. As I stepped toward her, she put up her hands.

"He killed Gerald?"

"No. I mean…I don't know. I don't think so. But his cohorts did."

"Jody," she said, her voice cracking. "This is…too much…"

We stood facing each other in the darkness, the emotion so tense I could feel it. Ruth had put up with a lot over the years, and the long hours and weekends were only part of it. When I was younger, I treated the job like some extension of the war, where the objective was clear and the enemy obvious. But I was reaching an age where sheer stubbornness wasn't enough to offset the stress, and just ignoring it no longer worked.

After Jackson died, I had been next in line for captain. Everyone in the department expected it, and with Nessie in our lives, Ruth was looking forward to me working in a more managerial role, off the streets and out of danger. But an incident behind a triple-decker in South Boston changed the course of my career. While serving an arrest warrant to a man who had murdered his family, I chased him into an alleyway and beat him senseless. Even as I was doing it, I knew it was wrong, and I probably would have killed him if Harrigan hadn't shown up and stopped me. Despite the brutality of the suspect's crime, the newspapers ran the story, and the only reason it didn't cause more of a public outcry was that the next day Robert Kennedy was assassinated. The scandal went away, but my rage had cost me the promotion, ironic considering I probably would have been safer in an office.

CHAPTER 26

IN ALL OUR YEARS WORKING TOGETHER, I HAD SEEN HARRIGAN ANGRY, anxious, aggravated, and annoyed. But I had never seen him truly panicked until he ran over to my car while I was pulling into headquarters. He followed me as I parked like he feared I would turn around and leave. After finding a spot, I reached for my briefcase, which was once again empty after delivering the case file to Marcus.

"You waiting for me?" I asked, getting out.

"Lieutenant, we need to talk."

"Can't we do it inside?"

"No."

"Let me just go tell—"

"He's in a meeting with the chief."

Our eyes locked.

"Okay."

Both of us got into the Valiant and shut the doors.

"Delilah called me last night," he said. "She got a summons."

"A summons? What kind of summons?"

"To appear at Suffolk Superior Court. For harboring a fugitive."

Sighing, I reached for a cigarette.

"Can I talk to her?" I asked.

"She's home right now."

Without another word, I started the car, and we flew out of the lot. The anxiety he had was now mine, too. I knew Delilah would be exonerated once the facts were revealed. She had informed us about Kagan's location, making his arrest possible. But if it also came out that Harrigan knew and didn't tell the captain, he could face a reprimand or worse. He had never received a complaint, either from a superior or from a member of the public, and he prided himself on his integrity.

As we passed the Boston Common, protesters were getting ready for another day in front of the State House. With their signs still on the ground, I couldn't tell if it was about the Vietnam war, women's rights, black power, or sexual freedom. And although I probably agreed with a lot of their views, I hated their tactics, and just the sight of them made me drive faster.

We got to Delilah's in minutes and parked out front. When she buzzed us in, it felt like a repeat of the day we got Kagan. The elevator still creaked; the hallway still smelled like pot. The only difference was that her apartment was across from the room we found him in.

Harrigan tapped on the door, and Delilah opened it, inviting us in with a nervous smile. I hadn't seen her in weeks and forgot how beautiful she was, her smooth brown skin and penetrating eyes.

"Hello."

"Hello," she responded softly.

Inside was a standard student dormitory room with a bed, a bathroom, and a desk. On the walls, there were posters of Martin Luther King, Nina Simone, and Miles Davis. Through the small window, I could see the Citgo sign in Kenmore Square, only yards from where Duggan had been gunned down.

Harrigan and I took the only two chairs, and Delilah sat on the bed, which was neatly made with a striped duvet.

"I understand you got a notice to appear in court," I said.

Nodding, she bit her bottom lip. The tension I thought was from distrust was just nerves. I could tell she was scared.

"I received it last week," she said.

"What was your relationship with Neil Kagan?"

"I know him from the Student Alliance."

"Which is what, exactly?"

"A coalition of all the activist groups on campus."

"Is *Students for a Democratic Society* a member?"

She glanced over to Harrigan, who sat with a look of tender yet professional support. It was an awkward situation, and I sympathized with them both.

"Yes, they are," she said, averting her eyes. "So am I."

The admission seemed harder for her than for me. Knowing that she was a political activist, I didn't care if it was SDS or the Sierra Club.

"How about United Labor Front?"

"I never heard of them until Neil showed up. Everyone said they were like SDS, except they were going to take things to the next level."

"What's *the next level?*"

"They were more…determined," she said, although *extreme* was the more appropriate word. "They want to overthrow the capitalist patriarchy and bring about societal transformation through radical social and political change…"

It was the programmed response of ideological zeal, something that always irked me. In Korea, the prisoners we interrogated would spout similar phrases and slogans like brainwashed zombies.

I raised my eyes and said, "Seems like a lot for one man."

"The United Labor Front is small but growing. Kagan came to Boston to start a chapter."

"And was he successful?" I asked.

"He made some inroads with SDS and some of the other anti-war groups. But he was planning to go back to Berkeley."

The remark caught my attention.

"Why?"

"He said he was being harassed here."

"Harassed?"

"Like followed. Whenever he spoke at meetings."

"Who'd he think was following him?"

"I don't know," she said. "I only overheard him talking to some of the girls…"

When she looked toward the door, I knew she meant the students who had hidden him.

"I…I had nothing to do with that," she added.

Her tone had all the purity of truth, but I would have believed her anyway. She had informed on Kagan's protectors and was Harrigan's girlfriend, so I trusted her.

"And Leslie Lavoie?"

"I don't know her. She was active with SDS until he convinced her to join the United Labor Front."

"Thank you," I said, then looked over to Harrigan, signaling it was time to go.

I could have pressed for more, but Delilah looked upset, and I didn't know if it was fear over the court summons or embarrassment at being involved with Kagan.

We all got up and made our way toward the door.

"If anyone contacts you, police or FBI," I said, "call me before you talk to them."

I handed her a card, and she glanced down, running her fingers over the words.

"Thank you. I will."

She was confident but humble, something I had sensed the first time I met her, and I only wished I had been so mature at her age. Considering that I was a white middle-aged cop from Boston, and she was a black graduate student from Chicago, it was a strange envy. I had come there to clear up some questions about Kagan, but I was leaving with the feeling that Harrigan had made a good choice. And for that reason, I had every intention of protecting them both.

Before walking out, I stopped.

"Just curious. Do you believe all that stuff?" I asked.

I wasn't specific, leaving her to decide which *stuff* I meant. She looked up, fluttered her long lashes, and smiled.

"I just want the war to end."

......

As we drove, Harrigan stared ahead and didn't say a word. It was more like a simmering silence than his normal quiet, and I knew something was on his mind. But I wouldn't say anything because he was the type of person who would only talk when ready. And he was stubborn. We were almost at headquarters when he finally mumbled something, and I looked over.

"What?"

"I shouldn't have gotten involved with her," he said.

"Too late for that."

"Lieutenant, I apologize."

"No need to," I said, tapping my cigarette out the window.

In the tumultuous days of my courtship with Ruth, he had always listened to me, and I was glad to return the favor.

"She's too young for me anyway."

"How young?"

"Thirty next month."

"That ain't young," I scoffed. "A perfect age to settle down."

"I really don't think I can be with her."

I hit the brakes and pulled over, turning to him.

"Don't say that!"

He sat facing me, his eyes wide and his back against the door.

"Lieutenant, with all due respect."

"Don't give me that *all due respect* shit!" I said. "She's a great girl."

"But the job—"

"To hell with the job! For chrissakes, you think the job is more important than her?"

My reaction far exceeded the circumstances. I could never predict the things that would set me off. But having learned the hard way that work was no substitute for happiness, I was only offering advice I wished I had been given.

"If you insist," he said, like it was an order. "What if the D.A. looks into it?"

"The DA's got bigger fish to fry."

It was a corny phrase that Captain Jackson used to use, some sentimental tribute to the man who had taught us everything.

"How do you mean?"

"I saw Marcus with Stan Sokol...or his brother. I couldn't tell. Either way, they know each other."

"When, Lieutenant?"

"Last night I...I went down to the Polish American Club. I saw some guys leaving, so I followed them."

I stumbled as I spoke, and it was mostly out of guilt. Of all the unspoken rules about our partnership, never going out to investigate alone was near the top.

"What were they doing?"

Just the thought of what I had seen made me anxious.

"I don't know."

"Shall we tell the captain?"

I always loved how he phrased things, and his dignified speech could soften the most difficult subjects. But this was one time it wouldn't help. If the news was a turning point, I knew Egersheim wouldn't be able to handle it.

"I guess we have to."

CHAPTER 27

WHEN HARRIGAN AND I WALKED INTO THE CAFETERIA, IT WAS SO EARLY that officers from the late shift were still coming in, their boots and parkas wet from the rain. I recognized a few, but most were rookies, consigned to work overnights because they were lowest on the seniority list. Even those who weren't had been on a lot less time than me, young men in their twenties and early thirties with boyish faces and the shine of youth. Sometimes I missed those carefree days, but considering all the trouble in the country, I wouldn't have wanted to be starting a career in law enforcement.

While Harrigan went to get breakfast, I sat down, sipped my coffee, and tried to stay awake. Ruth had come home shaken up about something at work, and I had tossed in bed worrying about the case. It was a restless night for both of us, and the only one who slept was Nessie.

"Stay at Delilah's last night?" I asked.

Putting his tray on the table, Harrigan shook his head and took a seat.

"Why?"

"My mother needs care," he said.

"So does a woman."

He gave me a sharp look and then plunged his spoon into a bowl of Raisin Bran. Even after our talk, I could tell he was still having doubts about Delilah, and it had nothing to do with compatibility. I wasn't going to let the ethical problems of the case ruin his chance at a relationship. The job was temporary; love was eternal.

"Whether you are together or not won't change anything—"

We got distracted when some cops swaggered in, talking loudly and cracking jokes. As they passed, they raised their thumbs, congratulating us on the arrest. I smiled for their sake—the whole force was relieved that we got someone for Duggan's murder. But I had a hard time accepting praise for something I thought was a sham.

"But I knew she was in the anti-war movement," Harrigan said.

"So what? We're not obliged to avoid everyone we disagree with."

He looked up, and our eyes met.

"I don't necessarily disagree."

As conventional as he appeared, he often went against the grain, and I always wondered if it was because he was black or because he was an immigrant. He was the sole Republican in a department of diehard Democrats but had sympathized with petty criminals and drug addicts long before it was fashionable. His ideas about love and marriage were staunchly traditional, yet he was the only one to stick up for a queer waiter who was being teased at a department Christmas party. I could never tell if he was full of contradictions or if we were all just hypocrites.

"Neither do I," I said.

"You don't?"

I lowered my voice, but not because I was ashamed.

"No. I want us the hell out of 'Nam, too."

Rubbing his chin, he looked around, his tense face giving way to a smile.

"Sometimes, Lieutenant, you surprise me."

......

AS USUAL, we sat waiting for Egersheim. Sometimes it felt like we spent more time in his office than he did. When he finally walked in, he was drenched. After acknowledging us with a curt smile, he hung up his coat. Once he sat, he pulled out a cigarette, which took five tries to light because the pack was damp. He had a few drags, shuffled some paperwork, and jotted down notes, working clumsily like we weren't even there. After Jackson's death, getting him for a boss was like trading in an all-star for a bush league player. But Egersheim had enough bureaucratic savvy to get by, which was its own form of skill. When not sure what to do, he always knew the right people to call.

I could blame him for his incompetence, but not for his position because it was the chief who had appointed him. Also, he gave me and Harrigan enough freedom so that we didn't clash, which worked fine when investigations went smoothly. But undermining a prosecution that had the support of the leadership, the rank-n-file, and most of the city was a new level of audacity, and I wasn't sure I was brave enough to do it.

"Sir, we don't believe Kagan robbed the bank," Harrigan blurted.

The words sent a chill through my body. I glanced over at him with a subtle but proud smile. The captain put down his pen and looked up.

"Pardon?" he asked.

"I said *we don't believe Kagan robbed the bank.*"

"The grand jury has already convened. It's too late for this nonsense!"

Egersheim was visibly defiant. Sensing that Harrigan was losing his nerve, I knew it was my moment to jump in.

"Sir," I said. "I saw Marcus...Mark Marecki at the seaport last night."

"What were you doing there?"

It was the wrong question, and he seemed to know it.

"Just out for fresh air," I said snidely.

"Go on, Lieutenant."

"Stanislaw Sokol was with him..."

He looked confused, which made me think he hadn't even read the case notes. I didn't want to complicate things by adding that Sokol had a twin, so I said, "The guy whose car was allegedly stolen for the bank robbery."

"Marecki would have interviewed the guy. Maybe they hit it off?"

The explanation was weak, even for Egersheim. Just like I had predicted, he wasn't able to handle it. He paused for a moment, hands clasped, thinking.

"Anything on that missing girl?" he asked.

"Nothing."

"I'm putting you on the case. I know her mother works for you."

It was a clever change of subject, and I got a strange mix of gratitude and bitterness. Obviously, he did it to avoid talking about the Kagan case, but he was also being generous. Except for investigations where a suspect or victim disappeared, the homicide unit never dealt with missing persons.

"Yes, sir," I said.

As Harrigan and I got up to go, I had the feeling I had just been tricked. But with my instincts telling me Alina and the robbery were related, at least it would buy us some time. In the hard choices of police ethics, finding a girl who might be alive was more important than getting the killer of a cop who wasn't.

"Gentlemen," the captain said, and we both turned. "Just don't drag it out. I can't have my detectives out chasing runaways."

CHAPTER 28

IT HAD BEEN A WEEK SINCE ALINA WAS REPORTED MISSING. TO MY surprise, Captain Egersheim had done his part, notifying the district commanders, putting out an APB, and even contacting the FBI, which kept a national registry. But much of it was for show, and mostly because I had asked him. People went missing every day, and no department had the resources to track down every impulsive teen, unhappy wife, or disgruntled employee. Some turned up, others never did, and only a very few cases ended up being classified as suspicious. It was unfortunate that crime got more attention than despair, but in the rat race of American life, those who were left behind were less important than those who got in the way.

I had already stopped by twice to see Nadia, who was in a permanent state of mourning, candles lit under the framed portrait of the Pope, a bible open on the table. It was hard to reassure her since conversations about procedure and statistics were impossible with her broken English. So we talked about the past, that universal language of nostalgia and regret.

She and her daughter had arrived in Boston after the war, living first in a settlement house run by Polish Catholic nuns in the South End. Alina was just an infant, having been born three months before they left. Nadia's husband couldn't come because he was detained in some camp for POWs or displaced persons. He later died of typhus, something I realized when she coughed and pointed to her forearm, suggesting a rash. I didn't know much about those chaotic days after the war, but it sounded typical, the women and children all uprooted, the men languishing in a devastated nation. Nevertheless, it was sad to hear that Alina had never met her father which, coupled with their poverty, might have explained why she resorted to stripping.

Despite my concern for Alina, I didn't want to spend my days looking for her. If she was still in the city, staying with friends or living on the streets, then the beat cops were better equipped to spot her. But considering she was from The Polish Triangle, it gave us an excuse to dig further into Stan and Alex Sokol who, at this point, were the only links to Duggan's death besides Marcus.

"They were born in Warsaw, Poland, November 5th, 1946," Harrigan said. "Arrived at Ellis Island, '48 with their mother and sister."

"Jesus, did any of these kids have fathers?"

As we drove, he read from their files while I absorbed the news and made offhand comments. It reminded me of the old days before everything had to go through the records department. Back then, entire investigations—notes, evidence, forensics reports, and witness statements—were kept in expandable document folders. We would take them wherever we went, a traveling case docket, and when we didn't, they were locked in the file cabinet in Jackson's office.

"They graduated Dorchester High School, 1964—"

"I don't want their life stories," I said, and he frowned.

Harrigan never rushed anything, always proceeding with the care and delicacy of a surgeon.

"Stanislaw was arrested for shoplifting from Filenes," he said, "December, '59. Receiving stolen goods in March of '61. in July of '61..."

It was mostly petty crimes—nothing I wouldn't have expected from a poor kid from Dorchester.

"...June, '66. Assault & battery at a rally in Cambridge."

"Now we're getting somewhere," I said. "Was it on police?"

"No. It says he attacked some protesters."

I smiled to myself.

"Is that even a crime?"

I didn't look over to see Harrigan's expression; his silence was scorn enough.

"Alexander was arrested with his brother at the event," he continued. "Reckless driving in May of '64. Drunk and disorderly that same summer. Not much else."

Turning onto Dorchester Avenue, we went past blocks of small businesses with Polish flags in the windows. Even with the rain, people were out, congregating on the corners and waving to friends and neighbors. In front of a pub, several men stood smoking beneath an awning, and they glared as we went by. By now I was used to it, and even if the Valiant wasn't a standard police vehicle, we still looked like cops.

With the wipers on, I scanned the misty streets, looking for Alina. But the truth was, all women in their mid-twenties looked the same. And I didn't believe she was in her neighborhood. In a community so close-knit, it would have been impossible to hide, and I was sure people knew she was missing.

We continued through South Boston and into the seaport, the hulls of giant commercial vessels rising through the gray haze. I found the wharf where I had seen Marcus and parked on the street, the gutter overflowing with murky water.

As we walked along the pier, the moist air reeked of fish, and in the distance, I heard cranes and other machinery. Halfway down, an old cargo ship was tied to the dock, its lines stretching and creaking. It looked like it had been at sea for decades, streaks of rust running down its hull and sides of the bridge house.

We headed toward the main office, a shabby corrugated steel building with a warped roof and no windows. When I opened the door, a bell jingled overhead. The room was plain and dank, with a long counter and some notices on the walls about work regulations and labor laws. Moments later, a chubby man walked in with a cigar hanging from his mouth. His thinning hair was slicked back, and he was sweating despite the cold.

"What can I do for you fellas?" he asked.

I showed him my badge, and he just nodded.

"Does a Stanislaw Sokol work here?"

"Stan," Harrigan added.

"A lot of men work here."

"I think he's Polish."

The man snorted, raising his eyes.

"So are half these bums."

"Long dark hair?"

"Again," he said, shaking his head. "Gotta be more specific."

He leaned on the counter like it was a struggle to stay upright. Even though he was gruff, he was friendly, and I knew shipping was a hard line of work, whether you were a dockworker or a manager.

"Does much work go on here after midnight?"

He shrugged his shoulders and took the cigar out of his mouth. Only then did I realize it wasn't lit.

"We work when there's work. Depends on what's in port."

"Curious," I said. "That boat out there—"

"Ship," he said, then he pointed. "That is a boat."

When I looked, I saw a cartoon taped to the wall, Popeye in a rowboat in a lightning storm. Harrigan and I both grinned, and I turned back to the man.

"That *ship*," I said with emphasis.

"The Pulaski?"

"Yeah. Where's it going?"

He reached over to the table behind him for a clipboard, flipping through the pages.

"That there is going to…" he said with a dramatic pause. "Gdańsk."

"Poland?"

"Ain't Indonesia, brother."

"When does it leave?"

"Sunday."

......

HARRIGAN and I drove through the wet streets, the Valiant bouncing over potholes that were now big puddles. The rain had stopped, but it was so damp my arm got soaked as I held it out the window to smoke. It didn't discourage the protestors, however, and as we passed by the State House, I saw a small crowd. This one was for Women's Liberation, a refreshing change from the war demonstrations, and the signs were more amusing: DON'T CRY: RESIST and WOMEN ARE RAPED OF THEIR RIGHTS.

With rush hour starting, it was late enough that the captain didn't expect us back. Unlike Jackson, Egersheim never kept track of our time and only loosely monitored our activities. At first, I was flattered, thinking he left us alone out of trust. But the longer I worked for him, the more I got the feeling that he just didn't know how to supervise us. And considering that he had transferred from the mounted unit, he probably would have done better if we were horses.

"They're up to something," I said.

"Like what?"

"Stolen goods. Maybe they're running a racket. Who knows?"

"And you're sure you saw Mr. Marecki with Sokol?"

I hesitated, but it was fair to ask. My eyesight—all my senses— were waning with age, and sometimes even I questioned myself. But the reaction I had that night was unmistakable, and I had to go on first impressions.

"Sure as shit," I said, and he chuckled.

"What would he have to gain?"

"They grew up in the same neighborhood," I said. "It's hard to explain. Things were different back then. Loyalty went deeper than..."

I stopped short, not wanting to give him a lecture on the ethics of Boston street culture. It was hard enough being black in Boston, never mind an immigrant from the Caribbean, and I knew he always felt like an outsider.

"Perhaps they reestablished their friendship after the case?"

"Now you sound like Egersheim," I said.

"How do you mean?"

"Making excuses."

"I'm not making excuses. I'm exploring every angle until we find the one that is sharpest."

I smiled. It was something Captain Jackson used to say. The man had been gone for over two years, yet his spirit lived on through his small expressions and bits of investigative wisdom.

When we got to the lights of Massachusetts Avenue, I turned to Harrigan.

"Kenmore Square?"

"No. My apartment, please," he mumbled.

"Not Delilah's?"

"I prefer to go home."

The light turned green, but I didn't move.

"Is she home?"

"She is, but I don't..."

Behind us, someone beeped. I looked back and threw up my hands, the fury I always felt with testy drivers. But I didn't shout or otherwise escalate the situation.

Cutting the wheel, I went right instead of to Roxbury, and Harrigan groaned. I raced toward Kenmore Square before he could argue, and the fact that all the lights were green made it somehow seem destined. We got to Delilah's building in three minutes, and I stopped out front.

"See you in the morning," I said.

He didn't reply, reaching for the door with a slow reluctance and getting out. I watched as he walked up to the entrance, his collar up and his trench coat swaying in the wind. There wasn't a skip in his step, but he looked more upbeat, which made me glad for taking him. When it came to the whims and doubts of romance, everyone needed a little nudge sometimes.

CHAPTER 29

I AWOKE TO THE SOUND OF TAPPING AND THOUGHT IT WAS THE RAIN. But when I opened my eyes, I realized it was Nessie, the pitter-patter of her little feet. She was standing beside the bed in her pajamas, her Raggedy Ann doll in her arms, watching with a mischievous smile. In her hair was a yellow clip, something she hadn't gone to bed with. I wondered if Ruth had put it in when she got home, or if Nessie did it herself.

"You make something in breakfast," she said, the word *in* just enough to make it cute.

Getting out of bed, I put on my pants and threw a cardigan over my t-shirt. It was still dark out, the first streaks of dawn coming through the shades. I took her by the hand, and together we walked down the staircase. She sat at the kitchen table while I boiled water for coffee and oatmeal. I wanted to give her some fruit, but the bananas in the bowl were rotten, another sign of our busy lives. Some weeks just getting to the supermarket was a challenge.

Once everything was ready, I brought two bowls over to the table and sat across from her. Eating in the shadowy light, I watched while she pretended to feed her doll some porridge. Still sleepy, she didn't say much, but I didn't care. Those quiet moments of the morning were sacred because they reminded me of how simple life could be.

The floor creaked, and I looked over to see Ruth, arms crossed and leaning in the doorway in a robe. She had a seductive smile, or maybe I was imagining it. After a week without sex, the male mind did strange things.

"Don't let me disturb you," she said.

"Want something to eat?"

"I'll make it."

She went over to the counter and opened the bread box. Nessie and I traded funny faces, but now I was distracted; the tone always changed when Ruth walked into the room. I could never tell if it was some unspoken tension over things we needed to discuss and hadn't, or the guilt I had over having to leave them each morning. Dr. Kaplan had warned me about letting our communication lapse, and I realized why when I got up from the table.

"You're breaking our agreement."

I stopped and turned to her.

"I gotta go get ready," I said.

"We agreed to have breakfast every morning together."

We never raised our voices in front of Nessie, yet sometimes we spoke in ways that made her upset. Not wanting to argue, I left the kitchen and went upstairs. After a quick shower, I threw on yesterday's suit because I still hadn't made it to the dry cleaner. Coming back down, I had hoped Ruth was in a better mood, but when she charged into the foyer, it was obvious she wasn't.

"It's back!"

Glancing into the living room, I saw Nessie sitting quietly on the couch, brushing her doll's hair.

"What?" I asked.

"That look. You have that look again…like you're a thousand miles away."

I didn't ignore her, but I also didn't reply, worried that it would only provoke her. Then as I put on my coat, she grabbed my arm, and I was forced to say something.

"I don't know—"

"You can't even make eye contact," she said, standing close and peering up.

"What's the rush?"

Finally, I turned to her.

"I gotta go in early. I have my appointment this afternoon."

Her anger vanished as quickly as it had come on, and I even sensed some regret. I had agreed to therapy only after she threatened to leave, and she supported me without question. I was never one to use guilt or pity to win a fight, but this was one area where everyone benefitted. Our lives were hectic, working full time and raising Nessie, and the investigation only added to the strain. Some days, I thought that if I didn't have Dr. Kaplan, I couldn't go on.

"Go," she said, wiping a tear. "I'm sorry."

......

AFTER WORK, I walked to *Headcase Hotel* early and lingered in the lobby, where a black security guard stood whistling at the counter. There was none of the bustle of other corporate buildings, with just two or three people straggling in, their hats pulled down and avoiding eye contact for privacy, or maybe out of shame. Except for an accounting firm on the ground floor, it was all mental health professionals, and everyone knew it, from the janitors to the postman.

I finished my cigarette, stamped it out in an ashtray beside the elevators, and went up to see Dr. Kaplan. When I walked into her office, she sat behind the desk in a red blouse, chandelier earrings dangling from her lobes. She was writing in a binder, her hand wrapped in a tight fist around the pen, a consequence of her lost fingers. Considering what she had lived through in the war, the injury was mild, but any disfigurement was hard, especially for a woman.

"Mr. Brae," she said, looking up.

"Am I too early?"

"No, you're fine. Have a seat."

I took the leather chair, which by now had a familiar feel, almost conforming to my body.

"Now, I have to be completely honest," she said. "Someone called earlier to ask if you were being treated here."

A shiver went up my back.

"What did you tell them?" I asked.

She came around and sat down, reaching for her notebook.

"I said I was legally and ethically obliged to maintain the confidentiality of all my patients."

Although I appreciated her integrity, the news left me furious, and even a little panicked. Aside from Ruth and Harrigan, there was only one other person who knew I was seeing a therapist.

"It's Marcus," I said.

She stopped, tilting her head with a worried surprise.

"He knows about this?"

"I went to see him after our meeting last week and told him I thought the case was suspicious. He asked why I was seeing a shrink."

"How'd it come up?"

"Things got heated. He told me to just let it go."

"And?"

"I told him to go to hell."

Both of us smiled at the same time. She hadn't taken a single note, and I didn't know if it was because she was too intrigued or because she didn't want to leave a paper trail about something that involved crime and corruption.

"How would he know you were getting help?" she asked.

I liked that she always said *help* instead of *therapy*, a word that seemed to better describe what I was there for.

"Um, he's with the FBI," I said, and it required no further explanation.

"Do you think he was trying to intimidate you?"

"Of course," I said. "But it ain't gonna work."

"No?"

I shook my head with street cop bravado. But the truth was, I was apprehensive, something I had been struggling with since I first real-ized Marcus had played a role in the robbery. It took me some time to see that, even though we had grown up together, the loyalty I owed him as a friend ended with the violence used against a fellow officer. Justice for Jerry Duggan was all that mattered now.

Sitting up, I looked her in the eye.

"He crossed a line he shouldn't have."

CHAPTER 30

As I DROVE TO WORK THE NEXT MORNING, MY MIND RACED. I SMOKED one cigarette after another, my hands tight around the wheel, blowing through red lights. It was the same sensation I used to get in the war, where adrenaline was the only antidote to fear. I hadn't slept the night before, which always left me on edge, but that wasn't the reason I was so anxious. Somehow, my talk with Dr. Kaplan helped me clarify my plans, removing the uncertainty and even some of the guilt. For all my bad habits, quirks, and flaws, my instincts were superb, and I had to trust them. I was going to tell the captain that Marcus was involved in the bank heist that killed Duggan, and if he balked, I would take it straight to the chief. But the moment I walked into his office, I knew things had taken an unexpected turn.

"Have a seat, Lieutenant," Egersheim said.

Standing beside his desk were Chief McNamara and two assistants.

"Capt.?" I said, confused.

Everyone looked serious, almost somber. After a short pause, the captain looked at the chief, and then the chief turned to me.

"Lieutenant," he said. "We have unfortunate news."

"What is it?"

"It's come to our attention that you've been…um…under the care of a psychiatrist."

"Psychologist," I said, although none of them probably knew the difference.

"Regardless, you know the rules, Lieutenant," Egersheim said. "Any problems related to mental health are required to be disclosed—"

"For *job-related stress*."

I had read the department policy before my first session with Dr. Kaplan, knowing psychotherapy was still controversial.

"So, you don't deny it?"

"Why would I? I know dozens of guys who are seeing a shrink."

It was one of the boldest bluffs I ever made. I didn't say they were fellow officers, but I knew they would take it that way, and I wanted to see them fret.

"You can take it up with the union, but as for now, my decision stands," the chief said.

"What decision is that, sir?"

"I'm putting you on administrative leave until further notice."

I froze. My mouth dropped open, and I was seized by a wave of anger and disbelief. I could have argued, but I knew it wouldn't have changed things. And I wasn't about to give Egersheim the satisfaction of seeing me beg. He had always been jealous of me, and some small part of him probably enjoyed the censure.

"Starting when?" I asked.

"Effective immediately."

The chief looked agitated, his eyes darting, his forehead damp. I had known him since he was appointed in '62, and I'd always respected him. He seemed like he didn't want to do it but was forced to out of professional obligation, which was a little consolation for the humiliation. I realized then it was someone from the department who had called Dr. Kaplan. But that didn't mean Marcus had not tipped them off.

"In a couple of weeks, we'd like you to meet with the department physician," the captain said. "He will decide if and when you're suited to return to work."

Putting my career in the hands of a general practitioner was as improper as it was insulting. Even if my mental health was in question, the man had no expertise in psychology.

I just stared at the window, too bitter to look at any of them.

"Is that all?" I asked coldly.

Egersheim looked at the chief, then at me.

"I'm sorry. We're gonna need you to surrender your weapon."

......

I DROVE AIMLESSLY through the streets. Aside from being stunned, I felt defeated, but it wasn't the worst state I had ever been in. And I always got some strange relief in being down because it meant there was nowhere to go but up.

With the whole day ahead of me, I went back to my old neighborhood, the place where it all began. In moments of crisis or disappointment, I always found solace in revisiting the streets of my youth. Unlike many other parts of the city, which had been knocked down, plowed over, and rebuilt, Roxbury was much the same, the endless blocks of apartments and shabby three-decker homes. The corner stores were still there, but the names had changed, and I saw the same playgrounds and empty lots where, three decades earlier, I learned to play stick ball and had my first kiss.

I turned down a side street and stopped in front of an abandoned brick building where, just above the entrance, I saw the faded words: *Roxbury Home for Stray Boys*. With the window rolled down, I smoked a cigarette, gazing out, mesmerized. Somewhere in the breeze, I could still hear the laughter and cries of all the children. The institution had closed in the fifties, a victim of the changing welfare system, and its charges moved to more modern facilities across the state. I was always surprised that the structure remained, that it hadn't been torn down like everything else that was old and no longer of any use. In the new Boston, a metropolis of high-rises and highways, there was no place for the forgotten things of the past.

Flicking my cigarette, I sped off, down Blue Hill Avenue and into Roslindale. Finally, I pulled into Forest Hills Cemetery, a sprawling burial ground of elegant gardens, sculptures, and monuments. Founded in the mid-19th century, it was famous for its elegance and was the resting place of such luminaries as poet E. E. Cummings and the playwright Eugene O'Neill.

As I drove through the main gate, a groundskeeper was raking leaves and putting them in the back of a truck. But otherwise, it was desolate, an almost perfect silence, the only sound the chirping of birds and the distant rush of cars along Morton Street. I veered right and went up a slope to a section of newer graves, polished and shining in the afternoon sun.

I got out and walked, the grass damp and squishing under my feet. I came to an ancient elm tree where, in its shadow, I looked down to see a small granite marker, flush with the ground.

Ernest C. Jackson
1902-1968

STANDING OVER IT, my heart raced, and my eyes got teary, which I told myself was from the wind. I hadn't been to the captain's grave in months, the last time after a bad argument with Ruth. I never thought much about religion, and at the *Home,* our only exposure to it was a service twice a month in the auditorium. It was conducted by an Episcopalian minister, a benefactor of the institution, which was strange considering so many of the kids were the offspring of impoverished Catholics and Jews. I didn't know if I believed in God or heaven, but something about being there made me feel closer to Jackson's spirit.

"Lieutenant?"

I spun around, and it was Harrigan.

"What the hell are you doing here?!" I exclaimed.

"I knew you would be here."

"You did?"

He stepped closer, lowering his voice.

"Egersheim told me the situation," he said.

He never called the captain *Egersheim*, which made me think he was just as upset as me.

"Tough break," I said.

I looked away and reached for a cigarette, blinking to clear the moisture from my eyes. Harrigan came up beside me, and we stood over Jackson's grave, a token memorial that seemed so insignificant compared to the man.

"Do you believe Agent Marecki told them about your treatment?"

"I know he did. And I'm going after the bastard."

"That's a big risk."

I turned my head, and we locked eyes.

"Do you think I have a choice?"

I whisked by him, and he hurried after me, between the rows of headstones, the endless names, dates, and epitaphs. Even in all my distress, I got a strange comfort in being among the dead because it put the temporary troubles of my own life in perspective.

When we reached the road, I saw a black Ford parked behind the Valiant. I hated the standard unmarked cars, which were always so obvious.

"What next, Lieutenant?" Harrigan asked.

"If I can prove it wasn't Kagan, maybe the chief will hear me out about Marcus."

"Perhaps you could talk to the witnesses?"

"I wish I could. Marcus and Shine interviewed them. They've got all the testimonies."

He held up his finger, went over to his car, and pulled something from the trunk. As he walked back, he had a mischievous look on his face.

"This should have what you need," he said.

He handed me a binder, which was so heavy I had to take it in both hands.

"The case report?"

"The whole kit and kaboodle."

"You son of a bitch."

"Well, you always said I took good notes."

I smiled for the first time that day, but I wasn't surprised because Harrigan always came through and always at the right time.

"Thank you."

"Put it to good use, Lieutenant."

We parted with a handshake, and I walked back to the Valiant. Before I opened the door, I stopped and looked over.

"How's Delilah?" I asked.

"To be frank, she's quite nervous. She has to go to Suffolk Superior Court next Wednesday."

He spoke like he was concerned only for her, but I knew he was also worried about his own role in the capture.

"I'll get Marcus before then."

He responded with a vague smile, somewhere between optimism and doom. Then he got into the car, made a U-turn, and drove away.

CHAPTER 31

SITTING ON THE COUCH WITH THE BINDER OPEN, I SQUINTED TO READ IN the lamplight. Scattered across the floor were Nessie's toys, a plastic telephone, an Easy-Bake Oven, and the wooden puzzle of California that Ruth's aunt had sent us. With the shades slightly open, I kept one eye on the street, but only two cars had gone by all night—a brown Ford station wagon and a Chrysler Newport, '68 or '69. I wasn't paranoid, but I was hyperalert, a difference I had learned after years on the force. Paranoia was a form of psychosis, which clouded one's thinking and hence, one's judgment. Alertness was a state of mental readiness, as well as physical. The department had taken my service weapon, but I still had my Beretta, which I kept tucked in my waist. By investigating Marcus' link to the robbery and Duggan's murder, I was basically implicating the FBI, the most powerful law enforcement agency in the country. Even if he had acted alone, I knew they would do anything to stop me from taking the scandal public.

The case file was a combination of photocopied documents and notes, conversations with witnesses, and crime scene observations, all in Harrigan's perfect penmanship. I had already seen the forensics report and the bureau's dossier on Neil Kagan, which included the people he associated with, his political affiliations, and his employment history. In one folder, I found Duggan's autopsy report, a list of vital statistics, and a sketch showing bullet entry and exit points, one through the heart and another through the spleen. A stick figure was a poor representation of any human, but the longer I stared, the more I saw a resemblance, the lanky arms and hunched back. I couldn't help but chuckle.

The witness accounts were a mix of the handwritten testimonies taken by patrolmen and formal reports taken by the bureau, typed, stamped, and dated. Three foreign tourists were across the street when the shooting happened; a milkman had observed the getaway car after it almost hit him, although he described the '66 Ford Impala more as *a light beige* than white. The janitor who had discovered the stolen car in a parking lot in Harvard Square didn't think it was unusual because "lots of kids left hotboxes there." Marcus and Shine had documented their interview with Nadia's daughter, identifying her only as "Lena" and describing her account as "dubious and unreliable."

On the last page, scribbled like an afterthought, was a comment about a homeless man named "Geronimo" who had been behind the bank that morning. It said nothing about what he had seen, only that he had been "scavenging for food in a dumpster." I couldn't tell if it was from Marcus or a local cop, but the words broke off. It wasn't necessarily suspicious—case reports were always a messy assortment of legal forms, technical documents, and offhand notes. But overall the investigation was lazy, and there were enough mistakes and loose ends that I was still shocked the chief had closed the case.

"You look so serious."

Peering up, I saw Ruth standing on the staircase.

"How's Nessie?" I asked.

"Sleeping like a lamb."

I smiled to myself.

"Are you coming to bed?" she asked.

"No, I've gotta get some more work done."

It wasn't really true. I had gone through the report enough and had all the information I needed. But I was anxious and knew I wouldn't sleep. I hadn't told her yet that I was on administrative leave, and I didn't know what worried me more when I did, that she would be horrified or that she would shout for joy. More than once, she had mentioned me quitting to do something else. With my years on the force and my military time, I probably could have pushed for an early retirement. But for all the stress and crazy hours, I loved the job, and nothing was more frightening than returning to the ordinary life of a private citizen.

"Sure it can't wait until morning?"

When I looked up again, she had one hand on the banister, her gown opened to reveal a thigh. Her sensual smile was something I couldn't resist, so I grinned and put down the folder.

"Be up in a minute," I said.

As she tiptoed back up, I walked over to the bookshelf. I took out my gun, checked the safety, and reached up, placing it on the top where it was concealed behind the trim.

......

AFTER BREAKFAST, I got dressed and left like I did most mornings. I still hadn't told Ruth about my work situation, and I was in a race to get enough evidence to incriminate Marcus before I did. This was the first time I ever went out to investigate on my own, and I had to be careful. If anyone found out, whether it was a department official or a member of the public, I could get in serious trouble. Administrative leave gave me my full pay with benefits, but it also relegated me temporarily to a civilian, and I didn't want to be accused of impersonating a police officer.

The first stop was to where it all began: Kenmore Square. I drove down the small lane that ran along the Mass Pike and parked by the Piccadilly Lounge because it was more hidden than the main roads. As I got out, I watched two men open the door of the club and disappear into the darkness. When the bartender said they never closed, I thought he was exaggerating, and I wondered who went to see strippers at nine in the morning.

Crossing the street, I went around the corner, the Shawmut Bank building shining in the sun. With the grates up, I knew it was open, and I had on a hat and sunglasses so I wouldn't be noticed by the manager, Herb Shepherd, or anyone else. As I walked past the spot where Duggan had collapsed, I looked for blood or even the scuff marks from his boots, but there were none. The sidewalk was deceptively clean, the only imperfections a few hairline cracks and some cigarette butts. I wasn't one for mysticism, but crime scenes always had a strange allure, as if the spirit of the victim lingered long after the deed.

I continued down the alley beside the bank, which was covered with weeds and litter. I passed the side entrance, a steel door with a bent handle and a deadbolt, and I imagined the culprits waiting there that morning. It was an easy heist—too easy—and the fact that they made the narrow window of time between when Shepherd opened up and the Brinks truck arrived was too lucky for chance.

At the back of the building, a rusted fence was the only thing separating the high ground of Beacon Street from the Mass Pike below. With so much trash, it was hard to know whether the area was asphalt or dirt.

Ready to turn back, I heard a noise and saw someone behind a dumpster. A man was sitting on an overturned shopping cart, a duffle bag next to him.

"Geronimo?" I asked, almost instinctively.

He looked over with a grin, his long beard covering his face.

"Don't tell me…my long-lost son?"

When he let out a piercing laugh, I couldn't tell if he was drunk or just insane.

"Are you Geronimo?"

"The name's Martin Philip Mackenzie," he said, "but, yeah, that's what they call me."

"Why is that?"

"I'm 3/8th Apache," he said.

His genealogical math seemed off, but his skin tone was darker than even a bad liver could produce.

"Were you here the morning this bank was robbed?"

"Indeed," he said. "I already told you everything."

"You didn't tell me anything."

"But I told them other fine gentlemen."

When I stepped closer, he looked up, his face wrinkled but his eyes clear.

"You saw a man and a woman parked here?" I asked, nodding to the alley.

"Woman? I ain't seen no woman."

A tingle went up my back.

"No?"

"Guess it coulda been a woman. Looked like two men to me."

"Could you describe them?"

"I only walked by. I was gonna ask for a cigarette, but their windows were closed. They were young folks, long hair."

"You didn't think it was strange?"

He shrugged his shoulders.

"At my age," he said, "everything about the world is strange."

CHAPTER 32

After dinner, Ruth got ready for work, and I sat with Nessie on the couch while she watched television and played with her toys. She was chattier lately, asking me questions and telling me things about her day. I got the feeling she knew I was distracted, and as much as I tried to laugh and smile, beneath it was my constant obsession with the case. Out in the world, I could manipulate my mood and expressions like an A-list actor, but never around the people I loved. Ruth sensed it too, those telling glances and vague remarks whose double meanings told me she was concerned. She never asked me outright what was wrong and had probably given up trying.

Ruth stood in the foyer in her nursing scrubs, fixing her hair in the mirror. Soon headlights came down the street, and I knew it was her ride. She came over and kissed Nessie on the cheek and gave me a halfhearted smile.

"8 o'clock bedtime," she said.

"I was hoping to watch *Love, American Style*."

"Me too, mummy!" Nessie said.

Her excitement was enough to ease any tension.

"You," Ruth said, getting her coat, "be a good girl for daddy."

"I will."

Ruth blew kisses at us both, grabbed her pocketbook, and left. The timing was close because, moments later, another car pulled up. When I looked out the window, I saw Nadia get out and wave to the driver. I assumed it was the man who was always at her apartment, and whether he was a close friend or secret lover, I still didn't know. Overweight, she struggled more than before, lumbering up the walkway, her shoulders hunched.

I had asked her to watch Nessie so I could go out. It wasn't completely selfish. Except for groceries, she hadn't left her house since her daughter's disappearance, and even the priest from her parish checked on her. If I was ever going to find Alina, I had to work at night, and Nadia would have to find the strength to carry on. And there was nothing more comforting than the company of a child.

"Hello," I said.

She smiled as she walked in, undoing her scarf and taking off her coat, the cold radiating off her body.

"Nessie," she said, looking over toward the couch.

Nessie got up and came over, and Nadia put her arm around her.

"She's already eaten," I said, patting my mouth.

Nadia gave me a funny look. I was never sure what she understood and what she didn't. Even at her house, our conversations were an awkward mix of hand motions and repeated phrases, nervous laughter and long nods.

While she took Nessie into the living room, I went up to the bedroom to get ready. As I dressed, I could hear them talking downstairs, Nessie's tiny voice and Nadia's broken words. However much they seemed to struggle to communicate, I knew they understood each other.

I put on jeans, a black turtleneck, and the leather jacket I hadn't worn in years. Looking in the mirror, I felt like a cross between Marlon Brando and Steve McQueen. I hadn't dressed so hip since my days working undercover. I was like an older version of my younger self, the onset of wrinkles with the same fiery spirit.

I grabbed my Beretta from behind the bureau. It had taken me five tries to get it from above the bookcase without Ruth noticing, and I felt like a spy in my own house. When I went downstairs, Nessie was surprised, her eyes wide, pointing at me. She ran over and I picked her up, blowing into her face and making her laugh. It seemed so playful, but inside I was torn because I hated to leave her.

I gave her one last kiss and then sent her back to Nadia, who sat on the couch with her hands on her lap. Even in the twenty minutes since arriving, she looked happier, or at least more relaxed. Smiling at them both, I walked out the door.

When I got to The Polish Triangle, I drove slowly along Dorchester Avenue, my cap pulled down. By now, I was sure a few people recognized the Valiant, and I didn't want to be seen, either by someone from work or by one of Marcus's associates. The pubs and diners were busy, cars double-parked on the road. The night was cold, feeling more like winter than fall, and everyone had on heavy coats and hats.

In the distance, the Polish American Club was lit up like a movie theater. There was a crowd out front, and people were waiting to get in. I had known about the fundraiser for Polish workers for weeks and would finally get to see what it was all about.

I parked half a block away and walked over. While I stood in line, I had a cigarette and glanced around. No one seemed to notice me, too busy talking, that familiar comfort of friends and neighbors. Everyone was dressed up, the older couples in traditional clothes while the younger folks wore modern styles, the men in pointed collars, the girls in maxi skirts.

As I got close to the doors, I peered in, and the room was packed. There were streamers on the ceiling, a banquet table at the back, and above the stage hung a large banner. My eyes drifted to the bar, and I immediately spotted the Sokol brothers, standing in long leather coats, drinks in their hands. It was the first time I had seen them together, which at least confirmed that they were twins and not one guy playing games. Between them stood a young woman, tall and lanky in an elegant black dress. As I strained to see, I realized it was Margaret Marie Kozlowski.

"Ticket?"

The doorman was glaring at me.

"Can I buy one?"

He nodded, so I reached for my wallet. As I opened it, the light caught my badge, making it shine, and I cringed. I wasn't sure he had seen it until he asked, "You here for a reason?"

"Just to help the workers of Poland."

When I took out a $20 bill and handed it to him, he shook his head.

"This is a private event," he said coldly.

"Are you serious?"

Ignoring me, he turned to the next people in line, and my temper surged. I went for the door anyway, and he grabbed my arm. I threw him off and he tried again, but I shoved him away. Bystanders yelled for us to stop, but I ignored their pleas, and I had the urge to throw him through the glass. As we scuffled, I saw a group of men coming across the dance floor, their arms flared and ready. Backing away, I put up my hands, more out of good sense than defeat. I snickered once at the doorman and stormed off down the sidewalk.

When I got to my car, I was out of breath, a combination of rage and exertion. I had a cigarette to calm down and then got in, starting the engine and driving away. Worried someone might have called the police, I turned at the first intersection to stay off main roads, and I would have zigzagged my way home through side streets if I had to.

Suddenly, headlights appeared in my rearview. At first, I thought it was obnoxious teenagers, but when it swerved side to side, I knew it was intentional. At the next crossroads, I cut the wheel and punched the gas. The Valiant swerved, and I could smell burnt rubber. My heart raced, and my senses were sharp from adrenaline. The car stayed on my bumper, the engine revving, and although I couldn't see it, I could tell it was a V-8. Not knowing if they wanted to run me off the road or just intimidate me, I was ready for the challenge. After weeks of lies and dead ends, the truth had come to me.

Ahead I saw neon, but I didn't realize it was Dorchester Avenue until it was too late. With a quick prayer, I sped across the busy road, leaving behind a mess of screeching tires and horns. Thinking I had lost them, I smiled, but when I looked ahead, the streetlights stopped. I hit the brakes and was jolted forward. Then blackness.

......

I BLINKED in the harsh white light, my head pounding and my body sore. Somewhere nearby, the sound of footsteps, people talking. Finally, my eyes adjusted, and I realized I was in a hospital room. I didn't know if it was midnight or the next morning.

"Are you awake?" I heard, and it was Ruth's voice.

I gazed up, wincing with embarrassment and even a little shame. It took a moment to recall what happened, but when I felt the bump on my forehead, I knew I had crashed.

"Nadia's watching Nessie," I blurted.

"I know. I called home the minute you arrived."

"She answered?"

"She knows how to use the phone, you know. She's not a Luddite."

I chuckled to myself, the fancy words of the college-educated. As she leaned over me, her face had that beautiful pout she always had when she was both mad and worried. Her dark hair was tucked into her nurse's cap, something I never saw because she only put it on at work.

"What's the damage?" I asked.

I meant it as much about the Valiant as my own condition because I loved the car like a dear friend.

"A mild cranial contusion, maybe a concussion."

I dropped my head back to the pillow with a sigh. I was getting too old to get hurt. But I had been through a lot worse, and although I was never officially wounded in Korea, I had survived machine gun fire and dozens of shell blasts. The war had done deeper harm, however, shredding my nerves and my mind, and some days I would have preferred an amputation over the lingering effects of shell shock.

When she stepped away, I thought she had left the room. Then I heard talking in the doorway, the faint voices of her and a man. Moments later, she returned.

"We're cleared to go," she said.

"We?"

"My shift is over now. And you have no way to get home. Janice will drive us."

As she helped me out of the bed, I still couldn't tell if she was upset or relieved.

The corridor was busy, with nurses rushing around, staff members moving gurneys. I had forgotten how hectic City Hospital was at night, and as the largest public facility, they got some of the worst cases: gunshot wounds, automobile accidents, fire victims, and more.

We went down the elevator and into the lobby, where I smoothed out my leather coat and tried to look presentable with a bandage on my forehead. Outside, Janice was parked in a line of waiting vehicles, her tiny Volkswagen wedged between a cab and an ambulance. I hesitated under the portico and looked at Ruth. I didn't know what repulsed me more, that the car was German-made or that it was a favorite of the hippies.

"What?" she asked.

"Are we all gonna fit?"

Taking my arm, she urged me forward.

"Sit in the front seat."

I smiled at Janice as I got in, squeezing into the small bucket seat. She put the car in gear and drove away, staring ahead with both hands on the wheel. For the whole ride home, she didn't say much, and I didn't know if she was nervous about what happened or was just shy. They had been carpooling together for over a year, but I had never gotten to know her. Like me, Ruth had lots of acquaintances but few close friends. And now with Nessie, our social lives consisted of the annual department Christmas party and a week in Hampton Beach every summer, where a group of her coworkers rented cottages. I didn't have any relatives, something I thought about more whenever I came close to death or grave injury. Ruth had a small family, but with her parents in California and her younger sister in Arizona, we seldom saw them.

When we pulled up to the house, all the lights were on. The clock on the dash read 2:20 a.m. The same car that had dropped Nadia off was parked out front, and I felt bad that they'd had to wait.

As I edged out, I thanked Janice and then hobbled up the walkway the same way Nadia had when she arrived. I was no longer dazed, but I was sore, that full-body aching that always came after a collision. I had been in lots of accidents over the years, mostly in speed chases and a couple of times in traffic. So far, I had been lucky, but not every cop was. Back when I was a patrolman, we lost an officer after his cruiser slid on ice and went off the Northern Avenue Bridge. Another time, a rookie went into the wrong lane in the Sumner Tunnel and was crushed by a freight truck.

Ruth unlocked the door, and we walked inside. Nadia quickly got up from the couch, her friend standing beside her, his hat in his hands. He looked older than before, or maybe he was just tired.

"How's Nessie?" I asked, but Ruth had already rushed upstairs to check.

"Good baby," Nadia said, and the man just smiled.

I wanted to apologize and explain what happened, but I was sure they either already knew or preferred not to. So we said goodnight, and as I led them to the door, I slipped Nadia a twenty-dollar bill for her time. At first, she wouldn't take it. But I insisted, and when she finally agreed, she leaned up and kissed me on the cheek.

I watched them as they got into the car, heading back to Dorchester. Ruth tiptoed down the stairs with no shoes on.

"You're dressed like an art student," she said.

"I'll take that as a compliment."

Frowning, she went into the kitchen. I sat on the couch, sinking into it like a warm bath, worried I wouldn't be able to get up. Ruth came back in with two glasses of water, handing me one before taking the seat beside me, curling her legs beneath her.

"How's your head?" she asked.

"I need aspirin."

"You've already had 2000 ml of it."

"Is that a lot?" I joked, then I took a sip.

We sat in silence, the only sound the hiss of the radiators, but I knew it wouldn't last.

"Want to tell me now or wait until tomorrow?" she asked.

I turned to her.

"Do I have a choice?"

She nodded.

"Let's wait until tomorrow."

CHAPTER 33

I woke up on the couch with Ruth in my arms. Outside it was still dark, but I could see the faint glow of dawn shimmering off the homes across the street. When I moved, she shuddered awake, looking into my eyes with a tired longing. Smiling, I pulled her close, but it was too late.

"Gotta go check on Ness," she said.

She got up and ran upstairs. I heard the bedroom door open, the little voice of Nessie, excited as she was each morning. Moments later, Ruth carried her down, but she was no longer an infant, her legs and arms looking more like a little girl's.

"Booboo," she said, touching my bandage.

"Daddy bumped his head. He's fine."

I forced a smile, but her wary look made me uneasy.

"How 'bout we watch *Captain Kangaroo*?" I asked, and she smiled and clapped her hands.

While Ruth went to make breakfast, Nessie sat on the couch, and I turned on the TV. The morning news was almost over, the last ten minutes an overview of world affairs. A group of Polish university students seeking asylum had hijacked a plane in Warsaw and forced it to land at the American base in West Germany. I leaned forward, staring at the screen, the images of the frightened young men and women standing before a crowd of reporters. I never followed international events—two years in Korea had been broadening enough for me—but I knew life in Poland must have been hard under the Soviets if people were willing to take such risks to escape.

The story was over in a flash, on to something about polar bears. Still, the incident struck me, and my eyes stayed fixed on the screen long after the news had ended and *Captain Kangaroo* began.

"Breakfast is ready!"

Nessie ran to the kitchen, and I went upstairs, quickly putting on slacks and a shirt, combing my hair back. After a night out dressed *like an artist*, it felt good to have regular clothes on again. I peeled off the bandage, and there was a red bump above my right eye and a hairline cut, already scabbed over. I wasn't sure yet about the Valiant, but the damage to me was minimal. My head had hit the steering wheel, and the only reason I knew was because it had happened before in my career.

When I came down, they were at the kitchen table. Nessie looked up with a big glass of orange juice in her hands, and Ruth didn't bother to acknowledge me. I knew she was still upset about the previous night, and I owed her an explanation. But Nessie was old enough to understand our conversations, so I wanted to wait until she was asleep.

I sat down and started to eat, winking at Nessie while I chewed.

"Don't you think you should cover that up?" Ruth asked, looking at my forehead.

"Naw. Makes me look tough."

She frowned.

"You're a pirate," Nessie said.

The remark was enough to break the tension, and Ruth chuckled.

I had just finished when I heard a beep. Glancing at the clock, it was eight-thirty. I kissed Nessie, and walked around to Ruth, wrapping my hands around her from behind in an awkward attempt at a hug. When I walked out, she put down her knife and fork and followed me into the hallway.

"We have to talk," she said.

I put on my coat and gave her a tight smile.

"We will."

"When?"

"You're off tonight, right?"

"Yes."

"Tonight then," I added.

I turned to go out the door, but she grabbed my arm. Standing on her toes, she leaned up and surprised me with a kiss.

"Be safe," she said, and I shrugged it off with a smile.

As I went down the path, I glanced back, and she was still in the doorway. I waved, and she waved back. In her expression, I saw the tragic longing of a policeman's wife, and it gave me a twinge of guilt. Although unaware of all the details, she still knew something was wrong. Since the day I met her, she could read my thoughts, fears, and feelings like no other woman could, and that was why I loved her. Just because she understood my problems, however, didn't mean she should have to endure them. I wasn't young anymore, and with her and Nessie in my life, I wasn't the only one who paid the price for the job. At times, I told myself that if I got out of this one last jam, I would pull back and maybe ask to work inside headquarters. But I had been saying that for years.

I walked up to the black Ford, where Harrigan sat stiffly behind the wheel. He always looked funny driving, his back arched and staring ahead like a butler or bodyguard. As I got in, I felt soreness in my back, but it could have been from sleeping on the couch.

"Is that from last night?" he asked.

I touched my forehead, and it stung.

"It wasn't from breakfast."

Frowning, he put the car in gear, and we drove off. When I had called earlier for a ride, he tried to refuse, using all his typical politeness and charm. I wasn't supposed to be working, and he didn't want to break the rules. With Delilah due in court on Wednesday, he was worried enough about his own job. But there was an old saying among cops, when your partner got a cold, you got the flu. We were both in too deep to back out now.

"I think it was Marcus," I said.

"You couldn't see the car?"

I shook my head, the frustration of getting old.

"You know I can't see anything at night. It sounded like a Charger."

"Why would he stir up trouble?"

"To rattle me? Who knows?"

"You didn't see him in the club?"

"No, but it happened so quick."

"Then maybe he just got lucky."

"Or maybe he was waiting for me."

He pulled into Sonny's, a gas station and garage at the corner of Massachusetts Avenue, and I got out. On one side was a graveyard of tires, piled ten feet high behind a metal fence. On the other was the yard, where a dozen cars sat waiting to be repaired.

As I approached the office, I had the same anxious anticipation of someone going to visit a loved one in the hospital. I had bought the Valiant on a cold November morning in '60, the same day Kennedy was elected and my first week as a detective. It had been with me through everything, from my first bust to my first date with Ruth, and it had the sentimental significance of an old friend.

I walked in, and a mechanic looked up from a water bubbler.

"Can I help ya?"

"You have my car?" I asked.

"We have a lotta cars."

"A green Plymouth."

"Oh, right."

He waved me into the garage, where I saw the Valiant up on a lift. Cringing, I looked at the front and was amazed to see it wasn't crushed in. The man grabbed a flashlight, and we went underneath, the rusted exhaust pipes, drive train, and wheel wells a filthy contrast to the car's shiny exterior.

"Is that how that happened?" he asked, looking at my head.

"No."

I should have told him the truth—there was no such thing as a single lie. But rumors spread fast on the streets of Boston, and I didn't want anyone to find out.

"What did you hit?"

"How bad is it?" I asked, avoiding the question because I didn't know.

"Blew out your whole suspension—springs, tie rods, struts. Everything."

When he pointed the light, I could see some new parts, their polished metal glistening. They had already started working on it, which wasn't a surprise because the station was known for its service and quick turnaround time.

"No damage to the front?" I asked.

He gave me a curious look.

"Nope. You just bottomed out. Must've been a hell of a pothole, though."

"Yeah, it was. When will it be done?"

"She's almost ready. Give us a couple more hours."

I was so stunned I got emotional. I still couldn't believe the damage wasn't worse. When I woke up in the hospital, I was sure the Valiant had been wrecked, or at least in need of serious repair. By the way Ruth talked, I thought I had gone head-on into a cement wall. But she didn't know what happened, other than that I had been in an accident and was knocked unconscious. Someone had called, and fortunately, the ambulance arrived before the police. If word had gotten back to Egersheim or the chief, I would have denied I was working. But I would have had a hard time explaining what I was doing out on a Wednesday night in The Polish Triangle.

I left and walked down Massachusetts Avenue, the sidewalks bustling with morning commuters. I was never on the streets anymore, unusual for a kid who had grown up on them. I missed those carefree years when the entire city seemed like my playground, when I knew every building, park, and alleyway from Franklin Park to Faneuil Hall. Now I felt exposed, as much from my status as a cop as because I didn't recognize Boston anymore, the glitzy high-rises and growing slums. There were a lot of contradictions, or maybe I was just getting old. But sometimes I wondered if, as Ruth had suggested, we should pack up and move to Ireland.

I walked into a camera shop across from Symphony Hall, and an old man with glasses looked up from the counter.

"Good morning," he said with an accent.

"I need a camera."

Raising his arms, he made a comical smile.

"Then you are in the right place."

"Something cheap, instant."

Turning around, he looked through stacks of boxes, piled high on a shelf against the wall. He pulled one out and said, "This should do."

When I nodded, he moved over to the register.

"Where're you from?" I asked.

"Dorchester."

"Originally."

"Originally, I am from Poland," he said, ringing in the price.

"How are things back home?"

He paused.

"This is my home," he said, and I admired his patriotism. "But in Poland, things are difficult at present."

"The government?"

He glanced up, giving me a sharp look. I couldn't tell if he was reluctant to talk politics or wanted to make sure no one was around before he did.

"Let's just say that the Russians are not the gentlest masters," he said, and the cash drawer opened with a ding. "$19.95, please."

I handed him a twenty, and he gave me a nickel. As I walked out, I felt that our short conversation was some validation of my suspicions about Marcus and the Sokol brothers. It wasn't unusual for American ethnics to get involved in the problems of their homelands. After the war, local Jews recruited men and money to establish the new state of Israel. In the fifties, a group of Italian anarchists had been caught laundering money to support their compatriots overseas.

When I finally got back to Sonny's, the Valiant was off the lift. I went into the office and reached for my wallet, knowing that if and when I got my job back, I was going to have to do a lot of overtime. But the repairs were cheaper than I thought, two hundred sixty-seven dollars, which the mechanic then rounded down to two hundred fifty.

"We rotated the tires too," he said.

"Thank you."

"You're welcome, officer."

I smiled. It was something I never would have expected. I didn't know how the man knew, other than that he saw my badge when I paid or my gun in the glove compartment. People always said I looked like a cop, which I used to take as a compliment before law and order became so controversial. Either way, I was touched by the courtesy. At a time in my career when I was feeling ignored and unappreciated, it gave me some small reason to go on.

I walked out to the lot, and the Valiant was parked by the gas pumps, its front wheels turned and engine on, ready and waiting. I was glad to have it again, but I knew the moment I got in, there was no turning back. I was going after Marcus and the others, whether it cost me my job or my reputation or both.

CHAPTER 34

"THOSE BASTARDS!" RUTH SAID.

She sat across from me at the kitchen table, her hair in a clip, the faint gloss of tears in her eyes. Outside it was dark, the cold wind whipping against the back door. I hated to see her so upset but was comforted to know that Nessie was safe asleep upstairs. In a family of three, the odds of everyone being content at once were low.

"Getting help is a violation?"

"They said officers have to report *any problems related to mental health.*"

"Even for trauma from the war?"

"I didn't read the policy that way. It said for *job-related stress.*"

"Then they are wrong, Jody. We need to get a lawyer."

"There's more," I said.

As she leaned forward to listen, the top of her robe opened, and I was tempted to look.

"Marcus organized the bank robbery. I think I can prove it."

Her face dropped.

"Wha…?" she said, gasping.

But she looked more disappointed than shocked, which was actually a relief. One of the tragedies of being an optimist was that people always let you down.

"I know it sounds crazy."

"No. It doesn't. I don't like that guy—"

"You've never met him."

"Didn't he get thrown out for beating someone?"

"We thought he did. He got adopted."

"Didn't he stab an employee with a pocketknife?"

I could have told her it was a screwdriver, but it wouldn't have made a difference.

"A 240-pound adult was choking him!"

"Didn't he—"

"He was an angry kid!" I shouted. "We all were!"

I turned away, too furious to talk about the past. I couldn't believe I was still defending Marcus, some perverse loyalty that lingered like a bad habit. Or maybe it was guilt. Ruth's remarks made me think about my own behavior, the violent outburst in South Boston that had ruined my promotion to captain. There were others too, lapses of judgment and moments of recklessness that could have gotten me suspended many times over. Captain Jackson had warned me about my temper, but the incidents were just far enough apart that the administration didn't notice or think it was a problem. As for Egersheim, he was never involved enough to know.

"I'm sorry," Ruth said.

Suddenly, the phone rang.

We looked at each other. We never got calls at night, except for when her sister got drunk and was feeling sentimental. I stood up, walked over to the wall, and picked up the receiver.

"Hello?" I said, hoping it was a wrong number.

But it wasn't. And in those few short words, I felt my heart sink. When I hung up, I must have looked dazed because Ruth jumped up from her chair.

"What is it?" she asked.

"The chief wants me in tomorrow. I have to go before the disciplinary board."

......

WHEN I PULLED INTO HEADQUARTERS, the building was somehow different. It looked like the window trim had been painted, or maybe I was always just too distracted to notice. I plodded up the front steps, weighed down by despair. Walking down the corridor, I nodded to friends and coworkers, and if anyone was aware of my situation, they didn't show it. Unlike a suspension or termination, administrative leave was an occupational gray area, a consequence of anything from disciplinary action to illness. In my younger years, I would have been worried about my reputation, but one benefit of getting older was not caring what people thought. If they were nosey enough to pry, I would have told them myself that I was seeing a shrink. In the culture of police bravado, therapy was frowned upon, even mocked, but that didn't mean it wasn't necessary. There were dozens of cops still suffering from combat and other traumas, and the divorce rates and early deaths were only a few outward symptoms of a problem that was rampant.

I opened the door to the boardroom, and it was like facing a court-martial. Seated at a long table were Chief McNamara, Captain Egersheim, the department arbitrator, three men from the anti-corruption unit, a representative from the patrolman's union, and a stenographer, the only woman in the room. A couple of them looked up when I entered, but they weren't only there for me. The disciplinary board met twice a week to deal with cops whose infractions ranged from cheating on timesheets to extorting criminals. Many officers' careers had ended in that room, and, in the worst cases, it was one step before going to the D.A. for prosecution.

"Lieutenant Brae," the chief said.

As I approached the table, he waved for me to take the chair across from them. The swelling on my forehead had gone down, but the scab and bruising were still obvious.

"How're you doing, Detective?"

It was an odd way to start the proceedings, so I answered with the first thing that came to mind.

"Were the front windows painted?"

The men all looked at each other; a few of them chuckled.

"As a matter of fact, I think they were."

I nodded and sat quietly.

"Incident 2306," the arbitrator said, reading from a document. "Joseph H. Brae. Lieutenant Detective."

When the stenographer started to type, the chief looked up.

"Mr. Brae, are you aware that your status of administrative leave prevents you from working?"

"Yes."

"We received a complaint, confirmed by department sources, that you were at...um..." He paused to look at the notes. "...the Polish American Club in Dorchester two nights ago. Is that true?"

"Yes."

"It was also confirmed by department sources that while you were there, you displayed your badge, giving the impression that you were operating in the capacity of a law enforcement officer. Is that true?"

"No."

"No?" one of the anti-corruption officials asked.

"It was a fundraiser. So I took out my wallet to buy a ticket."

"Can you elaborate on that interaction?"

I glanced over to Egersheim, but he wouldn't look at me.

"I tried to pay. The doorman wouldn't let me in, so I left."

"Was there not an altercation?"

"Yes," I said. "He wouldn't let me in because I was a police officer. I told him to go fuck himself, and he assaulted me."

It wasn't entirely true, but it was in the spirit of truth. Either way, the profanity got the reaction I was looking for, and no one was offended. Except for the stenographer and the arbitrator, everyone was a cop, and when it came to people who didn't respect our profession, we were all united.

"Was the man questioned?" Egersheim asked.

"I don't believe so."

"I think he should be."

I couldn't believe the captain had spoken up. He never dared to go against anything the chief thought or wanted, which was why we were in the situation.

"Duly noted," McNamara said, then he looked over at one of the officers. "Have someone speak to the other party…"

He paused abruptly and motioned for the woman to stop typing. Leaning over, he whispered something to the arbitrator, who responded with a nod.

"Jody," he continued, and I wasn't the only one surprised he used my first name. "We can resolve this pretty easily. Stay off the streets until your other matter is resolved, and there will be no action taken."

I appreciated his kindness and the fact that he kept my therapy confidential.

"Understand?" he added.

Nodding, I didn't say yes because I couldn't guarantee it. The arbitrator reached for the gavel, tapped it on the table, and announced, "Incident 2306 is continued without a finding."

······

IN THE HALLWAY, I stopped at the bubbler, still stunned from the meeting. Suspending me for seeing a shrink was a sham, but I understood their concern about working while on leave. It set a bad precedent. Even when I had screwed up in the past, it never got beyond Captain Jackson, who always kept matters between his detectives. That didn't mean his reprimands weren't severe, however, and I would have taken ten meetings before the disciplinary board over one with him, mainly because I respected him so much I hated to let him down.

Passing by the captain's office, I heard a voice. When I turned, Egersheim was beckoning to me with his finger. I walked over and followed him into the room, where he closed the door and asked me to sit.

"Jody…" he started.

I could always tell the nature of a conversation by how someone addressed me, whether it was my first name, last name, or police rank.

"I'm sorry about what happened in there."

"Don't be," I said, but it was a lie.

"I am. A lot of this is outta my control."

I didn't reply because I didn't believe it, knowing that captains had a lot of power when it came to investigations and to their underlings. It wasn't the first time he had kowtowed to the chief or other higher-ups, and I attributed it to personal weakness and not his position.

"Tell me, off the record," he said. "What were you doing in Dorchester the other night?"

I looked across at him, my gaze strong and unwavering.

"Trying to solve a crime."

He nodded and looked down, humbler than I had ever seen him. I didn't know if someone had pointed out all the inconsistencies in the case or if he had realized it on his own. But he finally seemed willing to listen.

"Tell me what you think you know."

"What *I know*," I corrected.

"Very well."

"First, I know the evidence against Neil Kagan and his girlfriend is weak."

"Fair enough," he said.

"He wasn't anywhere near Shawmut Bank the morning of the robbery."

"And you can prove that?"

"Yes."

I didn't want to drag Delilah into it, but with the momentum on my side, I couldn't hold back.

"Two key witnesses were omitted from the official report."

"The missing girl?"

"Alina is her name."

"Who else?"

"Geronimo," I said, and he smirked. "A homeless guy. He told me he saw two men in that car."

"That doesn't absolve Kagan. Maybe it was someone else?"

"The Ford Impala was owned by Stanley Sokol."

"Would they be foolish enough to use their own car?"

"If they had an airtight crime and the Feds covering for them."

The conversation stopped—the room went quiet. Egersheim just stared at me, his face red. I knew it was a bold accusation, but I also knew I was right.

"Do you still believe Agent Marecki is involved?" he asked.

"Absolutely. I saw him with the Sokol brothers at the seaport last week."

"Brothers?"

"They're twins."

He sighed and looked away like it was too much information to take in. As stubborn as he had been, I understood his apprehension. Reversing a grand jury finding wouldn't look good for the chief or the department. And the only way to avoid humiliation would be to submit new evidence that was so shocking, so far-fetched, that no one involved in the case could have ever predicted it.

"What do you want, Detective?"

"To get justice for Jerry Duggan."

Leaning over, he wrote something down. In the tense silence, I could hear my breathing, the beating of my heart.

"You got it," he said.

"Pardon?"

"You heard me. I'm overriding your administrative leave, putting you back to work. If the chief has a problem with that, I'll deal with it."

A smile broke across my face.

"Jody," he went on, pulling the side of his mustache. "I know I haven't been the best leader..."

I wanted to stop him there—it wasn't the time for apologies or expressions of regret. But he sounded sincere enough that I didn't.

"When I was a rookie, we responded to a fire on Beacon Street…a house…the whole building in flames…"

As he spoke, he avoided eye contact, gazing instead at some blank spot on his desk.

"Firemen brought two bodies out a back window. Children. Boy and a girl. Siblings. Smoke inhalation. They looked perfect…"

The image sent a shudder through me—I had seen similar horrific things.

"My sergeant ordered me to stay with them until they could get the paramedics. Fire trucks were blocking the alley. My wife was pregnant at the time. It was the longest ten minutes of my life."

Despite the captain's flaws, his bumbling and incompetence, I had always pitied more than despised him. He didn't seem at heart a bad person, but I had never felt genuine sympathy for him until that moment.

"The reason I tell you this," he said, and when he sniffled I didn't know if it was from the dry air or emotion, "is that it affected me. Bad. Couldn't sleep for months. Irritable all the time. I didn't know what was happening. My wife noticed, everyone else too. So, I had to get help."

When he finally looked up, I knew what he meant.

"I didn't tell the chief you were seeking treatment, Jody. Someone else did. And I'm sorry."

I had always thought Egersheim was a civil service hack, becoming a cop not out of passion or some sense of duty, but because it was the easiest path to a pension. And the fact he wasn't a veteran lessened his credibility with me even more. But I realized then that everyone had their own battles, and nobody escaped the sheer trauma of living. I wasn't sure if he was someone I could ever admire, but I definitely had a new respect for the man.

"Thank you," I said, and it was for many things.

"Now go get this bastard Marecki."

When I stood up, he held out his hand and we shook, something we never did.

"Let me know if you need anything."

"Thanks."

"Oh, and Lieutenant," he said, and I turned.

"Sir?"

"Your gun is in the top drawer."

He pointed to the file cabinet, and I walked over and got it.

CHAPTER 35

EGERSHEIM HAD DONE THE UNTHINKABLE, REINSTATING ME AS AN officer and letting me continue the investigation without the chief's support or approval. In some ways, it was a private agreement between us, and it felt good to be trusted again. But I didn't want to make a spectacle out of it, so I stayed away from headquarters, knowing it would only cause gossip. Word had already gotten around that the Kagan case was being questioned, and I didn't want the chief to be reminded of it by seeing me around.

I sat alone in a booth in Victoria's Diner with a coffee, ashtray, and copy of the Boston Globe that someone had left behind. I usually never read the local news because I experienced it all on the streets. But at the bottom of the front page, an article caught my eye.

Chief Orders Stop to Protests

Boston Police Chief Edmund McNamara has ordered a temporary halt to public protests of more than ten persons in the city. The move comes in light of the recent shooting death of officer Gerald Duggan, and the subsequent arrest of two "radicals" involved with the protest movements. The American Civil

Liberties Union has called the order an attack on the constitutionally protected right to peaceful assembly and has filed a brief with the U.S. Attorney's Office. Boston Police spokesman Jerome Hutchings said, "We want to be clear that this is only a temporary measure, put in place until the department and its allies can adequately assess the risks and threats of demonstrations to the public..."

"LIEUTENANT?"

I looked up to see Harrigan looming over me. I didn't like that he could sneak up because it made me feel I was losing my edge.

"Have a seat," I said.

I told him to take off his coat too, but he was too anxious, almost breathless.

"Shepherd called," he said.

"Shepherd?"

"From the bank."

So much had been going on I had almost forgotten.

"And?"

He leaned closer and looked around before speaking.

"He said there was a Polish girl...a girl with a Polish-sounding last name. She worked there until last year. Małgorzata Kozlowski."

"Małgorzata?" I asked, struggling to pronounce the name.

"Małgorzata Marie Kozlowski," he whispered. "Małgorzata is Polish for *Margaret*."

Our eyes locked in a moment of startling revelation. If I had even a sliver of a doubt that Marcus and his cohorts from The Polish Triangle organized the bank robbery and set up Kagan and Leslie Lavoic, it vanished that instant. There was no way the FBI could have overlooked the connection by accident. I had never had to convince Harrigan about my theory; he trusted my instincts like I trusted his. If he had any hesitation, it was only because he wanted evidence, and theories were nothing without proof.

"Did she know about the money transfer?" I asked.

"She would have."

Leaning back, I reached for my cigarettes until I remembered how much Harrigan hated smoking.

"Looks like McNamara is making waves."

I tapped the article with my finger, and Harrigan glanced down.

"Yes. I saw it this morning," he said.

"Do you read the Globe?"

He frowned like it was an accusation, and in some ways it was. The Boston Globe was the preferred newspaper of the liberal business class and wealthy suburbanites; the Boston Herald was for everyone else.

"My mother reads it."

"No wonder the chief was in a hurry to get them under indictment," I said.

"Just in time for Halloween."

"Scary to think, isn't it?"

The exchange was funny but true. For months, the city had been practically under siege by student activists and other groups, and residents were getting tired of it. If the department could use safety as an excuse to clamp down on some of the protests, I wouldn't have minded. But I didn't want them to frame two innocent young people to do it.

"Why don't you have a coffee?" I suggested.

"I really have to get back to work."

I glanced at my watch.

"How about a sandwich? It's almost lunchtime."

"No, thank you."

When he shook his head, I pursed my lips in disappointment. For some reason, I wasn't anxious and felt in no great rush, which was strange considering the urgency of the investigation. But after months of frustration, the captain and I were finally aligned, and a job meant something more when you had the support of your boss. It was a confidence I always had under Jackson, and now I had it with Egersheim, at least temporarily.

"I'm leaving early today," Harrigan said. "Delilah and I are going to see a show."

"A show?"

"At the Wilbur Theater. *Hair*."

Looking at each other, we both laughed, a moment of humor in an otherwise tense time. It couldn't have been more ironic, a musical about hippie counterculture in New York with all the contentious issues of the day, women's rights, racial justice, the draft. Weeks before, I might have snickered, but I had come to realize that just because people were young and idealistic didn't mean they were the enemy. As a federal agent, Marcus had done more to disgrace the public trust than any flag-burning or sign-waving activist, and if anyone was a traitor, it was him.

"Hope you both enjoy it."

......

When I got home, Ruth was standing in the front yard, watching as Nessie and the two girls next door played in the leaves. Our neighbor Esther was on her porch, and I could tell they were chatting. I was glad to see Ruth socializing; she needed some new friends. Most of the girls at work were either young and single or older and near retirement. Janice was married but had no kids, and it was hard to relate to family life without them. I always worried Ruth was lonely, knowing that motherhood wasn't the same without close female companions.

I got out of the car, and she glanced over. I dreaded that first look she always gave me, the transition from dread to relief when she realized I had made it home safely. Or maybe it was my own guilt. I was the only one who truly understood the dangers I faced each day. But I couldn't dwell on them, or I wouldn't have been able to work.

Ruth waved to the neighbor and walked over to me, her arms crossed and squirming.

"Dare I ask?" she said.

"The captain reinstated me."

Her face beamed.

"Temporarily," I added.

She didn't have time to respond because Nessie came running over with her arms out. Picking her up, I spun her around, and she giggled.

"C'mon," Ruth said to her. "Tell your friends you'll see them tomorrow. We have to eat."

We walked up the steps, Nessie between us, and when we got to the foyer, she ran upstairs. She came back down with a colorful box, the word *Batgirl* written across the top.

"What's this?" I asked.

"I'm Batgirl!"

"For Halloween," Ruth said. "We got it at Zaire's."

After dinner, Nessie went into the living room to watch TV, and I walked upstairs to get ready. When I came back down, Ruth had already had a glass of wine, her lips wet and cheeks rosy. She made me coffee, and we sat at the kitchen table, a conversation that I thought would be serious but not tense. But I was wrong.

"I don't understand why you can't contact those people," she said.

As we talked, she kept referring to the FBI as *those people* like Nessie would know or the house was wiretapped.

"I need evidence. Even if Egersheim takes it to the division head, he's gonna ask for proof. It's a huge allegation."

She nodded and looked away, her mascara smudged. Her concern was getting me worried.

"Couldn't you just talk to Marcus yourself?"

I was tempted to laugh but didn't, knowing it would sound dismissive.

"Momma, what's wrong?"

We both turned and Nessie was standing in the doorway, holding her Raggedy Ann doll by the arm.

"Nothing's wrong, honey," Ruth said, getting up and walking over. "Daddy just has to go to work for a little while."

"Will you come home?"

I understood what she meant, but the way she said it got me choked up. I was losing my nerve, which had never happened before I was married and had a child. I knew I had to go, so I picked Nessie up, and we all walked to the front door.

"Daddy, will you be batman?"

I looked at Nessie and then at Ruth, who raised her eyes with a smile.

"Of course I will," I said.

I kissed her on the forehead and put her down. She ran into the living room to watch the end of *Flipper*, leaving me and Ruth facing each other in the silence.

"I'll be back before midnight," I said.

She made a sour smile.

"I'll be up."

As I turned to go, she grabbed my hand and pulled me toward her, kissing me so hard I got aroused. Finally, I tore away, and we stared into each other's eyes, breathless.

"Be safe," she said.

"I will."

"Promise."

"I promise."

CHAPTER 36

THE VALIANT RODE BETTER WITH THE NEW SUSPENSION, WHICH GAVE ME a small boost of assurance on a night of uncertainty. I drove downtown with the radio off, staring straight ahead, my hands gripped to the wheel. As I came over the Northern Avenue Bridge, the lights of the city gave way to the darkness of warehouses and docks. With all the new construction in Boston, the seaport was like a ghost from the past, eerie in its desolation.

I parked a block away from where the Pulaski was moored, not wanting my car to be seen. I grabbed my gun, checked the chamber, and released the safety. Reaching to the backseat, I got the camera and tucked it under my coat. Then I got out and started to walk, my collar up, staying in the shadows where I could.

When I got to the wharf, I turned down an alleyway and came out behind the shipping office, where I had a clear view of the ship. I had to find out what was on it, which would either confirm or disprove what I suspected about Marcus and the others.

In the distance, I heard people working, the creak of forklifts or winches. Closer to me, the scuttle of rats in the darkness. Sneaking a quick cigarette, I chuckled to myself thinking how after all these years as a detective, my final investigation might be trying to prove a crazy theory no one in the department would believe.

As I came out from behind the building, headlights flashed, and I sprang back. A vehicle came down the pier and stopped. I peered around the corner to see a van with the rear doors open. Three men were taking out boxes and carrying them up the gangway. My heart pounded; my eyes were teary from the salt air.

Once they were done, they lingered by the van smoking, their conversation a mix of English and Polish. Marcus wasn't among them —I knew his voice and physique. And if the Sokol brothers were there, I couldn't tell because they all had long hair, denim jeans, and the swagger of young punks.

Finally, they got back in and drove off, and I was relieved because I had to piss. After I did, I stepped out and crept across the pier and up the gangway, peeking through an open door in the bulkhead. Inside, I heard the low rumble of the engines, powering the lights and other equipment even while docked.

The ship was small enough that it only had one hatch. When I looked in, the hold was lined with giant bags of sugar, rice, and flour. Along the floor were crates of condensed milk, coffee, and canned fruit. At that moment, I knew it wasn't a normal commercial shipment; no one exported dry goods to Europe anymore and hadn't since the Second World War. So it must have been for the Polish people, who had been experiencing price hikes and food shortages for years under the Soviets. I realized then that maybe I was wrong, and that it had been for charity all along.

I climbed through an open manhole and down a ladder to get a closer look. As I walked on top of the cargo, stowed tightly together, I read off the names Pillsbury, Domino, Carnation—all the major industrial producers. I reached the end and saw some unmarked boxes. I would have turned back except one of them was open. Peering in, I gasped. Stacked inside were M16s and handguns, grenades, and even a mortar. I held up my camera and snapped a shot, hoping to capture it despite the dim light.

I went back up the ladder and quickly headed out. But as I turned the corner, a voice shouted, "Hey, you!"

I spun around and a man was in the doorway. He was tall, dressed in striped coveralls and a cap, and I assumed he was either a crewmember or a guard on night duty. When he came at me, I dodged him and ran. He was faster than I expected from his size, and the moment I reached the top of the gangway, he grabbed me by the collar. In that split second, I had to decide whether to reach for my gun or not. Firing it, or even just taking it out, would raise the stakes of the confrontation, and with all the steel around, I feared a ricochet.

I struggled to break free, but his grasp was too strong. Pivoting, I punched him in the face. Instantly, he let go and fell back, groaning in pain, blood spurting. It was the luckiest shot I had ever taken.

I flew down the gangway to the dock, the camera swinging wildly around my neck, and ran up the pier toward the street, looking back every few seconds. I didn't stop until I got to my car, winded and sweating all over. I took one last look around, noting the quiet darkness of the warehouses and wharves, and then got in.

Pulling the tab on the camera, I waited for the photo to develop. Slowly, a picture appeared, the shapes of the weapons hazy but unmistakable. I didn't know if they were from the armory raid, but they were all military-issued, and I finally had proof. I started the engine and sped off into the night.

CHAPTER 37

I sat parked on Seaver Street across from the Franklin Park Zoo, the stone wall reminding me of the magical place inside. I spent many summers there, field trips with the *Home*, a hundred children separated into lines of girls and boys. Those were some of my best memories, seeing the tigers or having lunch on the picnic tables beside the giraffes. I even fell in love there or at least thought I did, a blonde girl with pigtails who smiled at me on the carousel.

But it wasn't all sunshine and happiness. We were as unruly as goats, often getting in trouble, and sometimes being sent back early with a chaperone. One time, I watched Marcus reach through the fence of the monkey cages, where he hurled peanuts mixed with rocks. Even in our mischievous youth, it seemed somehow cruel, the shriek of the animals getting pelted. It took me forty years and a homicide investigation to realize I had misjudged him or, even worse, to discover that maybe I was just as bad.

Startled by a knock, I looked over, and Harrigan was crouched in the window. I unlocked the passenger door, and he got in.

"Morning, Lieutenant," he said, like any other day.

As usual, he was clean-shaven, his pressed suit far more dignified than my wrinkled clothes.

"I got on the boat last night," I said, speaking low and glancing around. "It was lousy with weapons."

"What kind of weapons?"

I reached into my coat and took out the photo.

"Rifles mostly," I said, handing it to him. "Some artillery."

As he looked at it, his face tensed up.

"Were these taken in the armory robbery?"

"Don't know. The feds never showed us the inventory. It could be from other sources, too."

"So you think they're planning an invasion?" Harrigan asked.

I smiled, not sure if he was being serious or sarcastic. Nothing at this point would have surprised me. Although we could both deal with street crime, the politics and problems of the wider world were a mystery.

"There was food too. Crates of it."

"Sounds like they're expecting trouble."

"What do you know about Poland?" I asked.

"Only that they lost the war."

"I mean now," I said, and I rarely had to steer him away from humor.

"I don't follow events in Europe."

"Life is hard under communism."

"So I can imagine."

"What if they have a plan?"

"Who are *they*?"

"Marcus, the Sokol brothers—"

"What are you getting at, Lieutenant?" he asked.

It was strange how, whenever I reached a point where I had nothing more to lose, the truth descended over me like a warm blanket. So distracted by the *who* and *what* of the crime, I never had time to consider the *why*. No investigation was complete without a motive. Now it was clear—there was no other explanation.

"What if they robbed the Shawmut Bank to send aid to Poland?"

"I'd say it's the most outlandish thing I've ever heard," he said.

"They robbed the armory, they got weapons. That ship, the Pulaski. It's leaving Sunday."

Our eyes locked, and I grinned.

"So you think I'm right?"

"For the love of Jehovah, Lieutenant, I do hope so."

......

I STOOD beneath an overhang across from *Headcase Hotel* for almost a half-hour, scanning the crowds of pedestrians and looking for anyone familiar or suspicious. It wasn't people from the department I was worried about or even the Sokol brothers. By now, Marcus knew I was on to him, and he had the resources to trail me, which was why I had to make sure he wasn't. I didn't believe his partner Shine was involved, but I wasn't certain. And corruption in any agency was like skin cancer: you never knew its extent until you got beneath the surface.

Finally, I stepped out into the sunlight and scurried over, ducking into the doorway and then looking around again. It was more controlled vigilance than paranoia, my training from the military and those skills of survival learned in the war. As I entered the lobby, I nodded to the security guard, who stood smiling with his hands clasped behind his back.

Exiting the elevator, I knocked once before entering Dr. Kaplan's office.

"Mr. Brae," she said, coming out of the room where she had her desk and coffee maker. "What happened?"

I could go for hours forgetting about the bump on my head, but the moment someone mentioned it, the soreness returned.

"A fender bender."

"Are you alright?"

"Fine, thanks."

"Have a seat…please."

Sinking into the chair, I was instantly more at ease. Aside from my house, there was no place I felt safer.

"You look flustered," she said, sitting down.

"I feel flustered."

She smiled and reached for her pen and pad.

"Do you want to talk about it?"

Do you want to talk about it? I was always amused by the question, the phrase she used whenever I brought up some problem, conflict, or crisis. Although I appreciated her tact, I knew it was standard protocol in the business. Our sessions were one of the few areas of my life where I was asked and not expected to speak.

"Yeah," I said.

I hesitated, hoping she would start the conversation, and when she didn't, I continued.

"I…I was put on administrative leave…for coming here."

Her face dropped.

"Mr. Brae, I'm—"

"It's not your fault. Someone told the department. I don't know who, but I've got a pretty good idea."

"Marcus?"

I nodded.

"For how long?" she asked.

"They want the department doctor to evaluate me in a couple of weeks."

"I wouldn't advise—"

"I know," I said, not meaning to cut her off again. "They don't know a psychologist from a proctologist…"

When she grinned, it relieved some of the tension and encouraged me to go on.

"But I'm still investigating."

"Marcus?"

It was the second time she had said his name, and by now I felt like she knew him.

"Yes. They think it's someone else. A guy and a girl. Radicals, hippies…"

She didn't smirk, but her face tightened in a way that made me think she was offended. Of all the subjects we discussed, politics was the most sensitive. I had been seeing her for over three months and still didn't know her views, whether she was liberal or conservative, whether she had voted for Nixon or Humphrey.

"I read about it in the Globe," she said.

I gave a surprised look.

"It made a big splash."

"I saw your picture, too."

"Was I smiling?"

"You didn't see it?" she asked.

"No."

If I never liked publicity, I was even more uneasy about it when the arrest was a sham.

"Does this pose an ethical problem?"

"The attention?"

"No. Investigating your friend."

As usual, we spoke in circles about the case, which was safer for both of us. But by now she understood enough about it that we didn't need to be specific.

"There's more to it," I said. "Something more personal."

"More personal than Marcus?"

I squirmed in the chair, trying to get comfortable.

"There's a girl. Alina. She's missing…"

Dr. Kaplan's expression changed, but she continued to listen.

"She was also a witness to the robbery."

"Pardon. What was her name?"

"Alina. Alina Jankowski."

She started to speak then stopped, and for the first time, she seemed stumped. I always relied on her for her strength and wisdom, but everyone had their breaking point.

"You know Alina Jankowski?" she asked, finally.

I nodded.

"She's the daughter of our babysitter."

"Mr. Brae. This puts me in a very difficult position."

She had already given her speech about patient confidentiality and professional obligation, but I let her repeat it.

"I believe she's in danger," I said.

"She is…or was a client of mine."

As she spoke, her calm and steady voice began to falter.

"Not anymore?"

"She hasn't shown up in weeks."

Our eyes locked; the implication was clear.

"Any idea where she might be?"

It was a bold question, but by now we were both in too deep.

"She lives with—"

"Yes, I know," I said. "Her mother reported her missing."

"She…had a boyfriend."

"What's his name?"

"She never told me. We talked about lots of things. She's a very troubled young woman. Kind, but very troubled."

I thought back to the day of the shooting, the image of Alina crouched on the sidewalk and sobbing. She was dressed like a floozy, something that had struck me even with all the chaos around us. I had pitied her then, and I pitied her now.

"I know," I said. "Is there anything you can remember about the guy?

Dr. Kaplan shook her head.

When the timer rang, it was the first time I had ever seen her more relieved than me. Immediately, we both got up.

"Please, let's keep this between us," she said.

In her eyes, I saw strained indecision, like she didn't know whether to advise me, wish me luck, or pretend we had never discussed it. The fact that she knew Alina was a surprise, but it wasn't a shock. Boston was a small place, and Dr. Kaplan dealt with everyone from depressed housewives to delirious alcoholics.

As we stood facing each other, I handed her a check, hesitating before going over to the door. I hoped she would say more, but I couldn't pressure her. Her professional standing was on the line, and even with a young woman at risk, I wasn't sure how much she could tell me.

"Thank you," I said.

As I turned to leave, she said, "There is something else," and I stopped. "Something about the beach. Her boyfriend lived near a beach, I believe."

CHAPTER 38

Harrigan and I sat with Captain Egersheim in the back corner at Victoria's Diner. It was the same booth where I first met Delilah, and only a couple down from where Marcus and I had lunch, catching up after our years apart. The restaurant had a nostalgic charm, the location for almost every significant event, meeting, or conversation in my adult life. It was where my coworkers took me after I got promoted to detective; it was where I brought Ruth on our second date, and the fact that she didn't complain about the smoke and shabby décor told me she was worth getting to know. Finally, it was one of the last places I ate with Captain Jackson. I would never forget his shriveled frame and trembling fingers, picking at his Cobb salad to be polite, not because he had an appetite.

So when I called Egersheim and asked him to meet outside of headquarters, it was my first choice. Aside from being safe, it also signaled some kind of truce between us. He had come to my defense when the entire department seemed against me. That single display of loyalty, risking his own reputation, made up for the years of incompetence.

While I finally had his support, he didn't take the news well. I showed him the photo of the weapons and described my run-ins with the Sokol brothers. I reminded him that a key witness had gone missing and that another, Geronimo, had had his testimony omitted from the final report. I even told him about Delilah's role, something Harrigan wasn't prepared for, his look of momentary dread. But the captain barely acknowledged it. He was more troubled that a member of the FBI had coordinated a robbery that ended in a cop killing than that one of his detectives was dating a student activist.

"This is all…" Egersheim hesitated. "Beyond belief."

He leaned forward with his elbows on the table, eyes wide and pale white. In all my time working for him, we had never before had a case so shocking, and I was sure he wished, at least for a moment, that he was back to managing horses and parades. And I still hadn't gotten to the most bizarre part—the motive.

"We think they're sending it to Poland," I said.

For the first time, I was confident enough to say *we*.

"An arms deal?"

I shook my head but, before I could speak, Harrigan broke in.

"Possibly some kind of underground resistance. There's a lot of social unrest in the country, anger toward the Soviets. Two years ago, there were large protests against the communist government. The situation is quite unstable…"

He spoke with the authority of a pundit, and even Egersheim looked impressed. After I had told Harrigan my theory, he spent the night studying Poland and its politics. Now he was more informed than me, but I wasn't jealous because I always relied on him for specifics.

"It doesn't explain why the feds didn't make the connection that the armory witness had worked at the Shawmut Bank."

"They probably did. And it was quashed."

"So you think Agent Shine is in on it?" Egersheim asked.

"Doubt it. This seems to be about Marcus and his Polish Triangle gang. That doesn't mean Shine doesn't know. Ever find only one rotten apple in a barrel?"

He grinned, the first moment of humor since we arrived.

"And what about the missing girl?"

I looked at Harrigan, nodding for him to answer. While going over the case, it was he who had made the speculation, so he deserved to say it.

"We think she was a plant," he said. "Agent Marecki knows her. It's possible they were romantically involved. She works at a gentlemen's club in Kenmore Square."

"Then where is she?"

It was the question that had dogged me for weeks. In times of frustration, I was even tempted to chalk up her disappearance to coincidence. Only after my meeting with Dr. Kaplan did I realize there was a better explanation.

"I've learned that she's very troubled, emotionally fragile," I said. "When we talked to her after the robbery, she said something interesting."

Again I turned to Harrigan who, in his attention to detail, had recalled the remark and even made a note of it.

"She said *it shouldn't have happened.*"

I had thought about the statement a hundred times, and it still gave me chills. I could have been ashamed that I missed it, but I had been too upset about Duggan's death that morning to notice anything subtle or suspicious.

"We think she got cold feet and panicked," I said.

"They were afraid she was gonna talk?"

Harrigan and I nodded at the same time.

Egersheim rubbed his chin and pulled his mustache, either lost in thought or still too stunned to speak. When the waitress came over to see if we wanted more coffee, he acted like he didn't know she was there. I waited until she walked away before asking, "Where do we go from here?"

The question roused him from his stupor, and he sat up. For most of the conversation, he had been listening, taking everything in with a mix of dread and disbelief. But he was still the captain and the only person who could steer the investigation.

"When does the boat leave?" he asked.

"Tomorrow morning."

"We'll need a search warrant."

"But we have the photograph."

"Maritime laws are trickier. Probable cause doesn't always apply the same way."

"Even if the ship is in port?"

"It's still a foreign vessel. Let's not start a diplomatic crisis over a couple of rifles and some bags of rice…"

It was more than a *couple of rifles*, but I respected his caution. For once, I felt like he knew what he was doing, and I trusted his ability. For once, I felt like we were a team, united by the same goal. For once, he felt like a leader.

"Let me go now and talk with the D.A.," he added, his voice low but urgent. "Stay under the radar. Don't make any moves until you hear from me."

Taking out his wallet, he slapped a $10 bill on the table, far more than the cost of our three coffees and Harrigan's cinnamon bun. Then we all stood up, put on our coats, and headed for the door.

Outside, the cold wind whipped up and down Massachusetts Avenue, kicking up trash and other debris. We parted in the parking lot, and Harrigan and I went toward the Valiant.

"Gentlemen," Egersheim called, and we both looked.

"Sir?"

"Good work."

. . . . . .

WHEN I WALKED in the door, Nessie was sitting on the living room floor, brushing her doll's hair.

"Hi daddy," she said, too busy to look up.

"Hello, sweetheart."

Thinking she had been left alone, my temper rose until I heard voices, and realized Ruth and Nadia were in the kitchen. I hung up my coat and walked in, Nadia's eyes going right to the gun in my shoulder holster. Considering that she had lived through the war, I was sure the sight of a weapon brought out mixed feelings.

"You're home," Ruth said, looking over, her lashes fluttering.

She was having wine, and Nadia was drinking something hard from the liquor cabinet. They greeted me with smiles, but I knew they had been having a serious discussion, possibly crying. I could always sense the lingering emotion of deep or heartfelt conversation.

"Want me to get you some dinner?" Ruth asked.

Walking over to the stove, I looked in the pot to see a stew.

"Thanks. I can get it."

I filled a bowl and sat at the table, eating while they remained quiet. I knew the silence wouldn't last. I could feel Ruth's anxious anticipation like the vibration of the refrigerator.

"Is there any news?" she asked.

Leaning over the bowl, I looked up and cleared my throat.

"We're getting close."

It was one of the cruelest lies I had ever told in front of the parent of a victim, but I didn't regret it. Having Nadia there was awkward and, in some ways, unfair. Although I sympathized with her, I didn't want to talk about the investigation in my own home. The truth would have been harder, anyway. If Alina had been planted as a witness to the robbery and then lost her nerve, she was either dead or on the run. Either of those possibilities would have sent Nadia into a tailspin of despair.

After eating, I put the bowl in the sink. In the tense silence, I could feel them watching me. I was just ready to go into the living room to see Nessie when the phone rang. Everyone held their breath, including me, and I reached for the receiver.

"Hello?"

"Lieutenant," a voice said, and I was relieved it was Harrigan. "The captain wants to see us at his office in an hour."

"Why?"

"He wouldn't say."

But I didn't need to ask because it was obvious. No one got called into headquarters after hours unless it was urgent, so I was sure the chief had made a decision.

"See you soon."

Hanging up, I tried to hide my disappointment so I didn't alarm Nadia and Ruth. Some small part of me had hoped the operation would wait until morning; it was always hard to come home and go back out again. But with the Pulaski scheduled to leave the next day, we had to act now or risk the case turning into an even bigger scandal. If the ship made it out of port and had to be intercepted by the Coast Guard or Navy, politicians everywhere would be asking how the Boston Police could mistake two activists for the perpetrators of a crime that involved an FBI agent and weapons smuggling. If it wasn't such a disgrace, I would have laughed. The tension between law enforcement and college students had been building for years, and I always feared it was only one major incident away from a nationwide confrontation.

"I've gotta head into work," I said.

Ruth gave a sad smile, but she didn't argue, and everyone was too tired for questions and explanations. Leaning over, I kissed her on the cheek, and she seemed a little more reassured. I left the kitchen to go brush my teeth and, as I turned up the stairs, Nessie was coming down in her Batgirl outfit, so excited she looked ready to burst.

"Daddy!" she said. "Are we going to houses to get the candy?"

I smiled at the clunky speech of a child. But inside my heart sank because I had entirely forgotten about Halloween.

"I...I..."

"Daddy has to go trick-or-treating somewhere else tonight," I heard, and Ruth came into the foyer, saving me the guilt of having to explain. "Isn't that right?"

"That's right."

Nessie stood between us, gazing up with a toothy grin.

"Can I have some of your candy?"

"Of course," I said, rubbing the top of her head.

"What are you dressed as?"

I looked at Ruth.

"A police officer."

CHAPTER 39

Harrigan and I sat with Egersheim in his office and waited for Chief McNamara. It seemed like the captain had already had half a pack of cigarettes, smoking one after another. I could tell he was nervous, but we all were. He tried to stay composed, making small remarks, even a joke about a horse that walks into a bar.

Outside was dark, the lights twinkling in all the high-rises, and although the city looked peaceful, it was hard to relax. The time before an operation was always tense, that jittery dread, and the only reason I could handle it was that I'd had a lot of practice. The war had prepared me most, those nights on the line before a patrol or an attack, gathering our equipment and falling in for one last pep talk, usually whispered and always optimistic. I had discovered long before that, in most cases, the anticipation of something was worse than the thing itself.

The door opened, and we all looked over.

"Captain," the chief said, storming toward us across the floor.

Behind him were one of his lieutenants and two other younger officers.

When Egersheim got up to get him a chair from the corner, the chief held out his hand.

"Not necessary," he said. "This will be quick."

He stood beside the desk, and we turned to him.

"Paul told me what you found out about the bank investigation," he said, looking straight at me. For a second, I was confused, rarely hearing anyone call Egersheim by his first name. "First, commendable work, Lieutenant..."

The praise caught me off guard, and maybe I needed it because I got both choked up and reinvigorated.

"This is a damn disgrace," he went on, his face red. "I just got off the phone with the U.S. Attorney's Office. We can move in on the boat as long as we have the warrant."

Reaching into his coat, he took out an envelope and handed it to me. I thought it was for the Pulaski until I opened it and saw the words at the top, just under United States District Court: *Stanislaw Sokol and Aleksander Sokol, 19 Locust Street, Dorchester, Massachusetts.*

"The brothers?"

"I want you two to execute it," the chief said, looking at me and Harrigan.

"I doubt they're home."

It wasn't a joke, but everyone chuckled.

"Look around. If you can't find them it's most likely we caught them at the pier. The Harbor Patrol and State Police are working with us..."

The chief stopped, standing frozen with one arm out as if conducting. Then slowly he circled the room, looking everyone in the eye while a single bead of sweat rolled down his cheek.

"Are we ready, boys?"

"What about Marecki?" I asked.

"There's a special place in hell for that guy," he said, and for a moment, I thought he was going to avoid the question. "We've got a special task force driving up from D.C. They're due here within the hour."

I shivered from relief. Anything else we would achieve that night was a bonus. Ever since I first suspected Marcus was involved in the robbery, my biggest fear was that he would somehow escape prosecution.

McNamara waved to his entourage, and they left. The captain stood up, wiped his mustache, and walked over, staring at the floor like he didn't know what to say. Harrigan and I got up too, and we all stood in a circle.

"The chief has asked me to ride with him," he said.

His tone was somber, almost like he was ashamed for not joining us. But I wasn't offended. Jackson never went with us on stakeouts or arrests. The role of captain was more about leadership than action, a tradition I didn't want to break in case, someday, I came off the streets. Having been in the service and fought in the war, I respected chain of command. I believed in the idea of having someone in charge, even if it wasn't always the right person.

"If you don't find them," Egersheim said. "Come straight to the docks."

"Yes, sir."

We all shook, a flurry of crossed arms so chaotic that somehow Harrigan's and my hands ended up clasped.

"Now, be safe," the captain said.

His parting advice was strange, something a mother would say to her child, but I knew it was more out of innocence than ignorance. Except for his early years as a patrolman, he'd had a pretty comfortable career. I didn't resent him for it, knowing that he, like everyone else, paid a price for the things he avoided.

......

IT WAS A COLD NIGHT, the sky clear and just the whisper of a breeze. With the windows up and the heat on, I didn't smoke because I didn't want to suffocate Harrigan. But that didn't mean I wasn't craving a cigarette. I was nervous, my breathing shallow and my eyes laser-focused, that same heightened awareness I used to get in the war. Harrigan was anxious too, but he showed it in different ways, tapping his fingers or clearing his throat more than usual, those subtle quirks of character that had taken me years to know.

"Do you feel vindicated?"

"What?" I said, turning to him.

"That the chief relented."

"I don't think he's happy about it."

Turning onto Dorchester Avenue, we entered The Polish Triangle. By now, I felt a curious affection for the place. I no longer saw it as another anonymous section of the city, but as a distinct place with its own history and traditions. I sympathized with its residents, knowing the scandal was going to be difficult, a mark of shame on a people who, for the most part, were honest and hardworking. It was the immigrants' dilemma, always viewed with suspicion by the wider society and always stereotyped by the sins of the few.

As a child, I had never heard of The Polish Triangle, even though the *Home* was a mile down the road in Roxbury. The city was like that back then, a patchwork of small neighborhoods so separate they often didn't know the others existed. But in the modern Boston, the old world was fast being replaced by the new, and I doubted it would last.

I drove down Locust Street and stopped in front of the Sokols' house. With the lights off, it looked empty, but then all the rundown buildings in the area did. I looked at Harrigan and we got out, opening the fence gate and walking up the steps. Standing on the porch, I thought about when we visited at the start of the investigation, a day that now seemed like a lifetime ago.

While I knocked, Harrigan stood behind me with his hands in his pockets. I didn't expect trouble but serving a warrant always had the potential for resistance or violence.

Moments later, the door opened, and two eyes appeared in the crack. It was Mrs. Sokol, her expression somewhere between frightened and suspicious. I stepped back so she wouldn't feel intimidated.

"Ma'am," I said. "We're looking for Alex and Stanley."

"No home," she said, waving both hands.

"Do you know where they are?"

She looked at Harrigan then at me.

"No home," she said again.

We stared at each other for what felt like five minutes but was only a few seconds. I could have pressed her, even warned her about the penalties for harboring felons. But there was no honor in strong-arming an old woman, and she probably wouldn't have understood me anyway.

"Thank you," I said, and she shut the door.

Harrigan and I walked away, holding our conversation until we reached the street.

"You think she's lying?"

I looked back at the house, the dark windows and shabby paint.

"Doubt it."

Instead of going back to the car, I started down the sidewalk, and he followed. At the end of the street, an old fence with barbed wire looked out over the expressway below. A few yards before it was a ditch, three feet deep and filled with trash and dirty water. It was too big to be natural, so I guessed it had been cut into the asphalt by a backhoe when the road was severed to make the highway.

"Is that what you hit?"

"No, I hit a pothole," I said sarcastically.

But nothing about it was funny. I had come close to death so many times in my career that I'd lost count, and the only reason it didn't spook me was that I usually didn't know until afterward. I didn't believe in fate, but the older I got, the more I sensed I was using up all my second chances and that someday my luck would run out. I couldn't dwell on it, however, or I wouldn't have been able to work.

"Thank god for that pothole."

I turned and Harrigan was beside me, clutching the fence and looking down the embankment wall to the traffic below.

"Thank someone," I said, and I walked away.

As I went to get in the Valiant, something caught my eye. It was a notice, stapled to a pole and flapping in the wind. Tearing it off, I squinted to read it in the lamplight. The words were in English and Polish, but the picture was unmistakable.

MISSING

ALINA JANKOWSKI, 25, of 28 Rawson Street, Dorchester, has been missing since October 7th. She was last seen leaving work in Kenmore Square. If anyone has seen her, please contact the Polish American Club or the Boston Police Department.

ALINA JANKOWSKI, 25, z 28 Rawson Street w Dorchester zaginęła od 7 października. Ostatnio widziano ją opuszczającą pracę na Kenmore Square. Jeśli ktoś ją widział, prosimy o kontakt z Polish American Club lub Bostońską Policją.

THE PAPER WAS FLIMSY, the words and image smudged. I could tell it had been made from a cheap photocopier. The department didn't use posters, otherwise every pole and wall in the city would have been covered. So it must have been the community, banding together to find one of its own.

As we stared at it, I got a feeling of both panic and guilt. I didn't take Alina's disappearance seriously when Ruth first told me, thinking she was just another flighty young woman. But missing persons' cases were always trickier when it wasn't children. Adults had the right to do and go where they wanted. But knowing what I now knew about Marcus and the others, I feared for her life and wished I had started the search sooner.

We got in the car and drove off. There was no deliberation, no discussion about where to go next. As if by instinct, I headed for the one place that had been looming in the backdrop of all the intrigue: The Polish American Club.

We parked across the street and got out. As we approached the front doors, I checked the safety on my gun, and Harrigan did the same.

When we walked in, it was busy for a weekday night. Half the tables were full, and two dozen men were sitting at the bar. Some looked over, and I glared back, no longer worried about being careful or discreet. I would have whipped out my badge and shoved it in their faces if I had to. As with many investigations, I had reached a point where I was emotionally spent, and I wouldn't have looked at another incident summary, witness brief, or logistics report for all the time off in the world. I had agonized over the circumstances that led to Duggan's death long enough, and now was the time to act.

At the bar, a female bartender with long dark hair stood with her back to us, wiping down the counter and putting things in order. She seemed to linger, and I realized why when I called to her, and she turned around. It was Margaret Marie Kozlowski.

"You're a long way from Newburyport."

"Hello," she said.

She didn't seem thrilled, but at least she didn't pretend not to know me.

"You never told me you worked here."

"You never asked."

I stepped closer, speaking softly because I knew people were listening.

"How'd the fundraiser go?" I asked.

She smiled sourly, pushing her hair behind her ear.

"Can I get you a drink?"

Our eyes locked.

"Ginger ale," I said.

There was a quiet tension in the room, and even Harrigan sensed it, something I could tell by his posture. In times of danger or uncertainty, he always stood behind me, his back arched and feet apart, ready for anything.

She set the glass down in front of me, and when I reached for my wallet, she said, "It's on the house."

"Thanks. Where's your bathroom?"

Hesitant, she looked past me and nodded.

"Behind the stage."

I walked across the dancefloor and down a hallway, opening a door that had the word Mężczyźni and the shape of a man with a cane and top hat on it. As I peed into the urinal, I could hear voices and movement behind the wall. Coming out, I noticed another door at the end that was slightly open. I went toward it and peered in to see a storage room with boxes, mops, stage equipment, and more. Three men sat around a table. It took a second for my eyes to adjust and when they did, I realized what they were doing and gasped.

I reached for my gun, kicked in the door, and they all jumped up.

"Freeze!"

For a moment, time stopped, and no one moved. The Sokol brothers just stared at me while the other man looked at them. On the table was a pile of weapons, from small revolvers to double-barrel shotguns.

"Hands up!" I shouted.

Then all hell broke loose. While Alex ran for the exit, I saw his brother Stanley go for something in his waist. I shouted for him to drop it, but in that split second, it was too late. When he raised a gun, I fired, hitting him once in the chest, and he fell back onto a ladder. It took all my willpower to stop at one bullet, and I was proud that I did.

Harrigan burst in with his weapon drawn. Instantly, the other man put up his hands.

"Cuff him," I said, and I flew out the side door.

Next to the club was a small lot, wedged between the Southeast Expressway and the bridge over to South Boston. I looked around, but it was too dark, and I knew Alex could have gone anywhere. Then I heard a noise, the rattle of metal, and when I turned, I saw him clinging to the outside of the fence that bordered the highway. Putting away my gun, I walked over with my hands out, trying not to startle him. For the first time in years, I was more concerned with saving a suspect than arresting one.

"Don't move!" I said.

He struggled to hold on, his fingers tense around the links. He squirmed and groaned, his body dangling and long hair flowing. When I noticed a cross around his neck, I realized maybe it was Stanley and not Alex. But at this point, it didn't matter.

I crouched, moving toward him, the sound of sirens in the distance.

"Hang on," I said.

As I reached to take his hands, our eyes met. He gritted his teeth, shouted something in Polish, and I frowned in confusion. Then he let go. Cringing, I turned away. A half-second later, I heard the screech of brakes, car horns, and shattered glass. I didn't look over to see but prayed he didn't cause more death in pursuing his own.

I stood stunned, out of breath, and overcome by mild nausea. As I stumbled back toward the building, the police cars arrived, racing up from all directions, their sirens and lights cutting through the night. I had never felt prouder to be a cop. Harrigan met me at the door, his blazer open and his gun still out.

"Lieutenant?!" he said.

When he pointed at my arm, I was stunned to see blood, realizing Stanley had gotten a round off before I shot him. Feeling around the wound, I was relieved it was only a graze.

"Not as quick as I used to be," I said.

He laughed nervously and shoved his pistol back into the holster.

"None of us are."

We walked back into the storeroom, where paramedics were kneeling over the body of Stanislaw. The other man sat in the corner with his hands cuffed behind his back. I went up to him and asked, "Is that Alex or Stanley?"

"To be honest, sir, I can't tell them apart."

I snorted, and we continued back into the club. Everyone was standing, the room full of anxious chatter as officers walked around interviewing people. Behind the bar, Margaret was leaning against the wall, her hands over her eyes, sobbing while another woman consoled her.

I nodded to Harrigan, and we walked over.

"Miss," I said, and she looked up. "Where's Alina Jankowski?"

"I don't—"

"Don't lie to me!"

She swallowed, trying to catch her breath.

"With Marcus."

"Where?"

Our eyes locked, and although her expression was bitter, it was also honest.

"I don't know. But if you find him, you'll find her."

CHAPTER 40

I COULD HEAR THE SIRENS BEFORE WE GOT TO THE DOCKS, THE LIGHTS flashing behind the buildings and warehouses like the glow of mortar fire in an embattled town. We turned onto Northern Avenue and up ahead I saw a dozen police vehicles, standard and unmarked. We parked on the street and got out, running down the pier past cops and other officials. Considering the media wasn't there yet, I knew we couldn't have been too late.

In the distance, I saw the Pulaski, docked dramatically like some unwitting accomplice in a crime. All its floodlights were on, and officers were going up and down the gangway.

"Lieutenant?!"

I looked over, and Egersheim stood with a group of men by the office of the wharf. When we walked over, the chief turned to acknowledge us, the most deferential he had ever been.

"Brae," he said. "We heard what happened. Are you okay?"

The bleeding had stopped, but my shoulder still throbbed.

"Fine. Did you get Marcus?"

The chief paused and turned to the men beside him.

"These gentlemen are from Customs," he said. "And this is Matt Colleran with the bureau. He's just arrived from D.C."

The agent stepped out of the shadows, dressed in a long coat and hat. When he extended his hand, I was tempted not to shake it. But I couldn't blame an entire organization for the treachery of one man.

"Thanks for all your assistance," he said.

"Where's Marcus...?" I repeated, almost saying *Evans* instead of *Marecki.*

"We'll take it from here, detective."

Sneering, I looked at the others, as surprised as I was insulted by the smug reply.

"How about you answer my question?"

Colleran gave a tight smile but said nothing. If the captain and chief hadn't been there, I might have grabbed him by the collar and shaken a response from him.

"The Coast Guard has seized the Pulaski," Egersheim said, always changing the subject in tense moments. "We're gathering the evidence now."

"Jody," the chief spoke up. "I'm putting you in for a commendation. This will mean a lot to Duggan's wife and kids."

I tore my eyes from Colleran and turned to McNamara. It was a jarring shift from rage to gratitude, and too much was happening at once.

"Thank you, sir," I said.

I appreciated the honor even more because I knew it was humbling and, in some ways, an admission of all the department had done wrong in handling the case. A lot of people, including him, would have preferred that Kagan and Leslie Lavoie were the culprits. Everyone was looking for a reason to discredit the activists.

"What about Alina Jankowski?"

"Pardon?" McNamara asked.

"The girl who was reported missing," the captain said. "Allegedly a witness to the bank robbery."

The chief thought for a moment, biting his lip, and I could tell it was an inconvenient sidenote. Then he looked at his underlings, a sergeant and two detectives, who couldn't have been more indifferent if they sighed and shrugged their shoulders. With the bust of an international smuggling plot underway, everyone was too busy assessing how it would help their own careers. No one would get much praise for finding a troubled young woman.

A young patrolman came up, his cap tipped back, as eager as a kid running toward an ice cream truck.

"Sir," he said, out of breath. "State Police got an ID on the weapons. They're from the armory."

"All of them?"

"Most."

McNamara gave a satisfied smile. When the cop walked away, one of the detectives took out a cigarette, and the others did the same. The conversation moved on to small talk, gossip, and even some wisecracks. I was stunned, frustrated beyond belief. The captain seemed to sense it too because when I looked over, he averted his eyes. Jackson would have stood up to McNamara, Colleran, and the rest. But I had come to accept Egersheim for who he was, knowing that even if he wanted to be more assertive, he just wasn't capable of it.

While everyone talked, I stood at the edge of the group, my anger simmering and feeling helpless. I glared at Agent Colleran, but he wouldn't look back. Harrigan and I had exposed the scandal, and now we were being treated like minor participants.

When two officials from the Massachusetts Port Authority came over, it was a good opportunity to slip away. I had restrained my outrage long enough and didn't want to do or say anything stupid. So I walked off, and no one seemed to notice, back down the pier and out to the street, where several news trucks had just arrived. As I continued toward the Valiant, I didn't have to look back to know Harrigan was behind me.

"Lieutenant?"

I waited for him to catch up, and we walked the last few steps together.

"Do you think they have Agent Marecki in custody?" he asked.

Opening the door, I looked across at him.

"There's only one way to find out."

......

WE RACED down the Southeast Expressway with the city at our backs. With rush hour over, the road was clear for stretches at a time. The highway narrowed, and soon the dense suburbs were replaced by the quiet, leafy towns of the South Shore. Neither of us spoke, and the entire ride felt like a long meditation on all that had happened since Duggan's death.

Finally, we pulled off the exit, and I rolled up to a stop sign. Flicking my cigarette, I hesitated and looked around. Harrigan gave me a sideways glance, but I wasn't having second thoughts. Aside from a gas station, there were no lights, and I was mesmerized by the darkness because I wasn't used to it.

I cut the wheel, and we continued down a winding road toward the coast. I knew we were getting close to the water by the smell, the sour stench of seaweed and salt. We drove over a small bridge and into Humarock, a narrow spit of land that was connected to Marsh-field but part of the town of Scituate. With its ramshackle cottages and dusty lanes, it had long been a summer destination for Boston's working class.

The farther down the peninsula we went, the fewer the houses, plots giving way to wide swaths of beach grass and dunes. At some point, the street had transitioned to sand, and the Valiant rocked gently over the dips and crevices. Despite the cold, I rolled down the window, listening to the crash of the waves and wishing I was some-where else.

"I need a vacation," I said.

Harrigan turned and gave me a curious frown. Whether it was the long ride or my restless nerves, I had the urge to talk.

"You deserve one."

As we came around the bend, I could see the shape of a structure ahead, the lights of the few scattered houses around it. I thought back to when Marcus and I met for lunch at Victoria's Diner. He had mentioned living beside a military tower, and the only reason I remembered was that Ruth and I had gone to the beach there many years before, a fun but hapless day where she got sunburned and I lost my car keys.

"How 'bout you?" I asked. "You gonna take Delilah somewhere special?"

He chuckled and looked away, out to the blackness of the shore.

"First, let's see what the D.A. has to say—"

Boom!

The windshield shattered, and I was momentarily blinded. I lost control, and the car veered off the road, rolling into a ditch, the tires spinning on the sand. I sat up stunned and wiped glass from my eyes.

"Lieutenant," I heard.

When I looked, Harrigan had his hand on his chest. Leaning over, I ripped his suit jacket open and gasped when I saw blood. I didn't have to inspect it any closer to know it was a gunshot.

I looked around in a panic, but we were far from help. So I grabbed a handkerchief and crumpled it into a ball, pressing it against the wound.

"Hold this," I said.

He did what I said and didn't complain, which worried me even more. In those few seconds, I was paralyzed by indecision, my heart pounding. Yet, there was no more doubt or uncertainty—I knew what I had to do. Marcus had taken the coward's way out, and now I had to eliminate him.

"You go, Lieutenant," Harrigan said.

Our eyes locked, and he nodded, a look of quiet reassurance that gave me the courage to go. Reaching for his holster, I took out his pistol, undid the safety, and placed it firmly into his free hand. With a trembling smile, I patted him on the arm and opened the door. Leaving him there was the hardest choice I ever had to make.

I scurried up the embankment and peered over, where I saw a

small white cottage beside the military tower. All the lights were off, and in the driveway was Marcus's Dodge Charger, shining under the stars like a sinister beacon. There were also two dark cars, parked at angles with the doors open like the occupants had sped up and jumped out. I knew it was the feds, and the fact that there were no sounds or activity gave me an eerie feeling.

I stayed behind the beach grass and followed the road, crouched low with my gun out. Once I was opposite the house, I burst from the cover of the shrubs and ran across the street, landing between the two unmarked cars. Laying on the ground, I noticed shards of glass all around. When I glanced up, I realized some of the windows were blown out. Seconds later, I heard a soft groan and cringed. The agents had been ambushed.

Shimmying to the bumper, I looked at the house and saw a man lying on the walkway, his neck turned and arms out. The front door was open, but I wasn't going to take the risk. There was nothing harder than storming a blockaded building head-on, like trying to take a hill, and I would have to find another way in.

Then I heard a sound, a cough or a sniffle, some sign of a human presence amid the silence. Straining to see, I looked toward the tower and noticed a tiny glow on the observation deck. It was the tip of a cigarette.

I sat up and blew the sand off my gun. Keeping my eyes on the tower, I flew across the yard and collapsed behind a dune. Looking ahead, I saw a doorway on the side of the structure. Counting to three, I ran toward it.

Inside was pitch dark, the walls damp with salty air. I looked up the cement staircase and then slowly I ascended. Gripping my pistol with both hands, I turned on each landing like someone was waiting to pounce. I held my breath and listened for movement, cursing my eyesight, so tense I would have fired at the scuttle of a mouse.

I made it up the three flights, and as I approached the top, I could see a sliver of the sky. Stopping at the last step, I adjusted my grip and took a deep breath. Then I sprang forward and onto the observation deck.

"Hello."

I kept my gun raised but took my finger off the trigger. Standing at the edge and looking out to the water was a young woman, barefoot and dressed in a nightgown. With a cigarette between her fingers, she turned casually and smiled.

"Alina?" I asked.

"I wish you didn't come here."

I blinked at the strange remark.

"Your mother is worried about you."

"My mother always worries."

She spoke with a dreamy wonder, and I couldn't tell if it was from drugs or delirium. But with my partner wounded and several agents dead on the lawn, I wasn't interested in philosophizing.

"Where's Marcus?"

"He saved me, you know?" she said.

"He made you lie about Kagan and his girlfriend."

"Marcus didn't make me do anything. It was our idea."

Startled by the revelation, I slowly put my finger back on the trigger.

"Yeah?"

It was a short response, but the best way to keep someone talking was by not saying much at all.

"He loves me. I love him. We're going far away."

"To Poland?" I asked.

She took a long drag on the cigarette and blew the smoke out with a smirk.

"Poland is the past," she said. "We look to the future."

"Something tells me you two just ruined that chance."

She flicked her cigarette and faced me with a devious grin. Something wasn't right, and I knew it. The hair on the back of my neck stood up, that same sensation I used to get in the war if danger was close. When I noticed her eyes dart, I spun around. A figure burst from the shadows, and I stumbled back.

Suddenly, a gunshot.

I heard a groan, then a thud, and when I looked down, it was

Marcus. Alina screamed and ran toward him, but when I saw he had a gun, I tackled her to the ground. She shrieked and flailed like a lunatic, and the only thing that kept me from knocking her out was the vision of her mother Nadia.

Finally, I got on top of her, her arms and legs swinging wildly. I heard the click of handcuffs, and they weren't mine. Once she was restrained, I looked up to see Harrigan.

"You're...okay?" I said, relieved.

"For now."

He was breathing heavily, his forehead glistening with sweat. I knew the bullet hadn't hit any vital organs, but we still had to get him to a hospital. Scrambling over to Marcus, I put my fingers on his neck. Part of me hoped for a pulse, a few final minutes of consciousness to learn why. But when I saw the bullet had gone into the back of his head, I knew he was dead.

"Good shot."

Harrigan just looked at me, his eyes teary and nostrils flared. It was never easy being congratulated for killing someone. At other times, he would have extended his hand, but I could see he was struggling, so I got up on my own.

I walked over, grabbed Alina under the arm, and pulled her up. She was sobbing but calm, and the fact that she didn't resist was something I would note in the report because it might help her in court. As someone with my own mental problems, I sympathized with hers.

I pointed at the stairs, and she started to walk. Before I went, I glanced over at Marcus, his stout body lying in the shadows, a pool of blood around his head. He had thrown away his life for a cause I now realized he wasn't committed to. Considering all the unrest in the country and in the world, stealing money to help the workers of Poland would have at least been understandable. If I had learned anything about political movements, it was that even if the tactics were bad, the intentions were usually good. But there was no honor in greed.

When we reached the bottom of the tower, I heard sirens, lots of them. We walked out the side door, and flashing lights were coming toward us down the narrow peninsula. I marched Alina across the yard, just so she could see what they had done, and we staggered out to the road.

CHAPTER 41

WE SAT IN THE CHIEF'S OFFICE OVERLOOKING CITY HALL PLAZA, waiting for Egersheim to arrive. It was the first time I had seen Harrigan without a jacket, his bandage too thick to fit under it. The bullet had struck him just under his clavicle and lodged in the back of his shoulder, straight through soft tissue, missing every bone, artery, and organ.

When it happened, I saw blood seeping from his chest and was sure he had been hit in or near the heart. Only after he saved me from Marcus did I know he would live. No one with a grave injury could have walked from the car, climbed the tower, and fired with such precision. I was grateful but not surprised. Throughout our careers, we had both survived situations that should have killed us. And the more I thought about it, the more I got the mystical sense that someone or something was watching out for us.

Finally, the door opened. The captain walked in with some files under his arm. As usual, he was late and frantic, mumbling apologies before taking the chair beside me and Harrigan. We sat in a row, the three of us facing the chief, and it was the first time we were positioned as equals.

"The hospital called," Egersheim began, and I knew what he was going to say. "The other Sokol brother didn't make it."

The chief raised his eyes, Harrigan shook his head, and I just sighed. But none of our reactions were out of sympathy—we had all been in law enforcement too long to pity victims who had died trying to kill a cop. If anyone should have felt guilty, it was me because I shot him. But I didn't.

"Which Sokol brother?" I asked.

The captain smirked like he knew I was being sarcastic.

"They weren't sure. Relatives haven't identified the bodies yet."

"Regardless," McNamara said. "That leaves all the suspects dead."

"What about the girls?"

"Patsies, nothing more. We could get them on perjury, maybe accessory. But what judge is gonna lock them up?"

Egersheim seemed confused. As someone who had come over from the mounted unit, he still wasn't comfortable with the practical side of justice. Margaret could have been charged with accessory; Alina could have been charged with felony murder. But as two impressionable young women, it would have been hard to convince a jury they understood the consequences of their actions.

Margaret was dating Stanislaw Sokol, and Alina thought Marcus loved her. They had been persuaded to be false witnesses, pinning the bank and armory robberies on Neil Kagan and Leslie Lavoie. And it might have worked. But once Duggan got shot, Alina crumbled, and she couldn't hold up the act. The only reason it wasn't discovered by detectives on-scene was that Marcus had whisked her away.

"Oh," the captain said, looking at Harrigan. "I talked with the D.A. Your girlfriend has been cleared of any charges related to harboring a fugitive…"

We all smiled, although it was something we had expected.

"Moreover, he'd like to recommend a civilian commendation for her actions."

He turned to McNamara, who nodded and wrote something down. The district attorney, like any public official, could suggest such honors, but only the chief could issue them.

Harrigan cleared his throat and sat forward.

"Sir, she would prefer to stay anonymous."

McNamara looked stumped like it was something he had never been asked before. Or maybe he was just disappointed. In the aftermath of a bungled investigation, the administration was giving out awards like candy, if only to distract attention from all they had done wrong.

"I understand," the chief said.

And I did too. Delilah had taken a big risk informing on Kagan, probably motivated more by concern that he was innocent than because she thought he was guilty. But I knew she had no intention of stopping her political activities, and I didn't blame her. As a country, we were entering our sixth year in Vietnam. With a hundred American soldiers dying each week and no victory in sight, everyone had the right to be questioning the war. I had plenty of gripes with the younger generation, but this was one area where we agreed.

"Well, gentlemen," the chief said, leaning back, his hands clasped around his gut. "If there are no more questions, we can finally put this case to rest."

I still had plenty of questions, but I knew they wouldn't get answered there. So I responded with a smile and then looked over at Harrigan. We both got up, but Egersheim stayed seated, and I was sure he still had things to discuss with the chief. If the investigation had achieved anything, it was to make us a more cohesive team. And although I didn't have complete respect for him, it was moving in the right direction.

"Take the rest of the afternoon off," he said to us.

"Thank you, sir."

It was something I had intended anyway, but I let him think he was doing us a favor.

When Harrigan and I walked out, I got lightheaded and went over to the bubbler. I could have attributed it to sitting too long, but it was more likely the sudden realization that the case was finally closed. For weeks, I had agonized over it, so torn between the department's incompetence and my loyalty to Marcus that I thought it would break me.

"Are you okay, Lieutenant?"

Hunched over, I drank some water and splashed some on my face.

"Yeah," I said. "Just parched."

As we passed through the lobby, people looked over, secretaries stopped typing, and colleagues nodded. In any incident where a suspect was shot and killed, the praise was always more subdued. But at least it was deserved, something I hadn't felt after Kagan's arrest.

We went through the doors and down the front steps. The sky was clear, the air was crisp, and it felt like a new day. We walked across the lot and Harrigan stopped at one of the unmarked cruisers parked in a line against the fence. With the Valiant in the shop getting a windshield, I was once again without a car.

"Need a lift?" he asked.

"You going by Downtown Crossing?"

"Delilah's place, actually."

Our eyes locked, and I smiled.

"You go," I said. "I'll walk."

......

I SAT SLUMPED in the chair with my hands on my lap. The cushion was gentle against my arm, which was still sore from the graze. The room looked different, or maybe I just noticed things I hadn't before, like the aloe plant on the desk, the rusted outlet on the wall, and the stack of books in the corner. All my life, whenever I got through some traumatic period or event, I always came out with a new awareness. Or maybe I was just no longer distracted.

"Do you think she'll go to prison?"

For the first time, Dr. Kaplan had more questions than answers. She wasn't taking notes either, covering her maimed hand with her good one.

"Doubt it," I said. "She didn't hurt anybody. She's mentally unstable. My guess is they'll send her to a psychiatric ward."

Her expression didn't change, but she seemed relieved. As a professional, she was concerned for the welfare of her client, and prison was no place for a vulnerable young woman caught up in the allure of a sociopath.

"And how are you taking Marcus' untimely passing?"

I chuckled to myself. Only a therapist could describe getting shot in the head after ambushing federal agents as an *untimely passing*.

"With relish," I joked.

She averted her eyes and shifted in the chair. I could tell she didn't know whether to laugh or not.

"The hardest part of any of this," I added, "is not knowing."

"The moral unclarity?"

"If I know who the good guys are and who the bad guys are, I can do my job."

"And was Marcus a bad guy?"

While I had the urge to scoff, I trusted her enough to know all her questions had a deeper purpose.

"I don't know about back then," I said, the image of the *Home* coming into my mind. "But he sure was now."

"As long as you understand that. As long as you are certain. That's what matters."

A wave of emotion hit me, and I struggled not to get choked up.

"I am," I said.

She responded with a satisfied smile, letting a minute of silence pass before continuing.

"How is Ruth taking all this?"

"She feels bad for Nadia."

"And you?"

I thought for a moment and then looked up.

"I feel bad for humanity."

She rolled her eyes like I was being dramatic. When the timer rang, it only added to the impression that I was getting off easy, although it was the truth. In the past, hard cases always left me more bitter, and hatred, deceit, and cruelty never inspired much faith in the world. But for once, I wasn't angry.

We got up, and she walked with me toward the door. As I went to give her the check, she put up her bad hand, which I found significant.

"You keep that," she said.

"Free?"

"This session is *complimentary*. We've had too many conflicts of interest for me to accept it in good conscience."

"Then next week I'll tell you how I'm investigating your rabbi."

She laughed out loud, something I had never heard her do. We said goodbye, and I left, down the elevator and through the lobby, waving to the black security guard who, by now, knew me.

I walked out and into Downtown Crossing, which was crowded with pedestrians in the midday rush. Before, I would have kept my head down, but I was no longer worried or ashamed to be seen leaving *Headcase Hotel.* The captain and chief were now aware I was getting help, and after two shootings in one day, they probably realized why I needed it.

At the subway station, a blonde girl in hippie clothes stood by the entrance, a man playing guitar next to her. There was a sign too, something about Nixon and a picture of a Vietnamese village. After my session with Dr. Kaplan, I was in too good a mood to think about the war or any other global problems. I tried to avoid her, but she got in my way.

"Flower power," she said.

She held out a rose, flawless white with a long stem. As I reached for my wallet, she stopped me and giggled.

"No money. It's for peace."

I smiled awkwardly and took the flower, realizing how little I understood about their movement. Having grown up in an era where everything was a hustle, I always assumed they were doing the same.

I thanked her and headed down to the platform, holding the rose gently because I was going to put it to good use. After weeks of waiting, I was finally going to visit Duggan's family.

CHAPTER 42

DECEMBER

OUTSIDE IT WAS COLD, the wind rattling against the windows. We had just finished eating, and Ruth and I sat on the couch with Nessie between us. In the corner stood our new Christmas tree, decorated with ornaments and covered in tinsel. It was thin and misshapen, and I would have chosen a heartier one. But Nessie had picked it from the back of the bunch, saying it looked lonely and needed a family. And considering we were both orphans, I couldn't have agreed more.

Waiting to watch *Flipper,* we had to get through the evening news first. I always thought it was cruel that a children's show followed an hour of learning about the worst of mankind. Thankfully, Nessie was too young to understand any of it, and the only time we covered her eyes was when they showed graphic footage of Vietnam or some third-world atrocity.

After a long day, I had no interest in politics or national events. I tilted my head back and was just ready to shut my eyes when I heard the word *Poland* and looked up.

"In breaking news tonight, a sudden increase in the price of goods by the communist government has led to protests in cities across Poland…"

I sat forward, hands on my knees, my eyes fixed on the screen.

"At Lenin Shipyard in Gdańsk, thousands of dockworkers have walked off their jobs…"

I saw crowds of angry men facing off with police, who responded with tear gas and water cannons. As I watched, I got a sickening feeling, and I didn't know if it was from compassion or outrage. I glanced over to Ruth, and she was looking back.

"In Szczecin, at least four workers have been killed in what experts are describing as the worst unrest since the Poznan riots of 1956…"

The camera cut to another city, scenes of chaos, buildings on fire. People were running through the streets, smashing windows and looting shops while Soviet tanks rolled in.

"In a speech to the nation, Premier Cyrankiewicz has vowed to restore order, blaming the present crisis on 'thugs' and 'enemies of the state…'"

Something touched my arm, and I jumped. When I saw Nessie peering up, it was like I came out of a spell. The situation in Poland was tragic, and it explained why the community of The Polish Triangle was so concerned for their brethren abroad. I would never forgive Marcus for what he did, but when it came to the Sokol brothers, I at least understood their motive. In the world of crime and treachery, sometimes that was the only closure you got.

I got up from the couch and turned off the television.

"Let's play Chutes and Ladders until *Flipper* comes on," I said.

When Nessie's face beamed, Ruth smiled. I walked over and got the game off the shelf.

The story continues in *Love Ain't For Keeping*…

At a time when everyone is running from something, crimes often get lost in the scramble.

1972. After almost a decade of war, protests, and race riots, American cities are at an all-time low. In the rundown streets of Boston, people go missing all the time, and the police are too busy to look for them.

Detective Jody Brae already has his hands full, but when a young mother at his daughter's preschool vanishes, he has to help. Considering her troubled past, it seems like she is just another runaway. Unable to convince his captain that it's suspicious, Brae decides to investigate on his own.

The case goes cold until the body of a female is found a hundred miles away in the woods of New Hampshire. While badly decomposed, it has the same clothing as the missing woman, even her purse and license.

The only problem is…it's not her.

Pre-Order Your Copy Today!
https://www.amazon.com/dp/B0BGQHSZ58

ALSO BY JONATHAN CULLEN

The Days of War Series

The Last Happy Summer

Nighttime Passes, Morning Comes

Shadows of Our Time

The Storm Beyond the Tides

Sunsets Never Wait

Bermuda Blue

Port of Boston Series

Whiskey Point

City of Small Kingdoms

The Polish Triangle

Love Ain't For Keeping

Sign up for Jonathan's newsletter for updates on deals and new releases!

https://liquidmind.media/j-cullen-newsletter-sign-up-2-jody/

Enjoying the Port of Boston series? Pre-Order the latest installment, *Love Ain't For Keeping*, **coming to Amazon on August 1, 2023!**

https://www.amazon.com/Love-Aint-Keeping-Boston-Crime-ebook/dp/B0BGQHSZ58/

BIOGRAPHY

Jonathan Cullen grew up in Boston and attended public schools. After a brief career as a bicycle messenger, he attended Boston College and graduated with a B.A. in English Literature (1995). During his twenties, he wrote two unpublished novels, taught high school in Ireland, lived in Mexico, worked as a prison librarian, and spent a month in Kenya, Africa before finally settling down three blocks from where he grew up.

He currently lives in Boston (West Roxbury) with his wife Heidi and daughter Maeve.

CPSIA information can be obtained
at www.ICGtesting.com
Printed in the USA
BVHW050204010623
665222BV00012B/325